A BOUQUET OF CHARM

A BOUQUET OF CHARM

STARLING BAY, BOOK 8

SIENNA CARR

AUTHOR'S NOTE

A Bouquet of Charm is a STANDALONE romance in the
Starling Bay series. While you do not need to have read any of
the earlier books in this series, it might enhance your reading
experience if you do because many of the characters in this book
appear in the other Starling Bay books.

Starling Bay Series:

Whirlwind Kisses
Winter's Kiss
Maid for Him
Love Letters
Escape to Starling Bay (Books 1-3)
From Faking to Forever
Winter's Vow
Guarded Hearts
Table for Two
A Bouquet of Charm
Christmas Hope

CHAPTER 1

"You won't be the odd one out."

"I've always been the odd one out," Mackenzie disagreed. Her friend Leigh meant well, but Mackenzie was damned if she would be cajoled into attending another dinner party with three couples and her all by her lonesome self.

"We're going to have to find you someone." Leigh moved the coffee cups off the tray and the slice of lemon drizzle cake and set it down on the table. She liked this cozy little book and coffee shop that Leigh owned. When her workday finished, this was where she sometimes liked to end up, not just for the female company but because Leigh being a small business owner meant the two had some business matters they often discussed.

"As easily at that?" Mackenzie quipped. "Like finding a set of keys or a pen?" She dug her fork into the moist piece of cake and plopped it into her mouth. "This is a taste of heaven."

"I'm glad you like it." Leigh dug her fork into the other side. They shared the huge slice which Leigh had placed in the middle of the small table. "It's one of my bestsellers."

"Every cake you sell should be a bestseller."

Leigh pointed her fork at her. "Rourke doesn't have any single friends, otherwise I could have set you up with—."

"Don't. Stop. Please," Mackenzie begged. "I'm not looking, and I don't need a dinner date just to even up your numbers."

"But I don't understand why you're still single. Look at you." Her friend gestured with her hand at Mackenzie, who shook her head. The ugly duckling had grown up and the long legs and arms she had once hated were now the thing that got her noticed, as did her height and her long, strawberry-blonde corkscrew curls. Her freckles weren't something to disguise under layers of foundation. In Adult World, these were things to be prized. Things weren't so bad now. She was older and understood. It was all so different than the misery she had endured during her school years.

"I choose to be single. I *choose*. Besides, Bloom takes up a lot of my time." Leigh meant well, but her friend was deliriously in love and viewed life through rose-colored glasses. She could not, and would not, understand—in her heightened sense of being in love—how anyone would want to spend their life alone.

Mackenzie didn't plan to spend her life alone, but for now, she wasn't interested in taking on the headache of meeting a man and going through the assault course of a new relationship.

"What about at Jenna and Reed's engagement party?"

"What about it?"

"Did no one catch your eye?"

"I was *working*." It had been an honor to have been chosen to do the flowers for such an event; one of Starling Bay's most eligible bachelors had gotten engaged a few weeks ago, and to a woman who had once been his maid. It had been the highlight of her time here in Starling Bay. "I didn't have time to bat my eyelashes at anyone. Nor would I have. It's so unprofessional."

"But that's the perfect opportunity to meet someone! I'm sure both Reed and Jenna would have had plenty of single male friends. You do so many parties, Mackenzie. I don't understand why you've never met anyone."

Mackenzie laughed at the idea Leigh had in her head, as if she sat around, twiddling her thumbs and pouting at any single male guests at these events. She usually finished up her displays before the parties started. "Meeting someone isn't a major goal in my life, and I'm not going to rely on anyone, any man, to make my life better. It didn't work out for my mom, and, anyway, you should know better than anyone."

Leigh looked away, her lashes lowered, making Mackenzie wince.

"Sorry." It had been a low blow to mention Leigh's controlling and abusive ex. Over time, Leigh had slowly confided in her and told her everything. The picture Leigh had painted of that vile bully had given Mackenzie a sense of kinship with this woman who had quickly become her good friend soon after she moved to this coastal town and opened her florist shop.

But unlike Leigh, Mackenzie hadn't ever dated a man who had treated her badly. She'd just never allowed herself to get too close to people; she never fully believed them when they said they loved her.

It wasn't the bullies who had stripped her self-esteem and seeded the doubts. No. It had been much closer than that. Mothers weren't supposed to be cruel. She'd been unlucky in that way, but her beloved grandma, the rock of her life, had more than made up for the lack of parents in her childhood, and it was to this woman that she owed everything.

She had named her florist shop, Bloom, after her grandma's mantra, 'Be like the one and only Mackenzie.' The letters of each word making up *BLOOM*. Those words had lifted Mackenzie through the misery of bullies who unleashed their vitriol at her, telling her that she was a freak, and that her long skinny legs had been stretched by a torture device, that her long neck looked like a giraffe's.

You're hideous, they told her. The words had remained imprinted on her brain for many years while she had been in school. But life after school, out of her teen years, had mostly been good. It had shown her that people could be good, and nice, and caring, and that the ugliness and name-calling she had suffered had been caused by a small but loud minority who had drowned out all the good things.

Yet her mother's words she never forgot, no matter how hard she tried. When she had returned, not so long ago, Mackenzie decided it was time to leave. She'd moved to Starling Bay to start over, but would still visit her grandma as often as she could, even if that other woman now also lived there. She said she had changed, and asked for forgiveness. She said she'd been in rehab, and that she was now clean and had sorted herself out. She said she regretted everything she'd done but for Mackenzie, it was many years too late.

The only person who mattered, who had ever mattered to her was her grandma, and Mackenzie wanted to repay her by making her life easier and more comfortable now that she wasn't so able. Arthritis plagued her knees and hands mostly, though sometimes she would have a stiff neck and shoulders as well. Mackenzie had an idea about adding in a small bathroom downstairs, as well as moving Grandma's bed to this floor, because Grandma was finding it increasingly difficult to climb the stairs.

In the hope of trying to earn more from her business, she had added a small gift corner to her shop. It was a small display shelf with candles and pretty pouches of potpourri and other nice smelling things such as bath bombs, in case people wanted a variety of gifts.

Unfortunately, it wasn't doing too well. Luckily, one of Leigh's friends had a gift store and he sold vases and other gift items to an upscale department store. Mackenzie had recently contacted them with a view of creating some arrangements for them.

"Maybe we need to get you the services of the Love Doctor? Though I think Reed said he's only helping the men."

"A what?" Mackenzie stared at the one inch of cake left on the plate, and set down her fork.

"A Love Doctor."

Mackenzie snorted. "What on earth is a Love Doctor?"

Leigh pushed the plate towards Mackenzie. "I can't eat that. You have it. You could eat a horse and you still wouldn't put on any weight."

"If you're sure you don't want it." But Mackenzie didn't wait for an answer as she stabbed the last remaining piece of cake onto her fork.

"According to Reed, he's a guy teaching other guys how to win women over."

"Are you serious?"

"Deadly serious. Haven't you heard about his book? It's gone viral on the internet." She typed away on her cell phone, then turned it around to show Mackenzie.

"*The Love Doctor's Ten Rules for Dating: How to Find the Woman of Your Dreams without Swiping Left or Right.*"

They laughed. "That's a mouthful for a title," Mackenzie exclaimed.

"His angle is for men to move away from using social media and those dating apps, and to revert back to the old-fashioned way of face-to-face conversations and relating."

Mackenzie groaned at the sight of the bright red cover with a man's face in a thinking pose.

"Isn't it gross?" Leigh agreed. "But this book is selling like crazy."

"Really?"

"He's making a small fortune. I wonder what he charges for coaching."

"Coaching?" Mackenzie's eyes almost popped out of their sockets. "You can't be serious."

Leigh nodded smugly. "Unfortunately, I am. His book is selling like wildfire. Reed said the guy is onto a great business. He'll likely make a good chunk of change and then disappear."

"Smart guy." If only it were that easy for her to ramp up her business. "Who is he?"

"No one knows."

"What do you mean no one knows"? Mackenzie asked. "So how does your friend know?"

Leigh shrugged. "He knew someone who used his services."

Mackenzie didn't know whether to believe her fully. It sounded like baseless rumors doing the rounds.

"There's no photo and no name. He calls himself the Love Doctor," Leigh continued.

"How does he do the coaching?"

"Reed knew someone who knew someone who had a friend who was getting coaching, and this guy said something about having to sign an NDA, a non-disclosure agreement, so that he couldn't reveal the guy's identity."

"That sounds bizarre." They looked at one another and burst out laughing.

"To think that he's making so much money. We're in the wrong business," said Leigh.

"It would seem so. Ugh, Men," groaned Mackenzie. "Only they would need a guidebook on how to attract women."

"Tell me about it. Reed and the guys were in hysterics talking about it."

Mackenzie almost choked on her latte. "Reed would know someone who knows someone." The guy had contacts everywhere. Although she wasn't in the inner circle of these couples, she had attended a few dinner parties, and of course had provided the flowers for Reed's engagement party, and so she had come to know this small crowd well. "But coaching? How? And for what?"

"He has one-to-one consultations with guys and he advises them on how to find and keep women."

Mackenzie made a face. "Ewww." She didn't like the sound of that. "That sounds sleazy. What does he teach them?"

"Tricks. That's what." Leigh raised an eyebrow.

"Have you read the book?"

Leigh wrinkled her face in disgust. "Lord, no! Who has the time?"

"Plenty of men, by the sounds of it."

"Reed and the guys were reading excerpts from it on Reed's phone. It had us in hysterics. Ten rules of dating, imagine that."

"As many as that?"

"I should buy it and we'll dissect it," Leigh suggested. "It would make for some great entertainment one evening over a glass of wine."

"I'd rather watch a romcom," replied Mackenzie.

CHAPTER 2

*A*dam examined the wedding invitation, his insides filling with pride.

Jake Parnell, a student in one of the first batch of students he'd taken under his wing, had succeeded. The guy had been a bit of a joker, and slightly coarse in his attitudes and opinions. Adam had doubts about taking him on as a student, but the guy had begged him. He said he'd gobbled up the book in a few hours and knew he needed to fix his game, that he'd been going about it the wrong way.

Adam had relented and had taken him on and in time Jake met and fell in love with the woman of his dreams. He had invited Adam to his engagement party next week. He set the invitation on the mantelpiece with pride.

As a self-employed advertising guru, he was doing well taking care of small businesses and clients. But his world had blown up —in a good way—recently when an idea he had tried on a whim had taken off and had now eclipsed the advertising business he'd been doing for years.

Love coaching.

It really was a thing. There was a demand for another way to meet women, for men who didn't want to try dating apps, and who couldn't navigate the keep-up-with-the-Joneses world of social media. There were men who were awkward, and who didn't look like male models, nor had the wit or gift of gab. It was something he'd stumbled on by accident when he'd come across an online article one evening, an article that linked to a new dating website, and which taught men how to spruce up their images—even Photoshop them so that they made one look completely different to how they were in real life. It encouraged men to write descriptions that would entice women to click on their profiles.

In his opinion, this was all wrong. Adam didn't agree, partly because he'd tried using the dating apps and they weren't for him. The idea of a quick hook-up didn't appeal. He wanted to get to know the person, find a connection, but these apps didn't lend themselves to that type of experience. He was careful, having been burned in high school where he was known as a nerdy, geeky teen with glasses and no street cred. His dating experiences even then had been miserable.

Intrigued, he'd started writing an article about 'the other way', the old-fashioned way of meeting someone and talking face to face, and how to determine whether a woman was interested or not. And if so, how to go about navigating this unknown world.

One evening, just for fun, he'd quickly put together an eBook on how to woo and win women the old-fashioned way, by being genuine, being nice, attentive, listening, caring and interested. "How to Find the Woman of Your Dreams without Swiping Left or Right" had been created half out of curiosity, and half because it had been so simple to put together. He'd created ten rules, all made up, but true, because they were what everyone knew. Common sense. And he'd decided on ten rules because from his experience people liked nice round numbers and rules. They liked cookie-cutter recipes to success, and so that's what he gave them.

What he hadn't been prepared for was the response. He'd then put up a website to sell the digital book directly and put up some ads.

The next morning, he'd woken up to over a hundred orders. Then two hundred the day after that.

Soon he was selling hundreds of books a day and the easy money rolled in, all without him having to do much. His little experiment, his foray into something frivolous, something he'd put up because he had been intrigued, had made his jaw drop.

It differed so much from his normal day-to-day job and yet, despite the money, he didn't feel as happy as he should have. The truth was, he didn't want to be known. His success was so new and so instant, he wasn't yet comfortable with it.

There was something cheesy, something uncool, something to be laughed at, in being associated with this piece of work. It reminded him of high school and his days where he would rather have been a jock and the envy of others, the one the cheerleaders ogled, the one the team lifted on their shoulders at the end of a game. Computer science geeks didn't reach those heady heights.

And so he kept his identity hidden, referring to himself as the 'Love Doctor' and not putting a name to his book.

Outside of school, his brains had been useful, and his entrepreneurial mindset meant he was a self-starter, willing to learn, willing to prove himself and to subsequently make good money. He reinvented himself. Adulthood allowed that luxury, and soon he turned from nerd to super smooth and assertive.

For years he had toiled and worked to make the advertising business a success, and it was, but it was hard work, too. In contrast, he'd thrown nothing at the love coaching business. No research had gone into his book. It had been comprised of common sense. Treat a woman with respect, listen, be attentive and make her feel special. These were the basics, the 101s of dating, things he assumed all men knew. Things his father had passed down to him. Basic human common sense.

Apparently not to most men, it seemed. After sales of the eBook had gone through the roof, he'd started receiving emails from men who were desperate to learn what he had to teach. Desperate to find a suitable partner without having to put themselves on social media or dating websites.

Who knew?

He felt at once exhilarated, and then sleazy and questioned his ethics. After all, Adam Hartman didn't have such a healthy romantic life himself. Who was he to be telling others how to lead their love lives?

But some men begged him to help. He'd never received emails such as these, and when he emailed back with advice, these people acted on it and reported back to him.

Then some men asked for one-to-one coaching. Having moved to a new town in recent months, he felt invisible and unknown, and therefore more prone to risk-taking. For those that were local, he decided to take a chance.

This was how he'd found Jake Parnell. He wasn't his first client, he'd had two before then, but Jake was his success story. As soon as he had signed the NDA, Adam had started coaching him. Within eight weeks, Jake had met and fallen in love with the woman of his dreams.

Bingo!

Success.

Jake Parnell's invitation to his engagement party provided one problem for the Love Doctor. He didn't have a plus one for the event, and he wouldn't know anyone there, but he was self-assured and confident enough to work the room and mingle with people.

He'd already made up his mind to show his face for a short time and then go home.

CHAPTER 3

A lot of time and effort went into creating her floral arrangements, and for this small but intimate affair held in a luxurious tent, Mackenzie had outdone herself yet again.

Just as she was finishing up with the displays, the newly engaged couple came over and complimented her on her creations. The fiancée then asked Mackenzie if she would do the flowers for the wedding, and she had accepted, even though they hadn't yet settled on a wedding date.

When the happy couple had ended up in a passionate kiss, getting a little too carried away in front of her, she felt like a waitress interrupting an intimate dinner for two, and discreetly slipped away.

She got into her van and drove off. It was late evening on a Saturday night. What would she do when she got back home? The answer to that was easy.

Nothing.

After a day at the shop, she was happy to have tomorrow off. Working six days a week left her completely drained by the end of her workweek but compliments and accolades from happy customers always boosted her ego and filled her with a sense of worth which had lately eluded her. Ordinarily she didn't dwell on her past too much until her mother had returned and reminded her of the things she hadn't had, and of the normal childhood that hadn't been hers.

As a teen, it had taken reading endless self-help books, and the indomitable love of her grandma, to make her feel worthwhile. Distrust and caution were woven into the fabric of her personality, so when a man, or a woman, told her that she was beautiful, she didn't believe a word of it.

Tonight, she would spend as she did most Saturday evenings, eating a quickly put together dinner in front of the TV and watching a romantic movie.

As she parked outside her apartment and gathered her belongings from the van, a slow dread started to build in her belly when she couldn't find her phone.

"Ugh!" She groaned loudly, remembering exactly where it was, outside the tent, in one of the big terracotta pots that were on either side of the entrance. The party hosts had asked her to create a beautiful arch of flowers around the entrance and she'd set her phone on the ledge of one of the large pots—a silly place, for sure. The happily engaged couple had come over to talk to her just then and she'd forgotten all about her phone.

She drove back, annoyed with herself for wasting more time when she was already so tired.

The party was in full swing when she returned. Rows upon rows of cars had lined the driveway. Music floated in the air, and fairy lights twinkled and glistened outside. Laughter rippled in the warm, balmy air and as she headed towards the tent, a group of well-dressed guests were standing outside admiring her flower displays.

She glanced at the flower pot, but her phone was nowhere to be seen. When the guests went into the tent, she rushed over to it. The pot was huge, coming up to her thigh, so she bent over and peered inside, but she couldn't see all the way down, so she stuck her head in and fumbled around frantically.

Her panic trebled when she couldn't locate the darned thing. Her phone was her lifeline. It was how her grandma got a hold of her, as well as her customers. Because the pot was so big, she couldn't feel all the way around the base from one position, so she maneuvered her way around it, walking slowly and with her head still inside, one hand feeling along the base while the other hand remained on the pot's rim to prevent her from falling inside. With no success, she dipped her head in further, her feet lifting off the ground until she was almost on tiptoes.

Then she screamed as she lost her balance and tipped right in, the ridge of the pot pressed firm against her stomach and now both of her hands inside the pot, on the base of it as she did a bendy-legged cartwheel. Her body froze, but she could feel her ears turning red. This had nothing to do with her being face down in the pot.

"Do you want a hand?" It sounded like a man's voice, and she was in no position to turn it down.

"Please!"

Hands appeared on either side of her waist, large hands it felt like, which pulled her back so that her feet could touch the ground again. She slowly straightened herself up and turned around, embarrassed, her face flushed, heat burning her cheeks, and the blush turning deeper as she found herself staring into the glittering eyes of a tall and handsome-looking man.

"Hey there," his voice was deep, his eyes filled with amusement.

C H A P T E R 4

It was like a scene out of a romantic comedy. Adam couldn't believe his eyes, witnessing the entire event, from the moment this gorgeous creature arrived on the scene and seemed to be looking for something. She'd looked around the pot, then inside, then she'd bent over completely and stuck her head inside.

It was her cell phone that was now snugly sitting in the pocket of his jacket. He'd been busy talking to Jake's parents, otherwise he would have rushed over and put her out of her misery and handed her phone back there and then. He might even have prevented her from tipping her head inside the huge pot. But when she'd fallen inside, with only her slim and delectable legs in dark-colored jeans sticking up in the air, he'd rushed over to help.

Even though he'd asked her permission for him to help her, he hadn't known what to do with his hands; didn't know how to help her up and out of the pot without laying a finger on her. As bold and as daring as it was to make such a move on a total stranger, he placed his hands on the woman's waist and gently helped her up.

She uncurled herself hastily before brushing her hands down

15

her shirt and her jeans, then moved her huge, curly locks away so that he could see her face more clearly.

He flexed his hands. "I'm sorry. I didn't know how else to help you out."

"Um … thanks … I was looking for my cell phone."

"Ah." He fished it out of his pocket and started to hand it over. But just as she was about to take it, he asked her, "How do I know it's yours?" It seemed prudent to check first. She seemed taken aback.

"It's mine. How else would I know where it was?"

She had a point.

"Why do *you* have it?" she asked.

"I heard it ring."

She opened her mouth in shock. "I need to check who called."

"Well, can you give me a phone number, or something else to prove it's yours?"

Her brows slashed together in indignation, and she stared at him as if he were an imbecile. "It's *mine*. I fell into a flower pot trying to find it. What else did you think I was doing in there?"

"I had no idea. Maybe like all the other guests, you were admiring the flowers, and somehow … I don't know how … you fell in."

Her lips twisted. "A guest? Dressed like this?" She pinched the fabric of her jeans.

"Yes." He searched her face, and her heart skipped a beat, or three.

"I'm wearing jeans."

He shrugged. "You still look like you came dressed for this party." She rolled her eyes at that. "I'm not saying that to creep you out. I'm stating a fact, that's all," he said, worried that he might be coming across as a loser who was desperate for her attention.

"Okay, detective. Please let me have my phone back. It's late, and I'm tired, and …"

He could sense her urgency. "What's the photo on it?" he asked, not because he didn't believe her, but because he wanted to talk to her, and he didn't want to risk that she might take off once she'd gotten her phone back.

"It's a photo of my shop, Bloom." She folded her arms, sulky teenager like. He almost expected her to roll her eyes again any moment now.

"Mind if I check?" he asked, before he pressed a button that would light up the display scene.

"It's been in your possession this entire time. Check away all you want."

He pressed a button and as he peered closer, he saw the front of a shop, exactly as she had described. "Bloom," he said, "is this yours?"

"Yes. I came here to do all the floral arrangements." She waved her hand at the magnificent arch over the entrance to the tent.

He had long admired the flower displays, because they were eye-catching and unusual, and it was a surprise to discover that this woman had created them. "You *made* those?" Not being good with his hands, he admired people who were. She nodded.

"I'm impressed. They're eye-catching." Just like she was. Tall and striking, with that mane of curls. She stood out, first because of her height, and then because of her gorgeous face. "They stand out, your displays. I can't put my finger on why."

"Thank you."

Roses and other flowers, and stunning colors, pink and white, with dashes of blood red. She had used lots of foliage and greens. As a man to whom flowers were of no particular significance, even he had stopped and stared in awe. Her story made sense now, and the way he'd found her. He gave her the phone back.

She quickly checked it. "My grandma called," she remarked, before rushing away quickly without even saying goodbye. He raced after her, but she was already on the phone talking to someone. Her grandma, he presumed.

Shamelessly, he followed her away from the house and across the large driveway as she weaved in and out of the parked cars, not ready to have her leave. He didn't know anyone here and talking to her was infinitely preferable.

He waited out of earshot, not wanting to eavesdrop, and as soon as she put the phone away, he raced over without knowing why.

She opened the door to her van. In the lamplit shimmering light, he could make out the name of her shop on it.

"Are you leaving already?"

"I've got my phone. That's all I came back for."

"Why not stay a while?"

She laughed. "I'm not invited. I was here to do the flowers."

She was striking to look at, yet unaware of her looks. Something about her drew him to her, but he couldn't place what it was. He wasn't fixated on physical beauty to the point that he disregarded all else, but the manner of their meeting, and the fact that she seemed humble, and coy, made him want to talk to her more. What type of woman would be so concerned about talking to her grandmother?

"Why flowers?" he asked, finding a safe topic to discuss.

Her eyes narrowed, she tilted her head, the light falling on her silky skin and highlighting her high cheekbones. She was a mesmerizing sight; too bad she was so eager to get away. "I like making pretty things. It was the one thing I was good at. I'm better at making things with my hands, and with flowers, I found a way to make something that I could earn a living with."

"I like the way you think."

"We all have to do something, right? I could never sit in an office, behind a computer, so this is how I ended up doing what I do. You're very inquisitive."

She didn't mince her words.

"I'm nosy, you mean."

She checked her phone again. "I was trying to be polite."

"I'm not good at making things," he confessed. "Which is why I'm intrigued by people who can. Artists, designers, sculptors, florists."

"Is that a pick-up line? Lumping florists in with highly creative people?"

"You don't think you deserve to be?" He lifted his chin, appraising her. "You have a talent. You should see what I would do, given a few flowers and some grass."

"It's not grass. It's foliage."

"You see, I know nothing. And, to answer your question, no, that's not a pick-up line." He hoped he wasn't starting to sound like the desperate men who came to him for dating advice.

"Okay." Her tone was wary. His gaze fixed on her friendly smile as she opened the van door again.

"You can't leave," he tried frantically to think what else they could talk about, but he was failing badly, and as a love coach, this was ridiculous.

"Why not?" This time she didn't close the van door but kept it ajar.

"Because I've only just met you. That was some way to meet."

Her brow wrinkled, and she stared at him as if she didn't know what to make of him. "One I hope to forget, and fast."

"I won't tell anyone." He took a step towards her and held out his hand. "Adam Hartman."

She stared at it for a few seconds tentatively before shaking it. "Mackenzie Jeffers."

"Mackenzie," he said, rolling the name around his lips. She

looked like a Mackenzie. Not a Susie, or a Kate, or a Chloe. Her name was different, and appealing, and it fit her like a glove.

"Nice to meet you, Adam. Enjoy the party." She climbed inside her van and drove off.

Mackenzie Jeffers from Bloom.

It was a name and a woman he couldn't forget.

She was used to seeing that look of interest in men's eyes. It often made her flinch, the way some men stared, their greedy gazes raking in her body from head to toe, as if she were nothing more than an object.

But with this man who found her phone and had done his level best to keep her engaged longer than she intended to stay, there had been nothing sleazy.

He had been refreshingly nice.

And he had found her cell phone, and that had been the main thing. She'd called and spoken to her grandma. She panicked each time she got a call from Grandma because she worried that something bad might have happened to her. Thank goodness everything was okay.

As she drove back, the sky an even deeper, darker color of ink, she wondered if she could have stayed. She hadn't been invited, but she could have hung around for another fifteen minutes instead of rushing back to an empty home with nothing but a leftover sandwich for dinner.

CHAPTER 5

"I need your help, dude. I'm begging you. I've read your book and I need to know your secrets! Please."

Adam tapped his pen on the table, mulling over the email that had been sent to the Love Doctor. It was becoming more difficult to juggle his time. Thank goodness he had a different phone line for the love coaching because it was one way of ensuring a split between his two businesses.

Even though he had business clients to tend to, the lure of the money from his new endeavor was impossible to resist. He couldn't make his mind up about what to do. Sometimes he was tempted to throw the towel in on his advertising business and go all in with being the Love Doctor. Jake had been his first success story and knowing that he had helped him to find and connect with someone special had been priceless. He'd felt a sense of achievement, as if he'd made a difference in someone's life.

But there were times, like now, when he was putting together a presentation for a business client who needed it urgently and yet this email stared back at him, taking all of his attention.

I need your help, dude. I'm begging you.

Those words reached into his soul and made it impossible for him not to do something. But as for secrets, there weren't any. It was all common sense. The guy was from around these parts, near Starling Bay. Adam huffed out a slow breath. He'd been this guy once. He'd needed guidance. This guy sounded desperate. He had to at least meet with him and, depending on what the guy was like, he could offer one-to-one coaching.

He closed the email, told himself he would reply later. As with Jake, he would make the guy sign an NDA and then he could rent out a small meeting room at the hotel in town, because talking about someone's love problems wasn't easy to do in the lobby of a hotel.

He sat upright, as a new idea blossomed in his head. If he met with this new guy, he could also pass by the florist's place. He'd already looked up where she was based, and it was not far from the hotel.

Yes, he could help this man. He opened up his email, attached the NDA and asked the guy to sign it.

A few days later, Adam walked into The Grand Hotel and could tell right away that the guy with the slightly round belly, wearing a security guard outfit and looking uncomfortable, was his potential new client.

He walked up to him. "Patrick?"

The guy's eyes turned larger. "You're the love coach?"

Adam put his fingers to his lips and looked around. "Remember what I said? Please respect my privacy."

"Sure, dude, sure."

Adam ushered him in into the room, eager to get this over and done with so that he could go drop in on Mackenzie. All casual like, as if he was just passing by, which he was. "It's *Love Doctor*, not 'coach'."

"Isn't that the same thing?"

"Technically, no."

"But aren't you offering me *coaching*?"

"It's a branding thing, let's just forget about it. What can I do for you, Patrick?"

"I don't know." Patrick raised his hands in a gesture of defeat. "I'm not having much luck with the ladies. I'm trying real hard but I don't know where I'm going wrong."

"That's your first problem. Don't try so hard. Women can tell when you're doing that because you come across as desperate."

"Don't try so hard?" Patrick repeated the words as if they were magical and with the power to transform his life. His brow furrowed as he seemed to concentrate. "Got it. Don't try so—"

"See, there you go again. You're trying too hard."

"Am I?"

"You're repeating what I've said."

"Huh?"

"Calm down." Adam got up and paced around the room. "Breathe. Chill. Relax. You're looking to attract a woman, not defuse a bomb."

"I'm looking to attract a woman. I'm looking to attract a woman."

Adam scratched his jaw. The dude was repeating it as if it were a mantra. "You've got this, Patrick."

"I've got this." Patrick breathed in, a deep, loud inhale, but beads of sweat had formed on his brow.

"Patrick?"

"I'm relaxing. I'm taking your advice."

Adam was perplexed. "Are you hot?"

"Women don't think so."

"Are you *hot?*" Adam rolled his eyes and opened a window.

"Now that you mention it." The guy wiped a hand over his brow, making Adam wince. "I'm not usually like this, but lately, I seem to get all nervous and fall to pieces. I'm losing my game."

"Your game?" Adam lowered his chin. "Tell me about the last time you made someone laugh."

"That's easy. We have a shop that sells calendars and fancy notebooks. They're real fancy and real expensive. More expensive than a notebook has any right to be, gold embossed and with gold on the edges…"

"Stick to the story, bud. Just the facts. Nothing else."

"Okay, so there's a woman who works in there, and she thinks I'm funny. I make her laugh, and half of the time I'm not even trying to."

"Then why does she laugh?"

"She says I have a funny take on things. She's funny too, she says things that are odd, but funny. It's cool."

Adam noted that Patrick seemed more calm and in control when he was reciting the tale. "When you were talking just now, you were calm."

"I was calm."

"You were telling it just as it was in your head. That's the kind of guy you have to be. Calm and cool."

Patrick nodded, then frowned again. "My friend is dating Hailey Ross."

Adam blinked at him. "Who?" The name sounded familiar.

"Hailey Ross. The actress. She was here some time a few months ago."

Adam tried to think. He'd heard of her. "The action heroine?"

Patrick nodded again. "Yeah, the one in the Monica Martins movies. My friend is dating her."

Oh, geez. Adam bowed his head into his hand. The 'my friend is dating' disturbed him. While he'd known that some of these men might be desperate, he hadn't been prepared for them to be crackpots. Delusional.

"I can't set you up with a Hollywood star. That's not the type of thing I can help you with."

"Uh … yeah, I know, dude. That's not what I want. Hailey's nice and all, but I know my limit now, I guess. I'm just an average guy, maybe a little less than average—"

Adam pointed his finger. "Stop that. Just stop."

"But a guy like me, I'm not going to get a girl like that," Patrick protested. Adam's patience was beginning to wear thing. He glanced at his watch. He had a client meeting online later today but before that he wanted to go see Mackenzie. For what, exactly, he didn't yet know. The temptation of walking into the florist's shop suddenly seemed like a better option compared to wasting time with this weirdo.

"I have to cut this short, Patrick."

"What? Is this it? I paid sixty bucks for this?"

"This was just a getting to know you meeting. To see if we could work together. There's no charge for this." It cost him to rent this room for an hour, but he'd have to write that expense off.

"Phew." Patrick wiped the sweat off his brow. "That's good, because I don't get paid a lot for what I do."

"What do you do?" Adam glanced at the guy's uniform again.

"I work at the mall just out of town." Patrick shrugged. "It's not fancy or anything. I don't get to suit up like you, but it's not bad. I get by. My friend, Jackson, he's living the high life now. Got his own security company out in Hollywood and—"

"Jesus." Adam muttered under his breath. "I'm really not sure I can help you, Patrick."

The man's face dropped, incredulity making his eyebrows shoot up like hairy caterpillars. For a moment Adam thought he was going to cry. "You can't help me? You've decided, just like that? You don't know what it's like, being a loser like me." He got up, disappointment rolling off him in waves.

Adam sucked in a breath. He did know because he had been a loser like that once. "Okay, Okay." He'd give the guy one more chance. "But I don't want to hear anything about your friends."

He air quoted 'friends'. *Hailey Ross, my ass.* "This is about *you*. About upping your dating game. I'll teach you how to approach women, and then I'll give you tips and advice about how to find and keep the woman of your dreams."

"I've already found her."

"What?"

"I've already found her."

"The woman selling the fancy notebooks?" Adam asked.

Patrick shook his head. "The one I'm interested in doesn't know I exist."

"She doesn't know you exist?"

"Not in the way I want her to. She's my boss, and I'm just another security guard at the mall."

Adam's eyes grew large. "Your boss?" Talk about making a huge mistake. "Are you sure you want to go there, buddy?"

"You don't think I can?" Patrick's expression resembled a wet fish. "Just because Jackson and Hailey—"

There he went again. "Okay, buddy," Adam said quickly. "That's what we'll focus on for lesson two."

"Lesson two. Okay. Gotcha."

"I'll be in touch." Adam hastily picked up his leather binder and made a move to leave. There was no way he could bill this guy at all. The meeting had barely lasted fifteen minutes. Now, onto the real reason for his visit to the town center today.

CHAPTER 6

She was arranging the tulips in a silver bucket when the door opened announcing the arrival of a new customer.

"Good morning!" she said, feeling the same surge of excitement every time a customer walked in. Though she'd been running her shop for a while now, this feeling never went away. People, strangers, were buying her flowers and her creations. She had her dream job, and she was doing the thing she loved, and she was getting paid.

This customer seemed to know what she wanted, so Mackenzie gave her space. The last thing such people needed was for a nosy salesperson to try to sell to them.

"These are pretty." The customer hovered around the shelf where she had arranged her scented candles. She picked up the candles and sniffed, sighing at each aroma. "I'll take these three."

This was music to Mackenzie's ears. Such a great start to the week. Three candles and a bouquet, and it was only Monday morning.

"That's a wonderful choice." She packaged everything into her signature pink and blue gift bags.

"For my mom," the customer explained. "She's been taking

care of me and my kids because I got sick and I just want to thank her."

Her face tightened, and the smile she offered the woman didn't come easily. "I hope your mom likes them."

"I know she will. Thanks so much."

Mackenzie stared at the woman as she walked out. *Lucky woman.* Having a mom who still took care of at her at this age. She didn't know what that was like, having a mom do all the nice caring things that moms were supposed to do.

With a heavy heart, she got back to arranging her displays again.

"Mackenzie." Her insides turned to brick at the sound of her mother's voice. What on earth was she doing in here?

"Mackenzie, at least acknowledge me."

That voice, knowing that *she* was in here and could not be avoided, made it all the harder for Mackenzie to face her.

"What can I get for you?" The enthusiasm she naturally felt when dealing with customers flattened.

"Sunflowers. I'll take some sunflowers. This bunch seems nice." Her mother plucked a small bunch from the silver bucket. "Your grandma likes sunflowers."

Mackenzie took the bunch of flowers and bunched them together with a pretty purple-colored gauze ribbon.

"How have you been?" the woman asked.

Small talk. Mackenzie didn't want to make small talk. Not with this woman who didn't deserve her time.

Mackenzie silently wrapped them up, taking extra care because they were for her grandma.

"The silent treatment? In your shop? Really, Mackenzie?"

Mackenzie glared at her. "What do you want me to say?"

But her mother was examining the items in the gift corner. "You're selling candles now?"

"Take one for Grandma." Mackenzie suggested. She walked

over to the shelf, picked up a candle she knew her grandma would love and popped it into a small bag.

Her mother took out her small battered-looking purse. "What's the damage?"

Mackenzie saw another customer enter the shop. She didn't want to take money from this woman, even though she knew she should. She suspected that her mother depended a lot on Grandma, and what she gave Mackenzie now would mostly likely have come from her in the first place. "Don't worry about it. It's on me."

"You don't have to do that—"

"Take it." Mackenzie held up the bag of gifts. Her mother grabbed it and left.

Mackenzie walked over to the other customer. "Good morning. Is there anything I can help you with?" She flashed her usual greeting smile, the one she reserved for all her customers, and then she realized who he was; the guy from the party the other night. The one who had rescued her from the terracotta pot.

"So, this is your shop." He wandered around, examining her displays. "Your arrangements are stunning."

"Thank you." Her insides were still reeling from her last encounter, and now, with this man suddenly showing up in her shop, she was a mountain of intangible emotions she could not put a name to. Unease and excitement swirled around her as she watched him walk around the shop giving her compliments. Her displays were lovely. They had enabled her to get noticed and featured in magazine articles. Doing the flowers for Reed Knight's engagement party had helped get a lot of publicity recently, and this in turn had made her last few weeks busier than usual.

"You have a flair for the artistic."

"Are you going to keep them coming? The compliments," she

said, when he glanced back at her. She prided herself on her designs. They were uniquely hers. Many people commented on it.

Before he could reply, the door flew open and her mother charged back into the shop, her eyes teary. "I'm trying. I'm making a real effort. What will it take for you to realize I'm sorry?"

Embarrassment stirred with anger. She was aware that her new customer was watching her intently. "Do you mind? I'm with a customer."

"I'm your mother, Mackenzie. Don't punish me forever." Sheer desperation coiled around the words, snaking and sliding and hanging in the air. Guilt was the color of her eyes. It was all Mackenzie could see as she stared at her.

"Please don't make a scene," she begged, her voice tight and restrained. She wished the ground would break open and take her with it.

"I'm trying to make amends, and I wish you'd give me a chance." Her mother stormed out, visibly shaking, banging the door behind her. Mackenzie swiped a hand through her hair, not wanting to know what Adam might be thinking.

They stared at one another for a short awkward moment until she asked him how she could help him. She wanted him to be gone, although it seemed to her that he was here more for the conversation than anything else. This wasn't new to her. Men often came in here hitting on her.

But this guy wasn't hitting on her, not in an obvious way. Though he also wasn't buying anything.

"What do you recommend?" he asked at last. She was grateful that he kept the conversation on the flowers.

"It depends on who you're buying for."

"A friend. A 'thank you' bouquet."

"Just a 'thank you' bouquet? For any specific reason?"

He shook his head. "No."

"What does your friend like? What are their favorite flowers, what colors?"

"I don't know. Something bright, classy, vibrant, and fresh."

She wrinkled her nose. "All of my flowers are fresh. I don't sell wilted ones."

He laughed. "I was thinking of ways to describe my friend."

"Do you have a color scheme in mind?"

He shrugged. "No idea."

"You don't seem to know much about your friend."

"I don't. What do you recommend?"

"Calla lilies are nice."

"Those will do."

"Any particular bunch?" She motioned with her hand. "You pick one."

He did and handed it to her. "I'll wrap it up for you." She took it over to the counter and wrapped it up.

"You sell candles and gifts," he commented. He seemed to be examining her shop with a magnifying glass.

"I'm hoping people will see them and want to add them to their order."

"That's the way to do it."

"It's going slowly, but I'm hoping sales will pick up there."

He gave her a look as if he was going to say something. Then after a few seconds, "Bloom. That's a really cool name."

"My grandma suggested it."

"You're really close to your grandmother. That's sweet."

"She's a sweet woman. She's had a great influence on my life."

"That's what grandmothers do," he said softly, so softly it seemed to speak directly to her heart. "Bloom," he repeated. "It's short, sharp, and easy to remember."

"Be like the one and only Mackenzie." She handed him the prettily wrapped bouquet.

"Be like the one and only Mackenzie?" he echoed.

"Yes." He'd caught her off guard with his easy smile and his easy manner, even after the outburst with her mother, and now the conversation had veered off into personal matters. She had no desire to unduly reveal anything more about herself.

"That's clever. *Very* clever."

"She's a smart woman. She's been my rock."

"Grandmas and moms. They're the bedrock of all families."

"Not all moms." She hadn't intended for her reply to be so quick, and her tone so cold, but in light of what he had heard, she had now given him more information than he needed. "Can I get you anything else?" she asked, looking over at the door, eyeing a new customer who had just walked in.

"No, thank you. How much?"

She rang up the amount at the counter. He slipped her the bills and just as she handed him the bouquet, he gave it back to her. "What are you doing?"

"For you."

"What? For me?"

"Yes."

"Why?" Someone else had done this a few months ago. Someone who had been eager to get her number. She clasped her hands behind her back, refusing to take it.

"Because I want to."

She didn't want another scene. The new customer was looking at a display of bouquets, but the shop was small enough that their conversation could be easily heard. "I can't accept it," she insisted.

"Why not? It's a gift."

"For what? I barely know you. You're the one who found my phone. If anyone needs to give a gift, it would be me, and I've already thanked you." She didn't have anything else to give him.

"There's no reason for this. I didn't get a chance to talk to you properly the other night—"

He seemed reluctant to understand. "You gave me back my phone. I said thank you. That should have been the end of it," she said, speaking slowly and deliberately, hoping the message would get through to him. It had been a morning of scenes. First her mother, and now this. She'd been foolish enough to think this was going to be a great day.

"You haven't taken this in the spirit in which it was intended."

"What do you want, Adam?" she hissed.

"I don't want anything. I was curious about your shop. There's nothing I want from you. No strings attached."

She didn't like it. This was cheesy. Desperate. But the new customer had glanced over at her a couple of times now and she needed *this* man to be gone.

"It's very kind of you but completely unnecessary." She took the bouquet and forced a smile.

He picked up her brochure and business card. "Mind if I take—"

"Take them. Thank you." *Now please leave.* She nodded at the new customer who had picked out a couple of bouquets. "I'll be over in one second."

He was still perusing her brochure. "If you ever want to talk about branding, I can help you. I'm an advertising guru."

"No, thank you." She walked over to the other customer, inwardly cringing at hearing him call himself a 'guru'. She didn't know anyone who referred to themselves as a guru.

That, right there, was a bright red warning light.

He gave himself a virtual kick as he left the florist's shop.

Guru.

The word had been on the tip of his tongue because a fan had sent him a glowing review for the dating book. He claimed that Adam's book had helped him to find love.

But advertising *guru*? Really?

He slapped his forehead in shame. He also hadn't intended to give the florist the bouquet. The action smacked of desperation. Buying flowers for a woman he barely knew? What had come over him? He was usually cool and classy. He knew better.

Being around Mackenzie turned his brain to mush and made him be someone not unlike Patrick.

But he'd also witnessed something alarming. He'd heard Mackenzie being rude to a customer, something he couldn't reconcile to the friendly woman he was starting to get to know. And when she had later returned to the shop, he'd discovered that she was Mackenzie's mother.

He didn't understand the dynamics of that relationship, it was all so different than his own.

But it explained a lot. He'd expected confidence and flirtation from someone like Mackenzie, but there was a vulnerability about her which he hadn't been able to put his finger on.

This tiny glimpse into her life told him that all was not well, and that, more than anything, drew him to her.

CHAPTER 7

"He insisted I keep the bouquet he'd just bought from me." She had just finished telling Leigh about Adam's visit to her shop, as well as the engagement party over the weekend. They were sitting in Books & Buns at the end of another long day.

"That's so sweet."

Mackenzie disagreed. "That is cheesy, and creepy. I didn't want it. I put it back on the display stand."

Leigh patted her hand lightly. "People buy you flowers, pay you compliments and you pretend it's nothing."

"It *is* nothing. I don't know these men, and they don't know me."

"But they want to get to know you."

Mackenzie rolled her eyes. She could feel another lecture coming on from her well-meaning friend. "I have no interest in getting to know them." She laughed as she remembered what Adam had said. "He called himself a guru."

"A guru?"

"Yes, a guru. Who does that?"

"Someone who thinks highly of himself?" Leigh suggested with a wink. "Or someone who knows his subject matter."

"You would say that even if a turnip asked me on a date." Mackenzie swirled the spoon around in her café latte.

"If you said 'yes' to the turnip, I wouldn't mind."

"You're being silly now." Mackenzie stopped stirring long enough to blink at Leigh as if she were a freak. "It's a creepy thing to do, you have to admit."

"It's not creepy. I love getting flowers."

"From Rourke, not from anyone else. What would you do if a stranger walked in and bought you a cup of coffee and a slice of cake?"

Leigh's face turned sober for a passing second. Her friend had now found love with a man who treated her with the utmost respect and loved her deeply. "I hear you. You have to be careful who you get together with."

"That's my mantra," Mackenzie agreed.

"Speaking of my wonderful man, we're having a dinner party and you have to come."

Mackenzie opened her mouth to protest. She didn't want to go. She had been before, when Leigh had been kind enough to invite her. Rourke and his friends and their girlfriends were a nice, sociable bunch, and Leigh sometimes invited Mackenzie along when she and Rourke hosted an event. But as kind a gesture as this was, unease rolled in her stomach. She would be the odd one out; number seven at a dinner party of three couples. Cruel memories twisted in her gut as she remembered how that felt, and she made a face, balking at the invite.

"And don't say you can't." Leigh wagged a finger at her. "You've always got some excuse lined up."

Mackenzie liked Rourke and his friends, Reed and Dylan, and their partners. Merry, one of the women, used to be a marketing manager in Boston, and had offered to help Mackenzie, but she'd never gotten around to asking, and now it was too late because Merry was pregnant and Mackenzie didn't want to trouble her. They were all nice people, she liked them. She really did. It was just that seeing them all together, in pairs, each of them with someone, made her feel even more left out. The contrast was stark. They had someone, and she didn't.

"I have …" But before she could make up a lame excuse for why she couldn't come, she noticed a familiar face by the bookshelves on the other side. Instinctively, she slid further down in her chair.

"What are you doing?" Not one to miss anything, Leigh glanced over her shoulder, following her line of sight. She turned to Mackenzie. "Is *that* him? Is that *the* guy?"

Mackenzie nodded. Was he following her? She'd never seen him and now she'd seen him for the third time in a week.

"Why are you hiding?" Leigh asked.

"Why do you think?"

"I know him."

Dread pooled in Mackenzie's stomach. "You know him? Why didn't you say?"

"I didn't know he was your guy."

"He's not *my* guy."

"He's a smart guy. Good-looking too, you failed to mention that," Leigh said, haughtily.

"I didn't notice."

"The heck you didn't. You could be onto a good thing there, girlfriend."

Mackenzie pulled herself up a few inches. Adam was at the counter and was paying for something.

"Books, books and more books. He's smart. If I remember correctly, he buys a lot of stuff to do with advertising, and psychology, and selling tactics."

"Do you have everyone's reading preferences memorized?"

"Not everyone's, only those whose reading tastes are worthy of me remembering. I'm telling you, Mackenzie, this guy is smart."

"Oh, God, he's coming over." Mackenzie covered her face with her hands, as if this would make her invisible to him. How had she gone from never seeing this man to seeing him three times in the space of a week?

"Good evening." He addressed both of them. Mackenzie nodded and Leigh acknowledged him as if he were suddenly her best friend. They talked about his latest book purchases while Mackenzie quietly died in her chair. She busied herself with stirring her coffee, even though there was only a little bit left in the cup.

"You know my good friend Mackenzie," Leigh's brazen attempt to include her in the conversation pulled her right into it. "What a small world we live in."

"We met at an engagement party," Adam answered, giving them another easy smile.

"Mackenzie said you brought her flowers. She loved them."

Mackenzie kicked Leigh under the table lightly, prompting her to make a pained expression.

"Yeah?" Adam tilted his head, disbelief twinkling in his eyes. He was going along with the façade.

"They were lovely," Mackenzie agreed, somewhat stiffly.

"I saw you were picking up some more books," Leigh commented. Mackenzie hated the way her friend encouraged him to continue the conversation.

"Some new ones came out, and I had to have them."

"Did you get everything you needed?"

"I sure did. I've placed an order for a few more. In my line of work, you can never know everything."

"What do you do?" Leigh asked. Mackenzie watched their exchange, her friend was all wide-eyed and eager, and Adam was very much at ease and obviously wanting to showcase his life and career.

"I'm in advertising. I offered to help Mackenzie," he glanced over at her, and she shrunk back further into her seat. "Not that she needs help, but if she did, I'd be happy to help."

Leigh beamed with happiness. "That's a *great* idea. I'm sure she'll take you up on that kind offer. Won't you?"

Mackenzie would have narrowed her eyes at her friend but she was conscious of Adam watching them intently.

"I'm doing perfectly fine." She'd said it a little too quickly, a little too eagerly. "But thank you for the offer," she added, not wanting to sound completely rude.

"Not a problem. It's just that you mentioned you were trying different ways of earning more income. I've helped small business owners shift to doing things such as online lessons. I think something like that would be perfect for you."

What was he talking about? "Online lessons?"

How? She didn't know the first thing about that.

"You could teach people how to put flower displays together. You just record yourself making something and then upload it online. The beauty of these classes is that you don't have to do them in person, and you can reach as big an audience as you want. It would be a win-win. These things take off like crazy, but I digress." He waved his hands and then shoved them into his pockets. "You said you're doing fine so, I'll stop going on about it, but here's my business card in case you ever change your mind." He handed one to each of them. This guy never missed an opportunity.

"You're clearly passionate about what you do." Leigh had fallen for it and was clearly enraptured. "I love that idea about online lessons! Why don't you—?" She turned to Mackenzie then stopped, frozen in place by the look Mackenzie gave her.

Adam cleared his throat. "I love your shop. Coffee and books, it's the perfect combination." If nothing else, the man had the sense to read the mood and change the subject, much to Mackenzie's relief.

"Thank you, but with so many people buying online, it's a worry," said Leigh.

"But online shops can't match this." He waved his arm at the setting. "This place has a nice, cozy, informal touch to it. You don't get that online. I'm new to this town but this is one of the places I like to hang out in."

"Oh, so you're new? That would explain why I haven't seen you around much before." Leigh glanced at her pointedly, as if this new revelation was something profound to absorb and reflect upon. "Welcome to Starling Bay."

He smiled, looking sheepish, and ventured another glance at her. Mackenzie wished he would leave them. He must have read her mind or sensed something because he told them he needed to be someplace else and quickly made his exit.

"He likes you!" Leigh exclaimed.

"He doesn't know me."

"Then give him a chance to get to know you."

She didn't want to do that either. "Why?"

Leigh looked daggers at her. "That guy was practically begging you to let him help you, Mackenzie. Why are you so afraid of people?"

"I'm not afraid, and he wasn't begging. You read too much into situations."

"Check your schedule about the dinner. We'd love to see you," said Leigh, getting up and walking away. "We know how busy you are."

With any luck, she'd have flowers to deliver to someone on that day.

But arriving home later to a rejection letter darkened her mood further. The department store had turned her down. The news kicked her in the stomach, adding more unease to an already difficult week. The store didn't want her flower arrangements and wished her good luck.

She'd hoped getting her upscale bouquets into the store might help her to spread the word about her business, but the department store not wanting to go forward with her deflated her spirits. Her heart sank. Every rejection hurt, even these ones.

She wasn't good enough. Her flowers weren't special enough. She'd been hoping to get another stream of income. The department store monies would have been a steady and guaranteed stream of income, and it wouldn't have required the time and effort it took to put together arrangements for special occasions. Sometimes she had to drive long distances after a long day at work.

There was only one of her and she could only do so much. And there were only so many bouquets she could sell. Her gift corner wasn't going to successfully explode sales overnight.

She needed to do something.

The advertising guru flashed through her mind. What he'd said about online classes caught her imagination.

She could teach. Heck, she'd held a little informal flower arranging class at Leigh's place one day, when she'd done a demonstration to a group of Leigh's friends. The women had loved what she'd taught them.

But online? She didn't know the first thing about teaching lessons online.

But that guru did.

She had to do it. She had to step out of her comfort zone and ask for his help.

CHAPTER 8

His inbox was full of glowing testimonials.

This man and his methods have changed my life!

Life had never looked better. His eBook continued to sell ridiculously well, and he was offering coaching to a small number of clients. There weren't enough hours in the day for him to take care of both businesses.

Something was going to have to give soon. There was also the slight problem of his secret identity. He wasn't ready to show his face. His clients knew that he was real and that he existed, but he'd started to get noticed by small news outlets. News about the Love Doctor was starting to cause ripples. His clients, the ones who'd found love using his methods, were super enthusiastic about him and wanted to tell the world about it.

He'd joined the Starling Bay online forum when he had first arrived in this town, and this was where he posted his services for his advertising business. But he had no intention of ever mentioning the Love Doctor services there. At the rate things were going, he wouldn't have to. He'd hit the jackpot. Word of mouth was the best form of advertising and it was absolutely free.

Who would have thought? He, a high school nerd, one of the uncool kids, had transformed into someone successful and self-assured? He leaned back in his chair, arms behind his head and grinned like the cat who had gotten all the cream, savoring the moment.

He continued to read through his emails and when his cell phone rang, he was so engrossed in the rave reviews that his fans were posting that he didn't pick up on time.

Instead, he played the voicemail while he copied and pasted the best glowing reviews into a file so that he could later post them on his website as testimonials to his system.

"Hi there, uh … Adam. It's Mackenzie. Um … I'm the one who you helped rescue from the, uh … plant pot. I was wondering if you …uh … I was interested about what you said about online classes or something. Could we meet to discuss?"

"I'll be damned." He listened to the message a few times. The smile on his face spread and stayed there.

She had called him, and she needed his help. He could do that. He could help her. She had lots of potential. He was in the middle of calling her back when his doorbell rang.

Damn it.

He'd forgotten about Patrick. *Eager* Patrick. The guy wanted a second consultation, and this time with 'actionable things he could do.' He opened the door to a smiling, slightly sweaty Patrick, and that's when Mackenzie picked up.

"Hey, I just got your message," he said. He put a finger to his lips as he ushered Patrick in. He had decided against renting a meeting room at the hotel and had asked him to come to his home even though having his consultations this way meant that he was blurring the lines between professional and personal life.

"Thanks for calling back." Her soft voice brought a smile to his face and he wished Patrick wasn't here.

"What can I do for you?" It was sweet, the satisfaction of having her call him for something. He'd felt like an irritating little pain during the few interactions he'd had with her.

"I wanted to know more about the online classes you mentioned, and I'd love for you to take a look at my marketing materials and give me your honest opinion."

He eyed Patrick—who was looking around his tiny apartment—as Mackenzie explained that she was interested in the online lessons he had mentioned. "I can do that. I'd love to do that. We should meet."

"How about on Saturday night?"

He almost choked. "Saturday night?" Did she not have a life? A date? A boyfriend? Anything better to do on a Saturday night?

"Or we can pick another date, if you have plans," she said hastily.

"No plans. No. I don't have anything else on Saturday. I can meet."

"Awesome. Let me check my journal and I'll call you back so that we can discuss where to meet and what time."

"Sounds good. I look forward to hearing from you." He fist pumped the air. What a win. That gorgeous creature who had caught his eye had called him because she needed his help, and now she was meeting him on Saturday night to talk about things.

He hung up feeling smug. That had almost been too easy. "That's how you do it," he boasted to Patrick. "You find something they need, something that's important to them and you work your way to them through that."

"I don't follow." Patrick's brow furrowed.

"Take this lady I just spoke to. I met her recently. She's nice.

She's gorgeous, but more than that, she's funny. She's interesting." He got up and walked around the room, hands in his pockets, talking more to himself than to Patrick.

"Is she your girlfriend?"

"No."

"Someone you're working on?"

"No." Adam's shoulder lifted. "And don't use that expression, 'working on'. She's not a piece of meat or a problem to solve. You want to be a friend first, Patrick. So, take this lady. She's worried about her business. Worried isn't the right word, she wants to do better. She has a need, and I can help her. If it's important to her, it's important to me, and helping her will make me feel good about doing something good for her."

"So you are working on her?"

"Patrick. What did I just say to you?" he wailed.

"But that's how you get her interested in you, isn't that what you mean?" Patrick asked.

"Yes. Kind of. It builds a connection, and that's what you want, a connection. How can you be interested in someone, how can you want to get to know her better if you don't even connect on that level to begin with? But she's not interested in me."

"Why not?"

"She probably has a boyfriend, or doesn't want to get close, maybe she has other things going on in her life. You have to gauge what's going on."

"But if *you* can't get a girl, dude, then how can someone like me get—"

"Patrick, stop." He could see that the main thing getting in Patrick's way was his self-esteem. The guy saw himself as a loser, and if that was what he thought, so would everyone else.

"My friend got the actress, but Jax looks like the kind of guy most women would—"

"Stop. Stop! I don't want to hear about your Hollywood

friends." Adam stared up at the ceiling, patiently counting the circles on the retro lampshade. He wondered if this was ethical—advising someone who was delusional. Patrick clearly needed the type of medical help he wasn't qualified to give. He sat on the couch opposite, a grave expression on his face. "I'm not sure I can help you."

"Not this. Not again." Patrick punched the sofa cushion.

Adam flinched. If Patrick was a psycho, he wanted to distance himself. He needed to get him to seek proper help.

"I had a meeting with my boss yesterday," Patrick continued. "I was talking to her, and asking her how she was and trying to find out if she had a boyfriend, and—"

Oh, geez. The guy was still chasing his boss. Adam stared at Patrick's face carefully. To all intents and purposes, he seemed normal. He seemed like just an average guy.

"Why would you do that?"

"Talk to my boss?"

"Ask her if she's got a boyfriend."

"Is that wrong?"

Adam tried to breathe slowly to calm down his frustration. "You can't just charge in and ask her what her status is. Women don't like that."

"Then what can I do?"

"You have to be subtle. First of all, Patrick, you need to relate."

"*Relate?*"

"You have to find what makes her click."

Patrick scrunched up his face in a ball of confusion. Adam wheeled his large whiteboard across the room. His living room doubled as his office space. "Today's lesson is about the ten rules of dating."

"Cool." Patrick's eyes turned wide and his posture indicated that he was alert and ready. "I read about them in your book," he said excitedly.

"Well, now I'm going to go through each rule one by one and we'll discuss each and every one."

"Dude, this is going to help me so much."

Adam pointed to his corkboard on which he had pinned up each rule on a brightly colored piece of paper:

1.Be nice! Treat her well, be kind, be courteous, be respectful.

2.Keep off social media. You don't need it. Be natural. Be you.

3.Act confident, and in time you will be.

4.Don't rush into things. Don't pressure her.

5.Call her, don't use email or text. Speak to her.

6.Connect. Find her Achilles heel.

7.You only have one chance to make a first impression. Don't waste it.

8.Look good. Dress to impress. Ooze confidence.

9.Give her all your attention. Turn your phone off when you're with her.

10.Don't talk about your problems or your past.

"Here they are. Nothing amazing, nothing ground-breaking or new here."

Patrick sat upright and watched as Adam wheeled his large whiteboard towards the middle of the room and started writing a few key words pertaining to each rule on the whiteboard.

"Number one, treat her well. Simple, right? Goes without saying."

Patrick raised his hand.

"Should I take notes?"

CHAPTER 9

She hung up, dread sinking heavy in her chest. What had she gone and done? How exactly would this so-called advertising 'guru' help her? He probably thought she liked him and was using the business help as a way to get close to him.

She called Leigh before she could change her mind and cancel the meeting with him. "I can't make it to your dinner party on Saturday. I'm meeting that guy …the advertising guy."

"You're meeting Adam?" Leigh shrieked, before ending the animated phone conversation with a "You go girl! And tell me all about it afterwards."

She was interested to meet with him and see if he was as good as he made out to be, but more than that she was interested in finding out more about the online classes.

He had left it up to her to decide where to meet, and she, not wanting him to come to her place, or for her to go to his, had settled for meeting in the hotel lobby of The Grand Hotel.

She couldn't fathom why but the thought of meeting Adam again made her jittery. This was just a business meeting, she told herself, and he was a marketing guy. She needed his opinion. What she didn't need was to keep thinking about him rescuing her that first night they'd met, or him coming by her shop for no reason and buying her flowers.

He seemed persistent, and now she'd somehow given him what he wanted. But she only needed him for his marketing expertise, that was all. She'd make sure he understood.

She had planned to meet him soon after closing the shop but when Saturday rolled around, and she'd called and spoken to her grandma to see how she was doing, she'd been concerned. Grandma hadn't sounded too well. Her voice was raspy and the exuberance Mackenzie was used to was gone. She'd been worried about her all day.

Risking being late for the meeting with Adam, she rushed off to check in on the one person who came first in her life.

"Mackenzie?" Her grandma's gray-ringed tired eyes danced with joy when she opened the door. Mackenzie hadn't told her she was coming over.

"Grandma!" Mackenzie hugged the elderly woman as tightly as she dared, not wanting to squash her delicate arms.

"What are you doing here? You didn't tell me you were coming over."

"I didn't want you to go to any trouble." If she'd forewarned her, she knew her grandma would have gone to the trouble of having dinner ready.

"Nonsense. It's no trouble at all, not for my Mackenzie. Come right on in."

"Mackenzie, this is a surprise." Her mother's voice pinched Mackenzie's insides. She had wished, against all the odds, that her mother might be out somewhere with a friend. Mackenzie didn't turn around to acknowledge her. "I'm not staying for long. I came to see Grandma."

"Still, it's nice to see you. I'm sorry about the other day."

Mackenzie ignored the apology and followed as her grandmother walked slowly into the spacious living room. This had been the family home once upon a time, and it was here that she had been raised, mostly by Grandma, since Grandpa had died way too soon before his time.

She sat next to her grandma and prayed that her mother would leave them in peace and let them be.

Unfortunately, no. Her mother walked in, a little hesitantly, as if she were trying to gauge Mackenzie's mood but, tonight, Mackenzie didn't have the time or patience to put up with her mom.

"I'm sorry about the other day," her mother repeated.

"You shouldn't have done that. I'm trying to run a business."

"I'm sorry, Mack—"

"Do you mind? I came to see Grandma." It was rude, and it wasn't the way a daughter should speak to the woman who had given her life, but this woman hadn't been a mother. She had given her life, had pushed her out into the world, but hadn't nurtured her or loved her. Hadn't even wanted her.

"I'll leave you two alone."

"That's good of you," Mackenzie snapped back.

"What happened?" her grandma asked when her mother had left the room.

"Don't worry about it, Grandma." Mackenzie rubbed her grandmother's gnarled hands gently. "How bad is the pain today?"

"It's not so bad. It's manageable."

Mackenzie didn't like the sound of that. She didn't want it to be manageable. She wanted it gone. "Are you taking your meds on time?"

"Yes, I am, now stop worrying about me. You always worry. Stop it. Your mother is taking good care of me."

"She is?"

"She is."

"It's about time she stepped up," Mackenzie grumbled under

her breath. She peered into her beloved Grandma's face, concern skewering a hole in her sides. "You don't sound too good."

"I must have caught a slight cold. I'm getting old and my immune system isn't what it used to be."

"Now *you* stop it." She hated it when her grandmother talked of age, and time, and how much she missed her grandfather. These words upset Mackenzie, because her grandmother had been a powerhouse, doing all the things that parents should have done, all the school things and then dealing with the teenage angst, boyfriends, and prom, and even the bullies, once Mackenzie had plucked up the courage to tell her. The love of her grandma had sustained her and each time she thought of her, a tidal wave of love swept over her. For all those who had made her life hell and made her go to bed in tears, all of that was forgotten the moment her grandma came in and kissed her. She would wipe away the tears and tell her that children could be cruel, that she was a beautiful girl who would grow up and do great things. "Be like the one and only Mackenzie, child." And she would kiss her and leave.

"Does she feed you?" If her mother hadn't lived here, Mackenzie would have stayed the night and visited more often, but she didn't want to inhabit the same place where that woman lived.

"She has been, yes."

Her mother coming back into her life after years of making random appearances was too little, too late. It wasn't enough. A simple apology wasn't enough. Attempts at communication would never be enough. The woman had never been a mother to Mackenzie, and there was no use in her pretending to be one now. She didn't have a maternal bone in her body.

"Your mother wants to turn her life around."

"It's a bit too late for that, isn't it?"

"She's a changed woman, Mackenzie. She's trying to make up for all the mistakes she made before."

Mackenzie didn't care. The woman could try as hard as she wanted; some things could never be rectified. Her grandma cleared her throat several times, as if something had gotten stuck in it.

"You need lozenges," Mackenzie decided. "Have you had any?"

"I'll be fine. It's nothing. At my age, this is what life is like, it's just a path of ailments and illness."

Mackenzie didn't want to hear such talk. "I don't like you saying things like that, Grandma." She got up and walked over to the kitchen where she rifled through the closets looking for medicines.

"What are you looking for?"

Mackenzie bristled at the sound of that voice and continued looking without answering her mother.

"Mackenzie? I've reorganized everything. If you're looking for the—"

But Mackenzie had found the small box of medicines and placed it on the countertop. "She's out of throat lozenges." When she'd lived here, she'd made sure it was stocked with everything that her grandmother might need. Now the box was only half full. "This is supposed to be full of medicines. Don't you ever check to make sure it's full?"

Her mother looked at Mackenzie. "She never told me."

"It's not for Grandma to tell you. Can't you see for yourself?" Mackenzie tipped the box so that her mother could see. "You're supposed to be the responsible one. You're supposed to look after her. That's why you moved back, isn't it?"

"I have all of her important meds, I just didn't think about the other ones."

"Grandma is becoming frailer, and her arthritis isn't getting better. Now she's got a sore throat. Could you tell? Did you notice? You need to be responsible, you need to be someone she can depend on."

"She's my mother, Mackenzie. You're talking to me as if—"

"I'm talking like an adult with responsibility. You don't even know what that word means."

Her mother's face crumpled. "I've made a lot of mistakes, and you have no idea how much I hate myself for—"

"Twenty years of mistakes?" Mackenzie hissed.

"Your father left and—"

"Don't keep blaming him."

"He broke my heart—"

"For twenty years?" She didn't want to engage in a conversation, yet these words that she'd never before said to her mother, now fell from her lips like unstoppable curses. "He left you for another woman and you were a hot mess for *twenty years?* Did you forget that you had a child? Did I not matter?"

Tears sprang to her mother's eyes. "You mattered. Of course you matt—"

She didn't want to hear it. Not now. Not ever. She wanted the regret to gnaw away at her mother from the inside and she wasn't going to give her the satisfaction of forgiveness. "That woman in there," Mackenzie pointed at the wall, "she's the most important person in my entire life. I can't have anything happen to her, do you understand?"

She grabbed her van keys and almost ran out of the door, shouting over her shoulder to let her grandma know she was going to the drugstore. She was going to be late for the meeting with Adam but her grandmother was more important.

She raced to the drugstore, picked up everything she needed then rushed back. "Here, Grandma." She opened the box and let her grandmother pick out a throat lozenge. "If this doesn't help after a couple of days I'll make an appointment for you to see the doctor."

"I can do that," her mother replied. She was hovering around the door.

"Will you?" Mackenzie asked. "Will you remember to, or will I need to check in and make sure?"

Her mother lifted her hand to her neck. "Goodness, Mackenzie. You're making out like I don't know how to take care of your—"

"That's because you've never taken care of anyone but yourself."

Her grandmother tugged at her hand, like a child wanting to get her attention. "Not now, Mackenzie. I don't want any fighting."

"Sorry, Grandma." She glanced at her watch, shock making her jolt as she saw the time. Adam would be waiting. "I need to go."

"Aren't you staying for dinner?" her grandma asked.

"Not this time, Grandma. Sorry. I have a meeting."

"A meeting?" Grandma's eyes sparkled with anticipation. She chuckled. "On a Saturday night? Is it a meeting or a date?"

"A business meeting." Grandma was as eager as Leigh for Mackenzie to find her soulmate.

"Are you leaving because of me?" her mother asked.

"I'm going because I have a meeting." Not even glancing at her mother, she enveloped her grandma in another soft hug and kissed her on the cheek. "I'll be back and I'll stay for longer next time."

CHAPTER 10

He wasn't sure what he should to wear. It was Saturday night, and this was a business meeting. He didn't know whether to go for a casual look, or a business one. If he wore jeans and a shirt, Mackenzie might think he wasn't being serious. Worse, that he might have assumed this was more like a date.

He was fully aware of what this was. He'd finally decided on formal attire; a dark suit and tie, but as he paced around the lobby floor, twenty minutes after the time she should have been here, he got worried. He checked his cell phone again in case she'd left him a message. She hadn't.

Was she backing out?

He put a finger inside his shirt collar, feeling the heat. Not a good look for someone who was usually so poised. The idea of Mackenzie backing out of seeing him tonight made him uneasy.

When another ten minutes had passed, he really didn't know what to make of it. A girl like that probably had many other and better offers for tonight. It was possible that she had completely forgotten about meeting him. He stared at the hotel entrance yet again, contemplating what to do.

But then he saw her. She rushed in and looked around, her face red. Their gazes locked instantly. She looked slightly disheveled; something he wasn't prepared for as she rushed towards him.

"I was starting to think you might not show up," he said, pleased to see her.

"Sorry I'm late. I had to go see my grandma because she wasn't well. I needed to get her some medicines. I would have called and told you but my cell phone battery died and I forgot my charger at home and—"

He tried to calm her down. "It's okay, Mackenzie. Don't stress. You're here now."

"I'm sorry."

"Stop apologizing. It's okay." Even late and obviously harried, she was a vision to behold with her corkscrew curls tumbling around her shoulders, and her large brown eyes making his insides melt.

"I was worried in case you had something planned later on."

He shook his head. "Nothing planned. This is the highlight of my evening."

She laughed at that, but it was the truth. "Shall we sit down and get to it?" he asked, eager to get down to business talk. He led her back to where he'd been sitting. "How is your grandmother?"

"She's fine. It was nothing serious. She's getting old and I worry about her."

"You're obviously very close to her." She clearly loved her grandma and was devoted to her, but it made him wonder more about that whole business with her mother in the shop a few days ago. Clearly, there were issues. He hadn't been able to reconcile the sweet woman before him now to the one who had been in the shop. The way she had spoken to her mother had shocked him, but as curious as he was, it wasn't something he would bring up just yet.

"I am. She raised me and I have a lot to thank her for."

"She raised you?" So much for him not talking about her personal matters. He hadn't been able to help himself.

"Yes." Mackenzie pulled out her marketing materials as they sat down. "These are what I currently use." She obviously didn't want to delve deeper into that conversation. He examined them carefully.

"That is actually very good," he said, looking at her brochures and her business card. She had a good concept of branding. "Did you use a company to get these ideas?"

"I did it all myself. I designed it online and then got everything delivered. It works."

"I don't doubt that for a minute. You have a great eye for design and color. It's not surprising given your line of work." At least she knew what branding was. Many of his clients had no idea. He liked the pink and black colors she used.

"I was more interested in hearing about the online classes you mentioned." She looked at him as if he had the answer to everything. She was eager and enthusiastic. Hard-working, too. All the traits he had and admired in others.

"Those would be a great way for you to supplement your income from selling flowers—"

"I don't only sell flowers, as you know. I do weddings displays and flowers for parties. I was trying to get my bouquets into the department store, but they turned me down."

"They didn't want you?"

"No." She made a sad face.

"That's their loss."

"But I was counting on it. I thought I had a chance,"

"Sometimes things are out of your control. Your designs are amazing, so I doubt it was that."

"Whatever it was, they didn't want me," she countered.

He sensed a hint of dejection in her words. They weren't so

different. She was selling gifts in addition to her flowers, in an attempt to make more money, as was he. Luckily for him his foray into the dating eBook market had taken off like a blast. Mackenzie was an expert, knowledgeable and talented in her line of work. He was not. He'd taken a chance by writing a book when he was no master of his subject. He was no dating god. He didn't even have a girlfriend. A few women had recently shown an interest in him, but he hadn't felt that way about them.

Mackenzie was different. Unfortunately for him, the tables had turned and she didn't seem to be interested in him. But she'd grabbed his interest from the first moment, even before he'd watched her fall into the flower pot.

"Don't take it so personally. You don't know what factors go into their decisions. I understand that you're upset, and I know that every little stream of income helps, particularly for small businesses like yourself."

"That's why I'm asking for your help. I want to look into doing online classes, but I'm not sure how that works, or if anyone would be interested in seeing what I have to offer. I also wouldn't know how to do one, you know, record it and put it up there." She pointed to the ceiling, as if the internet was mysteriously up there.

"Have you ever shown anyone how to make flower displays? Your work is so creative. I'm sure people would want to see how you do it."

"I have shown a few friends." She proceeded to tell him how she'd had a small class where she had demonstrated her floristry skills. Her face lit up as she spoke and her eyes sparkled, her voice tingled with excitement. Here was a woman who loved what she did. She created beautiful things, and she was beautiful herself, inside and out. But he hesitated to tell her that because Mackenzie wasn't a woman one could reel in with compliments, she didn't fall for pretty words and phrases. She didn't believe them, not if they were about her.

She was the type of woman who would run a mile, and he didn't want her to run a mile.

She loved what she did and she could teach others how to do the same. Her enthusiasm was infectious.

His line of work wasn't the same. He didn't share the same passion for his business work, and the dating side project wasn't his life's work. He certainly wasn't going to leave a legacy that would make him proud, even though the money would definitely help. His snobbery about the topic kept him in check, but at the same time, Jake had benefited, and Patrick would, hopefully one day, also benefit.

"If you can show people at a workshop, or a dinner party or any other live way, you can do it online and reach a much bigger audience. And you can go global. You won't be limited to just being local."

"But I don't know how to do it online." Mackenzie wrung her hands, flexing her slender fingers.

"Don't worry about that."

"That's good to know." The smile on her face looked more like relief.

"It's not too difficult provided you've got the right equipment. A smartphone or external camera for recording content, a microphone, lighting and video editing software."

The worry crept back into her features again. "I'm not techy. I can get by, but video editing software? I wouldn't even know where to start."

He rushed to reassure her. "I've got all of those things. I can show you. It's not that difficult once you know, I promise." He went on to explain the entire process because technology shouldn't get in the way of Mackenzie making the most of her potential, and he could see from her business, from her creations, that she had that in abundance. What he couldn't understand was her quiet, unassuming manner. Here was a woman who looked like a model, and yet, she didn't have the confidence or bravado of someone who could walk through life as if she owned it. This was a woman who had a fragility about her that made him want to not only help her, but to protect her, even though she didn't need protecting. She seemed delicate, not that she looked as if she'd fall apart any moment, but she had a soft and sincere air about her.

"That's it?" she exclaimed. "I talk and show them how to make a bouquet?"

"That's it. It's pretty simple. It's all about the content. Give your viewer a useful piece of content. Solve a problem, show them something, answer a need. You might need to think about it, how and what you want to do, so take some time and then we can discuss it further, if you like."

"Thanks, I'd appreciate that." She gave him a rare smile this time. One which lit up her eyes.

"I think your online classes could really do well. You focus on good content, and I'll work on optimizing it for the search engines, so that you'll be found online."

"I'd like to know how to do it all myself, eventually."

She didn't want to rely on him. An independent woman, wanting to make her own way. He liked and respected that.

"You'll get the hang of it in no time. I think you'll come across really well on the videos. People like to have a friendly face that they can relate to. They want to see the person behind the business."

She looked away, her brows pleating with unease. "But I don't want to show my face."

"Pardon me?"

"Can I only show my hands? So that the viewer sees just my hands and the bouquet I'm making?"

"Why would you want that?"

"Because I would." Her reply was slow, as if she was holding back on saying something.

"Viewers want to get a feel for you—"

A dash of fear skittered across her irises. "What do you mean by *get a feel?*"

"They want to see your face and get a glimpse into the personality behind the content." He didn't want to say anything about her looks, because she'd think he was hitting on her, but with a face like that, and her friendly manner, she would do exceptionally well. She suddenly looked uneasy.

"Are you camera shy?" With her pretty looks, she didn't need to be.

She evaded the question. "I'm guessing that people just want to see what I'm making."

"I think your views would go through the roof if they saw your face."

She chewed her lip. "But could we try it with just the hands?"

He didn't understand her reluctance to show her face. "Are you hiding from someone? Do you have a bounty on your head?" he joked. She could have been a model. Tall, slim, stunning. He didn't understand her hesitation.

He had been Adam with big glasses and retainers. A face full of zits too. Now he had no worries about his looks or his ability to charm people. Making a sale, attracting a new client, convincing strangers like Jake and Patrick that he could help them to find love—all of this was easy to do when you oozed confidence, and this he did in buckets.

Mackenzie was the same, or so he had at first assumed, and now she seemed hell-bent on sabotaging her success before she had even started.

"What are you scared of?" Her reaction alarmed him, but it served only to confirm what he'd sensed all along, a fragility that he hadn't expected from someone who looked as if life had handed her everything. How was it that this woman was so beautiful, but had no idea of it?

"I would just rather not."

She clearly didn't want to elaborate and he wasn't going to press her for an explanation even though he was dying to know. "We can do it your way. You can just show your hands. It's your call, Mackenzie. You can do whatever you want."

"And you'll help me?"

"I absolutely will."

They discussed the format of the lessons and the frequency of them, and he explained to her how it would work. He suggested she make a few videos which she would offer for free, and then, if she really wanted to do it, she could create a subscription site and monetize that.

"But that's for another day. I think we should start with the free videos first, and take it from there."

"I think so too." She let out a long breath. "You've given me so much to think about, I feel as if my head is going to explode." She smiled, and his heart did a little leap inside his chest. He'd spent time talking and discussing business matters, and he had enjoyed every moment of it. The fact that it helped her made him feel even better.

They arranged for the next time they would meet, when he would record her making a flower arrangement. She promised him that she'd think about what to do for the next few lessons.

He suggested they get something to eat. It was late, way after his dinnertime and he hadn't eaten. Neither had she, she replied, but she still turned him down, saying she had to get back.

He didn't push it, and he wasn't surprised. Mackenzie seemed determined not to blur the lines between her personal and professional lives and he wasn't going to push it.

CHAPTER 11

*A*dam Hartman hadn't turned out to be anything like she had assumed.

He was easy to talk to and pleasant, and he'd been a great help to her. But more than that, he hadn't pressured her into explaining the conversation with her mother, which he had clearly overheard in the shop the other day, nor had he pushed her to explain about her hesitation to show her face on camera.

She didn't want to be ridiculed anymore. She didn't want people commenting about her freckles, or her long, long neck. She didn't want people telling her she was a freak. Even though she no longer believed that, and was older and wiser, there was something daunting about having her face online. She didn't feel comfortable with that, and she most definitely did not want to invite trouble from nameless, faceless trolls.

She no longer believed the words that had fallen from the mouths of those nasty schoolchildren, but trying to forget what had come out of her mother's mouth had been almost impossible. Even as a child, she knew in her little heart that mothers were not supposed to say such things. Both parents abandoning her had created a type of hurt that had never gone away. That type of hurt lingered forever.

Adam had made her feel at ease, and that was a rare thing for her, to hit it off with someone so quickly. She didn't understand it, couldn't explain it. Not even when Leigh asked her about it a few days later when they met for lunch.

She told her that Adam had helped her with his concept of online classes. Leigh squealed at the idea. "You mean like the one you did for me, Jenna and Merry?"

"You liked it, didn't you?"

"You were so good. We loved it!"

"That's what I'll be doing. A lesson a week. I need to buy the proper equipment but Adam's going to help me do the first few shows."

"*Adam* is going to?"

"No need to sound so surprised. I'm paying him. This is a business arrangement. He's not doing me any favors."

"With the ad *guru* you didn't like," Leigh reminded her.

"What's the big deal?" Though she was all too aware of the big deal. She, Mackenzie, who never let anyone get close, who kept her distance, the woman who was friendly on the surface but would run a million miles if anyone—any guy—tried to get close, was now getting along well with Adam, so much so that they were making videos together. Sort of.

"It's a good thing you never found the time to ask Merry for help."

"Why's that?"

"Because then you wouldn't have needed to reach out to this guru." Leigh gave her a mischievous wink.

"This is purely business." Adam was helping her purely in a business capacity. There were no strings attached. It was all above board and Leigh getting all excited about it was going to be a waste of her time and energy.

~

Patrick was back in his apartment again, raring to get on with his third consultation in two weeks.

"I asked her out and she turned me down."

Adam slapped a hand to his forehead. "Your boss?"

"Who else?"

"Who the heck told you to go and ask her out so fast?"

"I followed your ten rules of dating."

"All at once?"

"I was nice to her, I was confident. We work together, so I see her daily. There's no need for me to contact her through social media. I didn't rush into things—"

"Given that she's your boss, I felt we needed to discuss things first."

"Yeah, but I was going by your rules."

"You're supposed to go through them slowly, Patrick. You're not supposed to go through them at the speed of light."

"I was taking a leaf out of your book. You hit it lucky with your florist."

"She's not *my* florist."

"But you said she was interested."

"I did not."

"But you're interested in her, right? Because you can't stop talking about her," Patrick pointed out.

Adam pressed his lips together, wishing he hadn't mentioned Mackenzie to Patrick at all. The guy was a loose cannon.

"I said she *wasn't* interested in me."

"But I'm getting the vibe that you want her to be," Patrick persisted.

Adam scowled, hissing under his breath. "Forget I ever mentioned her." His dealings with Mackenzie were off limits. He wasn't using his rules on her. He wasn't actively pursuing her. He was just being himself. She needed help and she'd come to him. He was in a position to help her and that's what he'd done.

Obviously, in the process of talking to her, he'd discovered that she was close to her grandmother, he'd figured out that there was some sort of issue with her mom. He'd stumbled upon her Achilles heel, but he was just being a human being, someone who listened.

Too many people didn't listen these days, in his experience, and that was the cause of many problems. From his experience, most people just wanted to be heard. Like Patrick. The guy seemed to live for his consultations. Adam didn't mind the guy so much now that he was getting to know him. Being relatively new to the town, he didn't have a circle of friends here, and this was a way of getting to know people.

But Patrick wasn't one to stop. "How are you doing with her, anyway?"

"Let's not focus on me."

"But did you see her?"

"See her?" He slapped a hand to his face. "When did I say that?"

"You said you had a date."

"It wasn't a date. I was helping her out."

"You spent Saturday night with her."

"I did not spend Saturday night with her," he snapped.

"But —"

"Give me a break, Patrick. I had a meeting and I helped her with an aspect of her business."

"Did you find her Achilles heel? And if so, can you explain how, because that's something I don't really understand."

No, damn it. He would do no such thing. "This isn't about me, Patrick. This is about *you*."

"Now you're angry with me."

"I am not angry with you."

"You're supposed to be helping me, Adam. I'm paying you all this money—"

"You don't need to come to me twice a week."

"I want results."

"You want a relationship and calling it a result is your first mistake. Your pursuit of a woman isn't a race, you're not a horse."

"I want something out of it. I don't mean that in a selfish or bad way, but I would like to have some company. Why can't I have that? What's wrong with me? 'Cause it sure as heck sucks being lonely."

Adam blew out a long defeated breath. "There's nothing wrong with you, Patrick. You just need to not be so intense. You want to woo a woman by making her feel special and caring about her. You want to be nice and treat her right, but you don't stand a chance with anything if she's not interested. There's something called chemistry and if you and your potential partner—your boss —don't have it, then nothing is going to happen."

"How do I fix it?"

"Fix what?"

"My boss. I asked her out and she shot me down. How do I get chemistry with her?"

Adam swiped his hand over his face in resignation. Patrick was no Jake Parnell. He was having to go back to the bare basics. "Maybe first we try to figure out what it is you like about this woman and why you want her."

CHAPTER 12

*A*dam was going to let her use his camera and equipment, and he was going to set up the lighting, and he'd edit the video afterwards.

He'd been so good to her. There was no way she would have been able to get this done without his help.

To get the recording underway, she had invited him to her shop on the Sunday, when it would be closed to the public. The pitter-patter of her heartbeat grew louder the longer she waited for him.

It was a business meeting, she told herself. It was just that and nothing else. She tried to still her beating heart as she glanced at her watch. There was no reason to be so nervous, and yet she was.

Promptly at ten o'clock in the morning, she saw Adam's face peering through the shop window. The sight of him, casual this time in dark jeans and a T-shirt, sent a tingle through her nerve endings. Something in her heart went POP!

Maybe she was coming down with a fever.

"I should have suggested a later time," she said, letting him in. Unlike her, he probably had a social life and might have had a late night. He shook her hand as he walked in. Something sizzled, coming off his warm palms, something real, causing her to steel herself from flinching.

"This is fine." He carried a bag which she assumed had the equipment. "It won't take too long to set up. Are you ready to make your debut to the world?"

She smoothed a hand through her hair. "As ready as I can be."

"Just be yourself. Forget that you've got a camera pointed at you."

The thought made her queasy, and it didn't help that he seemed more sure of her than she did herself.

"Where are we doing this?" he asked.

"In the room at the back." She had a large table and everything on hand in the workshop where she made all her arrangements. He walked in and gave it a once-over. "This is perfect." He got the camera out and started to set it up. "You still want it to be just your hands?" he asked.

"Yes."

He stopped and looked at her, disappointment and surprise lurking in his expression. "If you want my advice, Mackenzie, I think it would be better if we could see your face. Get a shot of you above the waist, behind the table. I can pan in and out onto the flowers as needed—"

"I'd prefer it to just be my hands, like we already discussed." She wished he would stop trying to get her to change her mind.

"Okay."

An awkward silence fell between them as she watched him adjust the camera. Her nerves were on edge at the idea of having to face the camera and demonstrate putting a bouquet together. Adam watching her added another uneasy dimension. "How long will this take? I don't want to use up too much of your time."

"Not long. Maybe an hour, maybe slightly more. I didn't have anything to do today, so, don't worry about using up my time."

"You haven't sent me an invoice," she reminded him.

"Don't worry about that—"

"I don't want you to do this out of generosity, Adam." She didn't want to feel obliged to him.

"The first consultation was free. I was figuring out what you were looking for. I'll send you the bill for this one."

Thank goodness. A sense of relief flooded over her. As nice and as helpful as he was, she didn't want to be beholden to him.

He rolled up his sleeves, revealing lean and wiry forearms, the sight of which sent her thoughts into a tailspin. She tried to look away, and failed.

"There, that should do it. Are you ready to start?" He caught her staring and probably saw the heat creep across her cheeks. The more he stared, the hotter she became.

"Now?" Panic set in and their gazes locked in a moment that seemed to slow down to half the speed. A hum, so low that it was wasn't audible, but it was definitely there.

From the periphery of her vision, she noted his shirt. Slim fit. Casual. Hanging out over his jeans. She didn't recall his shoulders being so broad.

"Now. If you're ready." His voice had dropped lower, it was softer, more like a caress.

"But what do I do?" She tried to shake herself out of this spell that they both seemed to be caught up in. He'd come to help her record a video.

That's the goal.

But she suddenly wasn't so sure.

"Just be yourself," he told her, his eyes not wavering from hers. "Pretend you're talking to your friends."

But this was different than doing a demonstration in front of Leigh's friends. Not only was she uncomfortable with the idea of the camera staring at her, and that this recording would be put online eventually, but Adam watching her closely made her skin heat. Her nerves coiled like binding vines and held her frozen. She didn't want to make a fool of herself, not in front of him.

He grinned. "Hey, don't worry about it. Just do your thing."

"My … my thing?" If he continued to stare at her like that, she wouldn't be able to focus. She'd come across like a fool, embarrass herself more than she had by falling into the pot. Dear God, why had she agreed to this?

Adam walked towards her, a move which caused her heart rate to spike. "Be like the one and only Mackenzie."

A shiver rolled over her. This man knew her. He understood her and he'd known exactly what to say to calm her nerves. Empowered by her grandma's mantra, a new belief set in. Those words had the power to move her, they inspired her to action.

"Hello, everybody …" The color crept up in her cheeks, warming them. She touched a hand to her face, conscious of every little move she made. "Should I say that? Or should I say something—"

"That's fine. Don't worry. You're doing great. We can edit things out, just be *you*, Mackenzie."

She blew out a breath. *Just be me. Just be me.* This man was channeling her grandma, and her grandmother believed in her. Maybe he did too.

She could do this. Taking a deep breath, she dove right in, telling the audience, the camera, Adam, who she was and what she was going to demonstrate today. She talked about the flowers and why she had picked them, and then started putting her bouquet together. It became easier. In that moment, she forgot about Adam, and the camera, and about the faceless and nameless people who might see this video.

Before she knew it, she'd finished making the bouquet. "And there you go, a simple little flower arrangement that is easy to do yet looks so stunning. This could be a perfect gift, or you can use it to brighten up your home."

Adam clapped.

"Was it okay?" she asked, her body tingling from an overdose of adrenaline. Her palms were suddenly sweaty, her pulse suddenly racing.

"Was it okay?" he echoed. "That was excellent! You're a natural."

"Tell me the truth, Adam. Don't sugarcoat it."

He frowned. "Didn't you hear me? It was brilliant. You didn't say um or uh a lot, many people do. You're a natural, Mackenzie. You had a bout of stage fright for a few seconds, but then you flipped a switch and you delivered it like a pro."

"So, it was good? We don't have to do it again?"

He looked at her as if he was puzzled. "We don't. This was really good. Your first time and in my opinion, it's good enough to edit and put up."

"Can we watch it?" She needed to see how she came across on the video.

"Sure." He stood next to her, real close so that their shoulders almost touched. Close enough that she could breathe in the familiar scent of his cologne. He hit play and at the first sound of her own voice, she flinched, bumping her arm against his, cringing with embarrassment.

"I sound awful!"

"You do not. That's how you sound."

"That's how I sound?" She was horrified. "I sound awful."

He seemed to think it was funny because he laughed. "No, you don't."

As the video continued to play, she couldn't bring herself to look at it. Thank goodness her face wasn't on display. Her voice was bad enough, and the hands she could tolerate.

"This is good, Mackenzie. This is great. It will only need light editing."

"Ugh." She squeezed her eyes shut in misery. She'd assumed

she'd had a slightly raspy, seductive voice, not this tinny, girlie aberration.

"Everyone hears themselves differently in their heads, but the truth is, what you hear on this recording is how you sound."

She wanted to put her finger in her ears but didn't. But when it got to be too much, she covered her face with her hands. This was excruciatingly embarrassing. How did he not think so? Adam pried her hands away. "You've done really well. There's no need for you to be so embarrassed."

He couldn't have felt it, but she did, the spark of electricity the moment his hands touched hers. She moved her hands away. "I'm not used to watching myself or hearing myself. It takes some getting used to."

"Have you ever done this before?"

"Never. This was my first time."

"That's hard to believe. The recording is almost perfect. Your content, and the way you presented it, it was all perfect."

He was paying her so many compliments that her usual believability detector kicked in. It had always been easier to accept cruel words than the compliments. Despite Adam pointing out that she very rarely used the 'um' and 'ah' words, she knew the only reason this had been smooth and polished was because she'd spent all day practicing it, out of the fear of looking like an idiot in front of Adam. It had obviously paid off.

"I'll get this edited and send you a link to the final version."

"How do I upload it? Also, you said something about the engine?"

"Engine?" His brows pushed together as he glanced sideways, looking momentarily confused. She couldn't help but take in his face, his neck, his shoulders. The way he looked in that shirt which fit him so well, outlining a physique she had never before noticed. Broad at the top, narrowing to a V towards his waist. "Oh, you mean the search engine optimization." He glanced down and caught her giving him the once-over.

Again.

Her mouth fell open, words, excuses, an explanation, vanishing in a haze of embarrassment. She stepped back, needing to put distance between them. Needing time and space to regulate the crazy beating of her heart. "Is … is that what it is?" She'd heard of the term.

"It's just a way for you to be found on the internet. I can take care of all of that for you." If he'd noticed her ogling him, she was grateful that he wasn't going to call her out on it.

"Thanks so much." She picked up the bouquet. "For you." She didn't know what else to offer him.

"For me?" he laughed.

"I don't know what else to give you."

"You don't have to give me anything."

"But you've helped me so much."

"That's more than enough for me. I like to help, and as I keep telling you, you have a great business, Mackenzie, and you can be making so much more money."

"How will *this* make more?" She didn't understand how she could make money from giving a free demonstration.

"It's free content. You reel people in by showing them how to make these stunning displays, and you don't charge a thing, and then—it's up to you—but you could open up a membership site, where you charge people for lessons."

Her eyelids flew open. "A membership site?"

"That's what I meant by online classes. Some call it a subscription model. You offer a service, in your case, how to make floral arrangements. I know of people who make thousands of dollars, some a lot more, every month from these types of sites. All you need to do is be an expert in something, and you clearly are."

"Wow. Thousands of dollars?"

He nodded, as if he was used to this type of reaction. "A couple of thousand dollars a month, you could reach even more, it depends."

"It would really help."

"Extra money always does. I would suggest that you make, let's say, five videos, and we offer these for free. So today's video would be the first one. You show people what you can do, show them how good you are."

She wasn't sure that people would pay every month to learn about how to make floral arrangements. Unless they wanted to set up a business doing such a thing. She suggested the idea to him.

"I can show them how to make the arrangements and all aspects of floral design, but I can also talk about merchandising, and how to set up the business and sell, because I've gone through this myself."

"That a great idea! You could definitely charge more to people who want to start a business, rather than if they just wanted to learn a hobby."

"I've been through the growing pains of getting Bloom set up, so I could pass on my knowledge." The idea lit a fire under her. All at once she could see the potential in such a model. She would never have thought of it had it not been for Adam.

"I'd be able to help my grandmother," she cried, seeing a way forward for the first time.

"You love your grandma." It was a statement, a fact, the way he said it.

"More than anything in the world. She's been the one constant in my life."

"Yeah?"

"My mom left when I was seven, and my dad left a few years before then."

He put a hand to his mouth for a second, but it was too late, she'd already seen the shock and confusion swirling in his eyes. "I'm sorry. I … I …"

"It's okay. Really, I'm okay." But he was trying to piece it together, the conversation with her mother that he'd overheard, and what she had just shared with him now.

"But your mother. She was in the shop—"

"I'd rather not talk about it. I'm sorry. I don't know why I told you." Why had she? She didn't do that. Talk to strangers, let them in, share her past, but Adam didn't feel so much like a stranger anymore, even though he wasn't what she would call a friend.

This was supposed to be a purely business arrangement, and why she had offered up a part of her life that normally took her months to tell anyone about was hard to fathom. She clasped her hands together. "I want to do this, the membership site." She nudged the conversation down a different path. An extra couple of thousand dollars a month for doing this? It was the answer to her prayers.

"We could discuss that today if you want?" His voice seemed softer, as if what she'd told him had made him see her in another light. "I'm hungry. How about we go to lunch and we can talk about this further?"

She would have taken him up on this offer, but she had promised to visit her grandma for lunch. The best part of it? Her mother wouldn't be at home.

She winced. "I'm going to see my grandma." She didn't like turning him down, especially after all that he had done.

"Lucky Grandma. I'll get this edited and you can let me know when you want to meet again, and we can discuss more about the membership sites."

"Thanks, Adam. I'd appreciate that. I know nothing about membership sites. I wouldn't even know where to begin."

"Don't worry. I'll help you."

"Thank you. That's exactly what I need. I'm glad you rescued me from the flower pot." She wanted to inject a touch of humor after the conversation had taken a more serious turn.

"Me too." His suggestion to have lunch together told her that he didn't want to leave. Neither did she. Something had shifted between them, but she couldn't yet define what it was or why.

"We could meet for lunch next Sunday?" she suggested, feeling bad for turning him down when he had been so gracious with his time and help.

"Next Sunday?"

"Unless you're busy," she added.

"I'm not busy. My calendar is free."

"Then let's do lunch." It was a forward move, something she never did, but with Adam Hartman, it just felt right.

CHAPTER 13

*W*ine glasses and pizza adorned the cozy little table in Leigh's kitchen. It was perfect for a Friday evening after work when the two women could catch up and unwind after a busy workweek.

Mackenzie had finished telling her friend about her recording session with Adam and the new video she'd made but Leigh was less interested in that and more interested in Adam.

"Is he charging you for any of this?" Leigh asked.

"Yes, he is. It's business and nothing else, so don't go getting your hopes up. I'll buy my own equipment if I decide to pursue this, and he'll teach me everything—"

"He'll teach you everything?" Mischief sparkled in Leigh's eyes.

Mackenzie ignored her friend. "I want to see how it works out first. Adam's got to edit it and then I'll see what happens once we've uploaded it online."

"Have you found out whether he's single or not?" Leigh picked up a piece of garlic bread.

"I don't know. Why would I know?"

"You could ask him." Her friend's eyes opened wide, into a why-would-you-not stare.

"Why would I do that?" Mackenzie shot back.

"Why not? He's smart and good-looking, interesting too."

"I should take a leaf out of your book, you mean?"

"You can write poetry, if you want," Leigh replied. "Adam might appreciate it with him being an advertising man. He probably has a flair for words." Leigh seemed eager for something to flourish between her and Adam, and she didn't mind her friend's matchmaking ideas.

As far as she could tell, Adam was single because, like her, he didn't appear to have anything else to do but work. He never had calls from anyone who sounded like a girlfriend, and he had been free every time Mackenzie had suggested they meet.

He'd been eager to talk to her when they'd first met and he'd shown up at her shop soon after and given her a bouquet. And now he was helping her with the business.

She was almost ninety-nine percent certain that he was single. Just like her.

But unlike her, he was smooth, confident and at ease. He was a lot of things, as she was beginning to discover. She found herself thinking about him more after that first recording, and her insides bubbled at the thought of seeing him again. He was a busy man, really busy, but they had agreed to meet at The Olive Tree this coming weekend.

"What did I miss at your dinner party?" Mackenzie asked, not ready for Leigh to continue dissecting her interaction with Adam.

"It was really good. Merry is as big as a house. Jenna and I are planning her baby shower."

"Already?"

"The Frasers haven't wasted any time. Merry was only supposed to come here for a short break a few Christmases ago. Now they've married and having a baby."

"Good for her." Mackenzie didn't understand the speed with which some people moved. How did you know that someone was 'the one'? How?

"Reed was giving us more anecdotes about the Love Doctor," Leigh announced.

"From *that* guy?"

"Yes, that guy."

"Go on. What did he say?"

"Reed's contact says that the guy he knows who used his services isn't so sure about him anymore."

"It's all very vague, getting news from a friend of a friend of a friend ..." Mackenzie reached for a slice of pizza and picked an olive off it. "It all sounds like a lot of rumors and no hard facts. I bet it's all hype." She plopped the olive into her mouth.

"But the book exists," Leigh countered. "We had it open on an eReader and the guys were reading out the rules."

"Tell me."

Leigh refilled their wine glasses, then massaged her temples. "Let me remember. There was something about being spontaneous. Uh ... giving a woman all of your attention. Not using the cell phone. Being nice—"

Mackenzie was flabbergasted. "Being *nice*? That's a rule? Seriously?"

"It's in the book, I swear. Something about being nice and treating her well."

"As opposed to?" Mackenzie cried, incredulous.

Leigh stared down at the table before reaching for her wine glass. "Not all men treat women nicely, not all men are nice. It's not automatic for some men."

Mackenzie swallowed, then put her hand over Leigh's. "I know. I know." The light and easy mood had dipped into solemnity. Mackenzie let her friend take a sip of her wine.

"Maybe there is a niche for this type of book after all?" she said softly.

"We should write a book for women," Leigh suggested. Mackenzie observed her carefully, glad that her friend wasn't languishing in echoes of the past.

"We should. But do women need to be told how to pursue men? You didn't."

Leigh had a way with words and she'd pursued Rourke in a romantic fashion. It had been really quite sweet.

"Agreed. We don't need to know how to find a partner," Leigh remarked. "But if there was a female Love Doctor, would you go to her to fix your romantic problems?"

Mackenzie shook her head. "No, but that's because I don't have romantic problems." She gave a lopsided grin.

"I wish to high heaven that you would," said Leigh, sighing. "Then you'd get to experience the little problems, like … I can't even think. Like him leaving the toilet seat up."

"That wouldn't be a little problem."

"And constantly underestimating how long things take. Like, Rourke will say it'll take him fifteen minutes to get some gas, and he comes back two hours later because he met Reed and Dylan on the way and they ended up in a bar."

"But, to answer your question," said Mackenzie thoughtfully. "I wouldn't seek the help of a Love Doctor. Women don't need to seek out other people because we have our own network of close friends to fall back on and talk to, and to get help if we need it. I have you, right?" Mackenzie raised her wine glass as if making a toast. Leigh touched her glass to it in agreement.

"Men don't talk like we women do," Mackenzie continued. "They don't even have coffee and cake time."

Leigh waved another piece of garlic bread at her before she took a bite. "We talk it out and get help that way. We find answers, and get advice, we know what to do, or we ask someone. But men…"

"They don't have such networks." Mackenzie finished the sentence for her. "Or close friends they can talk to about their problems."

"Men pretend they don't have problems," countered Leigh. "And yet they think nothing of going to a complete stranger …a *Love Doctor*, paying him for advice." Leigh wrinkled up her nose as if merely talking about the guy brought a rancid smell into the room.

In solidarity, Mackenzie did the same. Love Doctor was a sleazy name. Like something out of the '70s. 'The Love Doctor,' Mackenzie recoiled and shivered in disgust. The idea of a man who made a career out of advising men on how to court women sent shivers down her spine. She didn't even want to think about his ten rules of dating.

"Talking about his book made for good dinner conversation. I wish you'd been there," said Leigh.

"Maybe next time."

"Maybe next time you and Adam could come together, as a couple—"

"Will you stop it?" Mackenzie sat back in her chair, her stomach full, her head swimming with happy thoughts of Adam and all he was doing for her.

CHAPTER 14

"*I* want my money back."

"What?"

"Gayle and I broke up."

"What?" Shock stunned Adam. He'd only been to the couple's engagement party not so long ago.

"Yeah, you heard right. We split. We were having too many arguments and it was just getting to be too much. It wasn't working, so we called it off. I want my money back."

"You're not getting your money back," Adam replied calmly. Whatever it was that had gone wrong between this couple, it wasn't his fault.

"What the heck do you mean? It's because of you that I'm in this mess."

Adam's jaw was so tight he felt his muscles harden. It didn't surprise him that Jake was blaming him for his relationship breaking down. The guy had seemed to be a bit of a douche when Adam had first met him, and he now wished he'd followed through on his gut feeling and hadn't taken him on. "I didn't sell you a product, Jake. I gave you advice and guidance."

"I followed your dating rules. Fat lot of good they did me."

"You made progress. You maybe went too fast, but you made progress and you got engaged." Too fast most definitely. The guy had gone from meeting the woman to getting engaged in under two months.

"And what a waste that was. You tricked me."

Adam scoffed. This guy was hinging on ridiculous. "Tricked you? I tricked you into meeting and dating someone? Can't you hear how pathetic you sound?"

Anger marked Jake's face, twisting his expression. "We weren't a good match. We were like chalk and cheese."

"I only advised you on how to treat a woman, I had nothing to do with finding her for you. That's on you, not me, so don't try to twist it to be any other way," Adam snarled.

"Give me my money back."

"Keep your voice down," Adam looked around the lobby of the hotel. He pinched the bridge of his nose. If he'd known that this was why the guy had wanted to meet with him, he wouldn't have come here. He couldn't help this guy. "Calm yourself down. I don't offer money back. I don't offer a guarantee. Our agreement was for me to teach you the ten rules of dating in the hope of giving you a better chance of finding someone without all of that social media nonsense. You're hurting. I get that."

"Just cut the bull—"

Adam couldn't believe his ears. "You listen to me, and you listen carefully. My rules aren't what caused the breakdown of your relationship."

"But you—"

"What I told you is common sense. That's all it is."

"Common sense? Don't pass it off as common sense just because you don't want to pay me back—"

"Sue me."

Jake swallowed. "What?"

"Sue me."

"I might just do that."

"Adam?" The familiar voice made his heart flip. He spun around and found himself staring into Mackenzie's surprised face.

She fixed him with a questioning gaze.

"Hey. What are you doing here?" Fear clawed at Adam's belly. How much had she heard? He stood up placing himself in front of Jake, hoping to block him from view.

"Is that Jake?" She sidestepped his question. He remembered; they knew each other. Mackenzie had done the flowers for Jake's party. Memories of the flower pot and that first meeting with Mackenzie flooded back and Adam hung his head in resignation. This could not have come at a worse time or place.

"You're the flower lady." Jake's voice behind his shoulder told him that Jake was also now standing.

Mackenzie flashed a friendly smile. "That's right. I did the flowers for your and Gayle's engagement party."

"So you did." Jake looked and sounded less than enthusiastic.

"It was a beautiful party," Mackenzie enthused, standing unaware in a landmine of problems.

"What are you doing here?" Adam asked her, trying to step in and hijack the conversation.

"I was delivering flowers for a convention that's taking place here."

"Jake's a client of mine," he said, needing to explain.

"A *past* client." Jake's surly mood was impossible to cover over. He could see that Mackenzie wasn't sure what was going on. But she wasn't stupid. Anyone could see that he and Jake had been in an argument.

"We'd better get going." He nodded in Jake's direction. "We have a couple of things to discuss."

"Me too," replied Mackenzie. "Have a good day."

He exhaled a breath he hadn't even known he was holding.

"I'll see you on …" He tried to remember when they were next meeting, but he couldn't see beyond the fog of chaos in his mind.

"Sunday," she reminded him. "Sunday at lunch time at The Olive Tree."

He watched her leave the hotel, needing to make sure she had left before he continued the meeting with Jake, and wondered how much damage this meeting with Jake had done.

Hopefully none. He tried to convince himself that Mackenzie had been too far away to hear anything.

His secret was safe. For now.

"I see why you made me sign a piece of paper." The corner of Jake's lips curled up into a sneer.

"What's that?"

"I know why you keep your name and reputation as far away from this Love Doctor baloney as you can."

"Will you keep your voice down," Adam hissed. This guy was going to cause him big problems if he wasn't careful. "You've signed an NDA."

"NDAs don't mean squat," Jake threatened. Adam swallowed uneasily. Most NDAs didn't stand up in court, and there was nothing really stopping Jake from revealing Adam's identity.

He had to decide for himself if he wanted to be known as the Love Doctor. Was he ready to make the switch to his newfound accidental career? A vision of him in a cheesy afternoon chat show made his stomach gurgle.

Maybe this was his gut reaction.

There was nothing suave and sophisticated about being known as a Love Doctor.

And Mackenzie? What would she do if she found out who he was and what he did?

CHAPTER 15

That had been most odd.

Two grown men having a loud and angry disagreement in public. Goodness knows about what. The last time she'd seen Jake Parnell had been on the night of his engagement party and he had been the epitome of happiness. She'd felt slightly envious watching him and his fiancée. They had looked so happy and in love. She wondered if Jake and Adam were friends who had fallen out, or if theirs was a business meeting.

She pushed it out of her mind and looked forward to seeing Adam on the weekend, though a part of her regretted her suggesting that they meet for lunch. She was a sucker for kindness, and she'd felt obligated towards him because he'd helped her. This was her problem. This deal between her and Adam was a business arrangement, and she should have remembered that. He was doing his job and she was paying him for it.

It really was as simple as that. Complications, such as having lunch before they shot the second video, were unnecessary.

When the day of their lunch came around, she got ready,

spending far too much time than was necessary trying on different outfits. She wasn't sure if she should wear jeans or capri pants. Did she want to look casual? Or a little professional? Staring at herself in the mirror, with her black capris and white linen shirt, she decided that this ensemble was too fancy. It would look as if she'd tried too hard. The casual look would be better. Hastily climbing out of her pants, she put on a pair of faded jeans and headed for the restaurant.

In her haste, she'd arrived early, and so decided to wait for Adam at the table. Ordering a fruit juice for herself, she wondered if this was too informal a setting?

Lunch for two.

So cozy and intimate.

Was she sending out the wrong message?

Was she somehow implying that she liked him?

The last time they had recorded a video, she'd been left thinking about him, what he'd said to ease her, his words of encouragement, the way he'd left her feeling and thinking about him long after he'd left her shop. Her insides churned in turmoil, sparking a riot of unease inside. At this rate, she wouldn't have much of an appetite.

"Hey." A light tap on her shoulder made her look up and into Adam's smiling face. Her senses stirred, her breath caught in her throat and goosebumps popped up all over her skin. No one had ever elicited such a physical reaction in her as this man did. It was a conundrum her frazzled brain couldn't figure out.

"Sorry I'm late. I had a last-minute client call me as I was leaving." He was so relaxed, so jovial, so charming, that her doubts suddenly slipped away.

"Are you late? I think I'm early."

He sat down, and all her nervousness melted away. She lifted her glass of juice to her lips. "You always seem to be busy. You must work twenty-four-seven."

"Don't we all?" He summoned the server and ordered a soft drink for himself. "I bet you're always thinking about work," he stated. He was right. She was either working or visiting her grandma. Only Leigh's interventions by way of dinner, or a girlie catch-up, enabled her to have some social time.

They went on to discuss their businesses and the trials and tribulations of working only for yourself. Then they ordered their meals, and more drinks, and continued to talk. It seemed like a normal lunch with normal conversation.

Why had she been so worried?

She was touched when he asked after her grandmother and wanted to know if she was feeling better. These little things were important. They told her that he'd listened, that he'd heard, that he was interested in the things that were important to her. A lot of men, in her experience, weren't as attentive, so meeting someone like Adam was refreshing.

Settling into their camaraderie as if she were pulling a soft cashmere blanket around her, she was emboldened, as if she could ask him anything. So, she did. "You and Jake, are you friends?"

His smile dipped, only for a second. "Friends?"

"It sounded as if you were having a disagreement the other day."

"Ahh." He placed his arms on the table, folding them together as if he'd suddenly turned serious. "Not everyone is as easy to work with as you."

"So it was business? I wondered." She grimaced. "I must sound really nosy."

He refilled his glass with sparkling water from the bottle. "That's okay. I hadn't realized we were being so loud."

"I couldn't help but overhear." She hoped he wouldn't think she was being too inquisitive.

"I guess most of the people in the hotel lobby must have heard." The muscle along the side of his jaw twitched. "Did *you* hear what we were talking about? It was supposed to be a confidential business matter. I shouldn't have held a business meeting in the lobby."

She tilted her head, considering his overly long explanation, and shrugged. "I didn't hear a word, it was just the tone, the loud voices."

"I gave him advice and he … well, let's just say he didn't like it."

She sensed slight discomfort, as if he didn't like her talking about this. "It's nothing. I shouldn't have even brought it up. I was surprised to see you both arguing, that's all."

He waved it off as nothing to worry about. "That's the problem with some of my clients. They don't want to listen to my advice."

"Maybe they should. Your advice is gold. I would never have thought to do what you suggested. Online things aren't on my radar, although online shopping is! I can shop online for the world."

A smile crept on his lips. "The online revolution is the way of the future, so I'll do whatever I can to help you get some business that way." They shared a warm smile. She no longer saw him as a pushy salesman. Thinking about it, Adam had never been pushy. He wasn't trying it on. He hadn't dropped her any pick-up lines. He wasn't the one who had suggested they have lunch today.

"I really appreciate your help."

"You're welcome. This is a turnaround, huh?" He picked up his glass and brought it to his lips. "You didn't want to give me the time of day when we first met." His eyes were filled with amusement and his tone was light but, still, an uncomfortable laugh slipped from her lips as she recalled the first time they'd met.

"I didn't know back then that you'd have so much knowledge that I would need."

He nodded. "Glad to be of help. Always." He looked as if he'd been about to say something, but he looked away instead.

"What?" Too many lingering stares, short-lived silences made her curious. Did he think about her the way she had started to think about him?

"You seem really close to your grandmother."

"I am." An explanation was in order, she could tell from the unasked question percolating in his eyes.

"Do you want to talk about it? You don't have to."

"But you're wondering why my grandma raised me, and given that you heard the conversation with my mother, you probably have questions."

"I do, but you don't have to tell me."

"I've already told you that my parents left me. My mom blamed me for my father leaving."

"But it wasn't your fault." Adam's soft voice was filled with compassion as he stared at her, his face somber.

"She seemed to think it was. She said—and I remember this because some words you can never erase—she said she hated me because having me changed her, it changed her body and messed with her mind, and because of that, my father didn't find her attractive anymore, so he went looking for someone else."

Shock stunned Adam's face. He opened his mouth but was speechless to say anything.

"My mom also suffered from post-partum depression which made their relationship even more rocky. My grandmother said that he came back when I was born, probably out of guilt, and maybe because he'd realized he had a new child, and had responsibility. My mother forgave him, but things were never the same and they still continued to fight like crazy. It got to a point where he couldn't take it anymore and walked out a few years later, to return to his mistress. But, just before he left, he told my mom that he'd lied and he'd been seeing the other woman the entire time."

"I'm … I'm so sorry." The way he looked at her, his expression soft and sad, and ripe with understanding, made her want to get it all out, the dark cancer that had been harboring inside her. She didn't do this, open up, confess, share her past, but with Adam, it seemed harder not to. He reached for her hand, placing his big, soft palm over hers.

"I felt like it was my fault for a long time."

"But it's not. You know that, don't you? What happened between your parents was not of your doing."

"I know that now, but it took me a long time to realize."

"That's a heavy burden to carry." He squeezed her hand gently, his warmth sending waves of comfort, her hand absorbing them greedily.

"It can be. I try not to think about it. I don't know why I'm telling you now." Ordinarily, her past would have been off limits to anyone else, but it didn't feel difficult talking to Adam about it. She didn't open up to anyone, and here she was letting the floodgates open wide.

"Do you have any memories of him?" he asked.

"Just a few. Visits to the park. They're blurred. I don't remember clearly. I know we fed the ducks. I know we laughed. I know he bought me ice cream. He obviously wanted an easier life." She forced a laugh, even though her vision blurred, her eyes turning moist.

"Don't cry, Mackenzie. Don't get upset thinking about the past. It's gone. It can't hurt you now." He moved his chair closer so that they were almost sitting side by side instead of being opposite. "Hey." She shook her head, about to tell him that it was okay, trying to compose herself and avoid catching people's attention, but his arm reached around her shoulder, and he pressed her to him. In the blink of an eye, it was only the two of them here. The other diners and servers eclipsed out of her world. "Hey. You're not alone, and you're not that small and defenseless little girl anymore. You're so much stronger because of everything you have suffered."

"I feel sorry for that little girl who was so unwanted." She blinked, not wanting the tears in her eyes to overfill and fall. Tensing her muscles, hardening herself, she fought to regain composure.

"Not by your grandmother," he said quickly. "Your grandmother treasured you. I can almost see your love for her. It's in your eyes, in your smile each time you talk about her."

"Yes," she whispered, fighting for composure, but inside she was losing the fight to hold it all together.

"Why did your mom leave?" He looked so sad as he asked her, as if this was something personal to him. She wiped a finger under her lashes, trying to blot away the wetness.

"She turned to alcohol and got hooked on meds. She was heartbroken. I didn't know why at the time, but thinking about things now, it seems her broken heart never recovered. She'd gotten into bad company, tried to find that type of love again, but she never did. I don't think she ever stopped blaming me, just like she never stopped loving him. She used to say it was my fault she'd lost her figure and had suffered from depression. I never forgot those words. In the end, Grandma told her to leave before she damaged me forever. Grandma said some women don't deserve the privilege of being a mom. Anyway, my mom got a job elsewhere, and that's how she lived her life, only coming home every now and then. I didn't see her much as I grew older, but I didn't miss her either. I didn't have any strong connection to her. She didn't do for me the things moms are supposed to do. She wasn't a mom to me. My grandma was and she still is. She's my everything. She made me the person I am today. I love her unconditionally, above all else."

Adam was silent, and then slowly, the corners of his lips turned upwards. "She helped you to name your shop. It's such a fitting name, Bloom."

"I think so."

His eyes, soft and warm, took away the misery that remembering the past had brought back. "You're going to be fine, Mackenzie. You already have so much. You make beautiful arrangements, and you brighten up everyone's day."

Did she? She looked away when he held her gaze so intensely.

"We should get going," she said, glancing at her watch. "We've been sitting here for two hours." She'd only planned on an hour for lunch, and she'd ended up telling him most of her life story, opening up to him in a way she never had with anyone.

"I'm sorry I asked too much." His gaze slowly trailed over her face, as if he was checking her sadness, the concern in his eyes a salve to her brokenness.

"You didn't. It was me. I don't know what came over me. I'm not usually so open with … with …"

"With?" He stared at her expectantly.

She didn't know what label to use. "With people I don't know that well."

A laugh rumbled through him. "You'll get to know me pretty well by the time we've done all your videos." His expression turned somber. "How about we do the video another time?"

"You don't want to do it now?" Panic charged through her. She'd bored him. Or worse, he was filled with pity instead.

"I have a client I need to call, and we're running late, so … how about we meet tomorrow? After work, perhaps? I can come to your shop."

She wasn't sure if she believed him, but revisiting her past had drained her, and she wasn't in the mood to make a video.

"Tomorrow, then."

CHAPTER 16

She looked defeated, lost, alone.

He wanted her to know that she was none of those things. Each time they were together, the air between them changed, deepened, electrified. He couldn't put a name to it, couldn't explain it rationally, but this woman affected him like no other. He wanted to be her protector, her friend, her confidante. Something more, if she shared the same feelings.

He'd told her a little white lie about why they couldn't record the next episode. He didn't have a client waiting. Even if he'd had someone, he would have canceled that meeting and made room for Mackenzie instead. He wanted the best for her, and telling a little white lie had seemed like a good idea.

The truth was, he had seen how upset Mackenzie was, and no matter how much she tried to hide it, the pain of her past was so vivid in her eyes. The camera would have picked it up, and something would have been off.

A mother who said such evil words to her child didn't deserve to be a mother. Mackenzie's grandmother had been right about that. He couldn't imagine how much damage those words did when they burrowed deep into the psyche of a child.

Now he understood why Mackenzie doted on her beloved grandmother. That woman must have been the rock in the young girl's life, and he was glad she'd been there for her.

As they parted ways and he drove back home, he couldn't stop thinking about her story. It made everything about her fall into place. He now understood why she seemed unsure and hesitant sometimes, and the vulnerability he had picked up on before now made sense.

He turned the radio on, then switched it off again because the tune was too bouncy, too poppy, too full of life, and he didn't feel like that. Mackenzie's childhood story had left his heart feeling heavy. He'd been so lucky to have loving parents and a family life that had grounded him. A glimpse into Mackenzie's life had revealed the wounds of those who weren't as lucky. He was even more determined to do what he could for her.

The next day, when he had finished with his clients, he went to Bloom. The 'Closed' sign was on the door, but he knew it would be open. He hesitated, his hand on the door, watching Mackenzie as she swept the floor. She wore her hair up today in a thick ponytail swept back from her face, and it revealed her features starkly; the high cheekbones, the big eyes and full mouth. She was beautiful, inside and out.

The more he got to know her, the more he found himself liking her. It was getting so bad that she was taking up all his mental headspace.

Just then, she looked up and caught him watching her. Even from where he stood he saw the color creep into her cheeks. She tucked away a stray lock of hair behind her ear then clasped her hands on the broom handle. Their eyes locked for a few seconds more until he pushed the door open and walked in.

"You looked so deep in thought, I didn't want to disturb you," he said, feeling the need to explain while his insides tightened in embarrassment.

Lame line. Lame excuse.

"I'm only sweeping the floor, Adam."

"I know but …" *You caught me staring.*

"I was rushing to get everything clean." She put the broom away, and all he could do was marvel at the mane of curls trailing down her back. "Come on in." She beckoned for him to follow her to the workspace at the back.

He started to set up the lighting and his camera and tripod. "Did you want to see the first episode again?" He rolled up his sleeves as if he was about to get his hands dirty.

"Has anything much changed?"

"I've added an intro, a little music, I've done a few edits and I've added opening credits. I can take them off, if you don't like them, but I felt it needed something. Curious to know what you think."

"It sounds like a great idea, and I'm sure it's perfect." She rubbed her hands together and walked over to him. "Let's see what you've put together."

A scent of roses wafted to him, and he couldn't tell if it was from the actual flowers or if it was her perfume. He hit the 'Play' button and Mackenzie's head nudged closer towards the camera. It only had a small window. She was standing so close just in front of him that he could smell the zingy scent of apple in her hair.

This was torture, standing so close to her and thinking of her the way he now did. He'd sensed something deeper, something layered in her, but he'd never expected her childhood to be wrought with so much pain. It drew him to her, made him want to protect her from hurt like that again. She'd been a stranger when they'd first met, but he suddenly felt as if he'd known her for all his life. It was the most peculiar of feelings, to know her without knowing her.

"I like the music. Did you create that?"

He nodded.

"Is there no end to your talents?" she asked, glancing over her shoulder and giving him a side profile of a cute little upturned nose, her wild hair flowing out of her ponytail.

"It's easy enough to do. There's a website where you can quickly put these things together."

"I love it. Thanks, Adam."

"You're welcome."

They watched the rest of the recording silently. She made it look so easy, the way she brought different colors and varieties of flowers together, so that by the time she had finished arranging them together in a bouquet, tied together with a pretty ribbon, they all complemented each other beautifully.

When it finished, she turned around and stared up at him with her dark eyes.

"That wasn't so bad," she stated tentatively.

Talk about the understatement of the year.

"Are you kidding me? That was brilliant. You're so talented, Mackenzie. You shouldn't have such little faith in yourself."

He'd noticed before that she wasn't sure of herself, that something held her back, but now he had a better idea of what that might be.

Until she'd opened up to him, he hadn't known what to make of it. He wasn't used to seeing women who outwardly had so much going for them hide from the limelight.

Businesswomen. Women who looked the way she did. He had dealt with plenty of women who had confidence coming out of every pore. They were so sure, so full of themselves sometimes. It was a good thing until it spilled over into something else, something ugly and big-headed, bordering on smugness. A feeling of *I am better than you.*

Mackenzie was nothing like that. He had found her self-effacing ways sweet, but then later he'd wondered if it was an act.

That maybe like him she, too, might be hiding something. But she was hiding nothing. All that she was she let him see. If anyone was being dishonest, it was him.

He stopped the recording. "I can upload that as soon as we finish the rest of the videos."

"I'm working on those. Maybe we can record the others all on the same day, if you can fit me in?"

"I'll be able to do that, and that's a great idea." He worried that he was making his feelings for her obvious, and that was why she wanted this done quickly.

"You're a super busy man." Her doe-like eyes stared back at him and it was impossible to look away.

"I make time for my important clients." She was as fragile as glass, as soft as silk, a conundrum, a puzzle, a riddle for him to work out.

"Important?" She gave him a rueful smile instead. The things she had shared with him came back to him. Here was a woman who looked like a model but didn't see herself the same way. Here was a woman filled with hurt because she'd been rejected by the two people who should have made her the center of their universe, but instead they walked away and left her. He wanted better things for Mackenzie, he wanted to take her pain away, and he felt defenseless that he could do nothing.

"We should get started," she mumbled. "We don't want to run out of time like we did yesterday. Did you meet your client on time?"

"Client?"

"You said you were meeting a client yesterday." The innocent look she gave him made him feel even more guilty.

"We didn't run out of time." He couldn't lie. Not even a little white lie. The secret he was already keeping from her was bad enough.

Her brows knitted together as she waited for him to elaborate.

"You were upset, Mackenzie, and I didn't think it would be a good idea to shoot a video then. The camera picks up everything that the human eye can't."

A frown shuttered her expression, her eyes pinned to his face as she tried to understand. "That was … that was … that was very thoughtful of you," she said finally.

"I could see your pain, I didn't like it. I see you more as a friend now … instead of someone I'm doing business with." He let that sink in, waited for her response, curious to know how his words would be received.

"That's very kind of you," she mumbled, raising her hand to push back a lock of hair behind her ears. "Um … you don't have to worry about me. I shouldn't have mentioned it—"

"I'm glad you trusted me enough to mention it."

She gave a nervous laugh. "We should get started now though, because I don't like taking up too much of your time. I feel as if I'm always asking you for things."

"I don't consider it as taking up too much of my time. It's more like spending time with a friend."

Her shoulders sagged, her body relaxing. Those words made her smile. "Okay, *friend*. Let's get this next episode recorded." She moved over to the other side of her large table, brushing the conversation aside, refusing to delve deeper into it. In the blink of an eye, she reverted to business mode as she laid her materials out on the table.

He adjusted the camera on the tripod. She flapped her hands together, as if she was trying to get her nerves in order. "Do I look nervous?"

Now there was a question he had a million answers for. "No, you look perfect."

"Are you going to count me down? Maybe we should get a clapper board like in the movies?"

"How about I just do a one, two, three, and we roll on three?" he offered.

"Okay. Let's keep it simple." She brushed her hair away, pressed her lips together, even though she didn't have any lipstick on as far as he could tell. He was just about to start recording when he it occurred to him to mention it one last time.

"I really think you should let the audience see the real Mackenzie."

"The real Mackenzie?" Then she realized what he was referring to. "No, I told you before, just the hands."

"Okay." He wasn't going to push it. "One, two, three." He hit the record button and watched her. She barely umed and ahed. Her performance was so polished that he wondered if she'd spent hours practicing it and perfecting it.

When she finished, he stopped recording, and rewound to the beginning to have a look. He quickly ran through the recording, checking in different places, but what he saw looked just fine. "This will require minimal editing. You're that good."

"I practiced for hours," she confessed, as she started to tidy up the workspace, ignoring his compliments.

"You are," he insisted. He began to dismantle the props.

She walked over to him and held out the bouquet she'd just put together.

"For me? *Again?*"

"I don't know." She stared up at him through her thick lashes.

"You don't know whether you want to give it to me?"

"I don't want your girlfriend to get suspicious each time you go home with another bouquet."

"I assure you, that won't be a problem because I don't have a girlfriend."

"Then this is yours." He gazed at her outstretched hand, at the luscious arrangements of purple and white flowers flecked with green. As he reached for the bouquet, his hand brushed

Mackenzie's and held there longer than was necessary. Warm, and soft, and hard to let go of.

This shoot had been different, and with Mackenzie confiding in him, something smooth, soft, and velvety was unfurling between them. The touch of their hands sparking *something*. It became intimate, their proximity as they worked together, his quiet admiration as he recorded her, watching her as she created something magnificent in front of his eyes. Unsaid words and feelings swirled in the air with the promise of becoming much more.

"Whoa! Am I interrupting something?"

He glanced over his shoulder, the shock of a different voice jarring the moment. He recognized her. It was the owner of Books & Buns. Mackenzie pulled her hand away as if she'd touched hot coals. An awkward silence descended, killing the buzz that had permeated the air.

"We were recording another episode," Mackenzie explained, moving away from him and leaving him standing with the bouquet in his hand.

"She has a talent." He showed her the bouquet Mackenzie had gifted to him.

"She has bags of talent." Leigh reached for the bouquet and smelled it, gazing at it in awe. "It's insane the way she throws these things together." She went to hand it back to him but he didn't take it.

"You keep it. Mackenzie won't mind. I already have the first one."

"The first one?" Leigh stared at them both in turn, feigning mock surprise. "You mean to say she gives you all the things she makes?"

"I've only made two," Mackenzie replied defensively.

Her friend examined the camera.

"Careful. That's expensive," Mackenzie cried, raising her voice.

"Relax. I'm not going to break it. Can I see what you recorded?" Leigh turned to him for permission, but before he could reply, Mackenzie answered.

"Wait until it's edited and we've put it up on the internet."

"Why can't I see it now?"

"It won't need much editing," he stated, wanting to ease the tension he sensed between the two women, something he didn't understand. "Mind if I show her a sneak preview?"

Mackenzie folded her arms even more tightly. "If you must." He showed Leigh a few minutes of the recording.

"Why am I staring at your hands? Why aren't you showing your face?" Leigh asked her, perplexed.

Mackenzie made a groaning noise. "Not you, too."

"You're as bad as that creepy Love Doctor."

Leigh's words were like a Taser to his chest. *They knew about the Love Doctor?*

"Ugh, hardly," said Mackenzie. "Not even his customers know what he looks like."

"Who?" He tried to keep his voice level despite the rising level of panic creeping up from his stomach. This was the first time he'd come face to face with women openly discussing and, from the sounds of it, hating the Love Doctor.

"The Love Doctor, have you heard of him?" The angry look on Leigh's face indicated that she wasn't a fan.

"It sounds like the name of a movie or a song." He hoped to feign complete ignorance.

"If only. He's some guy who's sold a book on dating. I'm surprised you haven't heard of him." Mackenzie frowned at him. "Every guy your age has heard of him."

"I don't think it's just his age," Leigh butted in. "*Most* guys have probably bought the book. It seems to have gone viral. Him and his stupid dating rules." Leigh's sarcasm hit like a bullet.

"He's coaching men on how to find women," Mackenzie sniped. The women gave each other looks of disgust.

Leigh shook her head at him. "And no one knows who he is."

"I'm not as bad as he is," Mackenzie cried defensively. "Stop comparing me to him. Just because I choose not to show my face. I have a shop, my customers know me in person, there's a picture of me on my website. I'm not hiding. I'm just not sure about these videos going online and attracting new customers. There will be people I don't know, and you know how cruel trolls can be."

"You don't have to show your face. It's not necessary," he answered, desperate to change the subject. "We want to focus on what you're making, and the demonstration is the most important part of it."

"It is?" Leigh asked. "Won't it be more personable if the viewer can see Mackenzie's face?"

"I agree, but with a face like that, people won't be able to take their eyes off her." In his haste to stand up for her, he'd inadvertently told the truth. *His* truth. His thoughts. His opinion.

Both women stared at him as if he'd announced he was running for president.

"I'll, uh ..." Leigh started to walk towards the door. "I'll come back later," she said, glancing over her shoulder at Mackenzie.

"Leigh gave me a ride today," Mackenzie explained. So *that* was the reason her friend was here.

"Great. Then we're done for tonight." Her friend was her ride home tonight and he didn't want to get in the way of that. "You let me know when you're ready to record the rest," he said to Mackenzie.

"Let's set a date now," Mackenzie suggested. "I'm eager to get these recorded and uploaded."

She stared at him, an invisible thread running the length of the gap between them, maintaining a connection which had been almost broken when Leigh had walked in.

"You could come over to my place, if you want," he suggested.

"It would save you having to carry your equipment all the way here." She chewed her lip thoughtfully while twirling a lock of her hair around her finger.

"It would." But that wasn't why he'd made the suggestion. He didn't mind carrying his equipment anywhere, for Mackenzie. But at least if she came to him, her friend Leigh wouldn't show up unexpectedly.

"I'll check my journal and call you," she said, leaving him feeling hopeful.

$\sim$

"Don't say a word." Mackenzie turned her back to Leigh and started to clean the table.

Leigh had such bad timing sometimes. If she hadn't come, she and Adam would have talked for a while.

It had been some time since she had enjoyed the company of someone like him. A guy. A guy who might be interested in her. She sensed he was because of the way he looked at her sometimes, and the number of times she'd caught him staring.

Very few men made an impression on her, but Adam certainly had.

"I told you he's helping me. We were shooting the second video." Her cheeks heated as she swept up the leaves and petals that had fallen to the floor.

Leigh was being silent. Mackenzie put the broom up in the corner, then turned around and grabbed her bag, making haste to leave. "He's helping me. I'm looking for ways to increase my income and Adam has some good ideas."

"I haven't said a word," Leigh exclaimed. She opened the door and stepped outside. Mackenzie switched off the lights and locked the door.

"He's friendly and helpful." But that wasn't the reason her fingers still tingled from his touch. She had met plenty of friendly and helpful people during her time in Starling Bay, but she'd never experienced the light and giddy feeling inside that came from being around Adam.

It had been a while since she'd floated on air.

This meeting with Adam filled the empty hole inside her. She looked forward to seeing him again, yes, it was business but, somehow, their interactions seemed to be morphing into something else. Something warm, and soft, something which made her insides bubble.

"I told you he was nice when I saw him at my coffee shop," Leigh maintained.

"There's nothing going on."

"I didn't say there was."

"I'm just saying."

"You're being very defensive for someone who's only recording videos."

CHAPTER 17

*D*id she suspect?

More than ten days had passed and still he and Mackenzie hadn't been able to meet. Each time he'd called to suggest they get together, she'd said she was busy.

It was obvious.

Things had been going so well between him and Mackenzie that for her to suddenly start avoiding him indicated that she was suspicious. She'd put two and two together, from witnessing his loud disagreement with Jake, to her friend commenting about the Love Doctor. Since then Mackenzie had been low-key.

Desperate to find out for sure, he decided to pay a visit to Bloom; he had ordered more books so he needed to go to the bookshop to pick them up. It would be a good excuse for him.

On his way to Books & Buns, he saw Patrick walking out of Fellini's with a glamorous woman at his side. A guy in a biker's jacket walked alongside them, but it was the woman next to Patrick's side that caught his attention.

Adam blinked.

The woman was laughing, and she was talking to Patrick.

Patrick. Not the other dude. Patrick was making her laugh. Adam stopped walking, distracted by the sight.

"Hey, Adam!"

He flinched. Patrick had seen him. He lifted his hand in acknowledgment. It was too late to pretend he hadn't seen them. Patrick beckoned for him to come over, so he begrudgingly did.

Patrick slapped him on the back, obviously happy to see him. "Hey, dude. These are my friends I was telling you about." He gestured at them. "This is Jax, and this is Hailey. *Hailey Ross.*" Something about the way he said it made Adam take notice.

The actress flashed him a warm smile.

Holy cannoli.

She was absolutely stunning.

The guy hadn't been lying. He hadn't been making it up, and yet Adam had completely dismissed Patrick's words as fantasy. Not only did he know this woman, but he seemed to be good friends with her. Hailey Ross was Monica Martins in the big blockbuster Hollywood action movies.

He had doubted Patrick's words and considered them as hogwash.

"This is the guy I was telling you about." Patrick jerked his chin at the guy in the biker jacket. "He used to work with me at the mall."

"How do you know Patrick?" the biker guy asked, wrapping his hand around the actress's possessively.

"We're just … acquaintances," Adam replied carefully. Then changing the subject quickly, he asked Hailey Ross how she was finding Starling Bay, only to be told that she'd been born here.

"But I came back recently and fell in love with this place all over again," she replied. She and the biker guy locked hands and looked into one another's eyes, seeming to forget that he and Patrick were there.

She was a vision of beauty, all straight white teeth, full lips and beautiful eyes. But she couldn't hold a candle to Mackenzie.

Mackenzie,

He needed to go see her.

"It's been nice meeting you," he said, a phony laugh slipping from his lips. "I didn't believe Patrick when he told me he knew you."

Patrick's brows shot straight up. "You didn't?"

"But, now I see you're such good friends," he said, breaking out into a full smile. "I should have known you wouldn't joke about such things." It would do no good for Patrick to know what he really believed. "I wasn't sure." He'd assumed that Patrick was a fantasist, and now he felt ashamed. He was more determined than ever to help Patrick find the woman of his dreams.

Patrick beamed back. "We need to meet." He moved in closer so that only Adam could hear. "There have been new developments."

"What sort of developments?" Adam wanted to know. Now that he'd realized Patrick's friends weren't imaginary, that Hailey Ross was in fact *the* Hailey Ross, he needed to come through for the guy.

"Developments," whispered Patrick, his face lighting up. Adam dreaded to think what this might mean. "I'll explain later."

"Don't tell me you've gone and asked the CEO of your company on a date?" He glanced at Patrick's friends. The starry-eyed couple moved away and were talking, lost in their own conversation.

Patrick's brow creased. "I wouldn't do that, because the CEO is a *guy.*"

Adam slapped him on the back lightly. "You worry me. See you around, buddy. Call me."

"Sure will, dude."

Instead of heading towards Books & Buns, Adam went

directly to Bloom. Mackenzie's reaction would tell him right away if she suspected him of being the Love Doctor or not. That woman couldn't hide her feeling if she tried, and he liked that about her.

"Hey." She looked surprised to see him. "Long time no see, stranger."

He cocked his head. "You're calling me a stranger?"

She narrowed her eyes at him. "Ye-ees." It was a slow reply.

"It's just that you haven't been," he started to say, at the same time she started to talk.

"Everyone and her best friend is getting married or having a party. I've been crazy busy. The past few weeks have been insane."

"They have?"

"Yes. What's wrong?" She had a bunch of flowers in one hand and a ribbon in the other. He tried to gauge her mood, but it appeared to be genuine, and that soft look in her eyes told him she was pleased to see him. "So, you haven't been avoiding me?"

"No."

His paranoia had run loose. She didn't suspect. She had no idea. He cleared his throat. "I thought you wanted to get all of your videos recorded and uploaded as soon as possible."

"I was, I am. Nothing's changed."

"But I haven't been able to pin you down—not that I want to pin you down, not like that …that's not what I mean."

Her gaze turned quizzical, as he blubbered uncharacteristically. "Each time I called, you were always so busy…"

"That's what I've just told you. I have been busy, Adam. I wasn't brushing you off, in case you had that crazy idea in your head." When he didn't reply, she lifted a questioning eyebrow. "You really thought I was avoiding you?"

He had, yet again, embarrassed himself. He was supposed to

be in charge. He was supposed to have it together and be that cool, collected guy who knew how to handle these things. He charged clients for this stuff. People came to him to be coached on this.

He was the Love Doctor, for crying out loud.

But in this moment, he'd reverted to that high school nerd again, awkward and stilted. "I wasn't sure."

"Why would I do something like that when you've done so much for me?" She tilted her face up at him. Her smooth soft skin, those high, high, high cheekbones he was so tempted to touch. He took a step back.

"I don't know, Mackenzie. I don't know."

"What don't you know?"

He lifted his hand, as if he was going to touch her face. Except that he couldn't. There were boundaries to respect. She didn't think of him like that. It didn't matter what he thought—nothing mattered unless she felt the same.

"I assumed you were avoiding me."

"Why would I avoid you, Adam?"

Because you think I'm the Love Doctor. "Don't worry about it. It's a guy thing. You don't know what it's like when we have to make the moves and all you girls have to do is pick and choose."

Dig a deeper hole, asshole.

"Who's making a move?" Curiosity widened her eyes.

"No one. Not me, that's for sure. I'm not making a move on you."

"I know, Adam. Relax." Her full lips curved up into a smile, and he couldn't tell if she was laughing at him or with him. This woman brought out the high school geeky nerd in him. Around her, he reverted back to a blubbering, anxious skeleton of a man who said the first thing that came to his mind.

Her arms folded and her eyes fixed him with a let's-see-how-you-get-out-of-this-mess look.

"I thought we were getting along. I was just shocked that everything's gone so quiet now, that's all."

She stepped towards him. "We are getting along." There was a huskiness to her voice that hadn't been there before.

Oh, boy. Was it possible that she felt for him the same way he felt about her? "In that case, forget I said anything."

"Done." She flashed a smile that melted every ounce of worry away.

"I ran into one of my clients," he told her, eager to move to safer territory.

"Anyone I know?"

"I saw that actress, the one in the Monica Martins movies, with her boyfriend."

"Hailey and Jax?"

She referred to them in first-name terms. "You *know* them?" Every person in this place really did know everyone else. It was starting to worry him.

"Hailey always buys a truckload of flowers when she's here."

"When she's here?"

"She divides her time between LA and here, and her boyfriend, Jax, does the same now that they're together. He's Roxy's brother, the woman from the diner. Didn't you know?"

No, he did not. "I'm still a newcomer to this place," he reminded her. "Does everyone know everyone else in this town?"

Mackenzie laughed. "It's not that bad. Unless you have something to hide, in which case, forget it. Secrets are never safe here."

He forced a laugh. "Of course not." But a worry nibbled away at him. He'd picked the wrong place to move to. At this rate, his secret would soon be out. Maybe he should have considered moving to Alaska.

His secret hadn't seemed like such a big deal until now. He didn't like keeping anything from Mackenzie, and even though there was nothing between them, the thought of lying to her unnerved him. The woman had already been let down by so many people before and he didn't want to be another douchebag to add to that list.

A few customers walked into the shop and he stepped to the side to let Mackenzie tend to them while he waited. She was busy; this much he could clearly see, and this was just in the shop. With the added work of making and delivering arrangements to special events, Mackenzie clearly had a lot going on.

She came over to him. "How about we record the rest of the episodes tomorrow? If you're free, that is. I've prepared the content for them."

He was always free when it came to her. "Sure. We could do it tonight. I'm free tonight."

She winced. "I can't tonight. I've got a meeting."

A meeting, or a date? "A meeting?" he asked, his breath hitched as he waited for her reply.

"The SBWEB meetups."

"The what?"

"It's a small group of business owners and entrepreneurs who get together and talk about what they do."

It was only a meeting. Hope was not lost. "I haven't heard about those."

"That's because you're a man," Mackenzie pointed out.

"Pardon me?"

"It's short for Starling Bay Women's Entrepreneurial and Business." She went on to explain that there were informal meetings held every month or so by a group of women entrepreneurs.

"Someone like me can't attend?"

"No, but there are monthly meetings in the town hall—"

"I know. I've attended a few. Don't you go to those?"

"They're too big and not as effective, and I don't like them.

The women's meetings are friendlier and not as daunting, and we can discuss our own businesses in more depth."

"You have to do what works for you," he replied. The monthly town hall meetings were good for networking, and between that and the online forum, he had done what he could to advertise his marketing skills. "We can meet tomorrow. I'll come here again with my equipment," he offered, because it was obvious that her busy schedule made it impossible for them to meet. She was probably too tired after work to go over to his place.

"Are you sure? You'll have to carry your things over to my place again. I don't want to put you out so much."

"It's not a problem." She wasn't putting him out. He wanted to help her as much as he could, and with his eBook income doing so well, he wanted Mackenzie to experience greater success as well. She was capable of it, she deserved it. If he could do it with a dating book, he was confident she could do it with her business.

"You always say that," she threw back with a smile.

"Because it isn't, not for you."

CHAPTER 18

"And that concludes this meeting," said Francine, owner of the local recruitment agency, and the woman who usually chaired the SBWEB meetings. "Unless anyone else has anything else to share?"

Roxy raised her hand. "Have any of you heard about the Love Doctor?"

"You too?" Leigh cried.

A chorus of exclaim rippled around the table. Francine raised her voice. "Clearly we do have something to discuss! What Love Doctor?"

"I heard that he coaches men in the business of *lurve* ..." The women burst out into hysterics and the conversation soon turned to who this man was and what he did.

"Jackson says that one of his friends has the book and he swears by this guy," Roxy said. "He said something about the ten—"

"Rules of dating," Mackenzie and Leigh chimed in.

"But maybe some men need guidance," suggested Francine thoughtfully. The serious part of the meeting was over and the gossip and fun part had started. Half of the women had slipped away, leaving the regulars who were always slow to leave.

"It depends on what he's teaching them," Leigh shot back.

"He might be doing good," said Francine. "He might not be as bad as you think."

"Are you dating this guy?" someone asked, "because you're being pretty defensive about him, Francine."

The women laughed.

"No!" Francine cried.

"But she has a point," said Mackenzie. "Maybe this guy's intentions aren't so bad. Maybe he just wants to help these poor guys."

"Does anyone know who he is? I'd like to interview him." This request came from Lisa who worked at the local paper.

"Now *that* would be interesting!" someone cried. "You'd get to find out his identity for sure."

Cries of "Yes!" and "Do that!" rippled around the table.

"Why is he hiding?" Leigh asked, her eyes blazing with fire. "If he's doing such good work, *helping men*, as Francine seems to think—and goodness knows some men need all the help they can get—then why is he hiding?"

Mackenzie lifted an eyebrow when Leigh leveled the question at everyone around the table. She didn't know, but she had given more thought to Leigh's comment about her not showing her face. Was she hiding, too?

"Why don't you track him down, Lisa, and interview him, and we can discuss him at the next meeting?" Francine suggested.

Raucous laughter erupted. "Better still, we should invite him along to the next meeting as a guest."

"I'd sure like to ask him a question or two." Leigh took a final sip of her sparkling water.

"I'll do what I can," Lisa promised. "Watch this space."

"Great seeing you all." Francine started to say her goodbyes and they all followed suit, hugging and kissing one another on the cheek, saying their goodbyes. This group of women had become good friends.

When she had first moved to Starling Bay, Mackenzie had known no one, but setting up her florist's shop had been a fast way to get to know the townspeople and other businesses.

She and Leigh got into the van and talked about Lisa tracking down the elusive Love Doctor.

"She'll find him, make no mistake about that," mused Mackenzie. "If anyone can reveal who he is, Lisa can."

"Speaking of men, what's the latest with the advertising *guru*?" Leigh switched on the inside light.

"We're going to try to finish recording the rest of the episodes tomorrow."

"Nice. I can't wait to see them."

"Adam says he'll get them edited as soon as possible and then he's going to set me up with a membership site." She went on to explain it in detail. "He says if I provide free content to draw viewers in, then I can attract people who might be willing to pay for the—"

Leigh yawned, rather loudly and rudely. "I don't want to know about the business. I want to know about *you two*."

"There's nothing to say." She'd done nothing but think about that evening in her shop before Leigh had interrupted. She had walked in on something. There had been a shift in their friendship, in how she and Adam were around one another. Their conversation had slipped away from making videos to her childhood and they were getting to know each other, only, he seemed to know more about her than she did about him.

"You said he's been quiet lately, and you haven't seen him much."

"He came to the shop yesterday, said he needed to find out why *I'd* been quiet."

"Have you?" Leigh asked.

"I've been busy. You know how crazy things have been lately. Each time Adam called, I couldn't talk properly."

"Are you actively trying to stay single forever?" Leigh asked, crotchety irritation in her voice.

"No." And then, thinking about it, "I like him," she blurted out.

Leigh grabbed her hand. "Say that again, just so that I can be sure I heard you correctly."

"I like him." Maybe it was the darkness inside the van that made it easier for her to confess, to not guard her emotions as much. "I haven't liked someone in a long, long time."

"You can say that again. This is monumental, Mackenzie."

"But I'm not sure that he likes me. I kept him at bay, right from the start, and he was interested back then, at least I think he was. I don't know why I do that—sabotage things before they've had a chance to get started. I pushed Adam away before he'd gotten anywhere close, and now it's too late to give him another first impression."

"Maybe because of what you went through as a child," Leigh suggested. "You never really knew your dad, and then with what happened with your mom … We shouldn't believe the monsters. I'm sorry for calling your mom that, but—"

"It's the truth."

"But at least your mom is trying to make amends now," Leigh said softly.

Mackenzie sighed. "She shouldn't waste her time, and I'm not interested." Things were especially difficult now, what with the double whammy of the gift corner not doing so well and the rejection from the department store. Added to this she could no longer rush to the home she grew up in, could no longer stay over for days at her grandma's place whenever she needed to rest and recharge. But Adam provided some respite and for that she was grateful.

Leigh squeezed her hand as if to comfort her. "I'm not pressuring you to do anything about that situation. That's your call, but I'm here for you in case you need to talk about it. But I want you to know that what your mom said to you isn't the truth and letting it simmer inside you gives it a power it doesn't deserve. We allow those words to sink into our core and we start to believe them, but they're not true, Mackenzie. They never were, and they never will be. You thinking about the past only makes it more real to you in the moment."

Mackenzie stared straight ahead, her thoughts twirling into the darkness before her. "I've moved on. I have." She was a big girl now and she didn't care about the bullies, but the worry about trolls was on her radar due to that experience. She had become strong, because Grandma had believed in her. She'd become Teflon-coated, and cruel words could no longer stick and hurt, but her internal survival system made her react in a way that shut down her emotions. She'd done this with Adam, and she was starting to regret it.

"Adam sees what we all see in you, Mackenzie. You're gorgeous, funny and effervescent."

"Effervescent? That's a new one."

"You never seem down or upset about anything."

This wasn't true. She simply managed to hide it well, that was all, but with Adam lately, she'd started to be more of the real Mackenzie. No guard. No pretense. She didn't have to pretend. He'd seen her raw emotions, naked and vulnerable.

"But *effervescent?*"

"I'm sure Adam would agree. You said you like him, I bet he likes you back."

"I wish I could tell for certain. He's wonderful. He's ... everything all packaged up and –"

"And at your door, helping you." Leigh air-quoted the last few words.

"He's been amazing."

Leigh let go of her hand. "I've never seen you gush before. It's eye-opening."

Mackenzie swatted her friend lightly, then turned the ignition key.

"You have to stop believing hurt words," Leigh said.

"Hurt words?"

"The ones people throw at us like knives, to wound us, that's why they do it. Don't believe them, because they're all lies. I'm not just talking about the bullies and all the names they called you. Your mom hurt you too, but don't let the past get in the way of having a great future."

Mackenzie threw her friend a sideways glance. "Have you been reading many self-help books lately?" Her friend always had great advice to offer whenever Mackenzie needed it, but tonight she was overflowing with it, like a waterfall, gushing with no end in sight.

It was true. Adam made her feel good. He made her feel like she could achieve anything. The compliments he showered her with after each recording boosted her confidence. She was good at what she did, and she knew that because people told her. What Adam gave her was an inner self-esteem. He was unlike the men she had met before, and finding someone genuine like him, trusting someone not to hurt her, was a big step.

CHAPTER 19

The next evening, Adam returned and they shot the remaining episodes quickly. Maybe because she had practiced a few times at home by herself, she was able to jump in and get into the flow much quicker. As always, Adam was patient and full of encouragement, which helped. It also made her no longer feel shy in front of him.

"And it's a wrap," Adam stated in mock excitement as he turned the camera off.

"We worked fast." She noted the time on the wall. "We raced through that."

"Because you're a natural in front of the camera, and you love what you do, so your enthusiasm shines through. Those are stunning." He nodded at the three arrangements she'd created. One was in a vase of water, one was a horizontal display, and one was a wedding bouquet.

"Thanks. I've been practicing a little every day so it all flowed as if I was on autopilot."

He started to pack away the camera. "Your delivery is so professional. You come across as very polished."

"Thanks. If I come across as polished, it's because you're

always so inspiring, Adam. You make me feel as if I could do anything."

He stopped what he was doing. "You can do anything." He stared at her as if she were Wonder Woman, as if she really was wearing the tiara and the cape. The silent moment bloomed into something potent, and she could feel their conversation veering off again from business talk to uncharted waters.

"You see, there you go again. I bet you do that with all your clients."

He laughed. "Not all of them."

"Is Hailey Ross a client? Or is it her boyfriend?" She'd forgotten to ask him earlier.

"Uh … no … neither of them. Their friend is."

She started to clear away the table she'd been working on. "Anyone I know?" She risked being nosy because Adam didn't give much away even though she had opened up to him.

"I don't think so."

That was an odd reply. The chances were she wouldn't know the person, even though the network of connections in this town was like the roots of a tree—wide and deep.

"How's that going?" His glance shifted to her gift corner.

"Not too great. What I make from that would probably enable me to buy dinner once a week." Not as many people as she hoped liked to add candles or bath bombs to their purchase. This was why she now had her hopes pinned on earning from teaching floristry lessons online.

"Are we talking about a Fellini's dinner, or something from the diner?"

She laughed at his analogy. "A Fellini's dinner."

"That's not so bad, then." He gave her a look of encouragement.

"I'd hoped for better results, but it seems like getting people to buy more isn't working."

"This, what we're doing now, will work. Trust me."

"I hope so." She liked his confidence. He talked as if doubt never entered his mind. His words elevated her own ambitions, made her want to reach for more. For too long she'd felt alone. Running a business was hard, and having Leigh to talk things over with—as well as the women from the monthly meetings—helped quell the loneliness while enabling her to take her business problems to like-minded people. But having Adam advise her had been like having a magic tool in her arsenal. She no longer felt disheartened.

He believed in her. The way he spoke to her made her believe that she could achieve anything. He had no idea how much she appreciated him.

"As before, there's not going to be a lot to edit. I'll send you the link so that you can watch these recordings and then we can get together, and I can go through the strategy of how to get this onto the internet, how we can get you new customers and we can talk more about the subscription site, if you want."

He seemed so sure of this plan that she fully expected this to work. "How much difference would it make if I showed my face?" she asked, emboldened by the idea that she could do anything.

His eyes grew large with surprise. "In my opinion, I think it would help a lot. Why? Have you changed your mind?" He zipped up the tripod bag.

"Maybe..." Her inner belief was stronger because of the things he said, and the way he saw her. This man, who she hadn't gone looking for, hadn't been interested in before, had created such an impact on her that she'd confronted her fears.

"What are you afraid of, Mackenzie?" He walked towards her, his steps swallowing up the distance between them. "You look upset." His hand reached out, and she hitched a breath, expecting to feel his wide palm across her cheek. But then he dropped his arm to his side.

His voice turned low, like a soft whisper that only she could hear, reaching inside her tenderly. She wasn't going to tear up. She wasn't. She gazed at the ceiling, unable to face him.

"Tell me." This time his hand touched her cheek, and her insides jumped.

"I'm scared."

His hand became a caress, and she leaned into it, needing the soft touch and the connection. "Scared of what?" he asked, his voice a hoarse whisper.

"Of people leaving nasty comments and trolling me. Calling me a freak."

"Never. Why would you think they'd do that?"

"Because that's what they used to say before."

"Before?" His thumb gently stroked her cheek, and her insides bottomed out. For a quick second, she forgot to breathe. "What do you mean, *before*?"

"The kids at school."

Silence tiptoed around them. She didn't want to open that can of worms, letting the past wriggle out all slimy and caked in dirt.

"Kids can be cruel sometimes. They can be jealous, too," he said.

She stared at the floor. "They said I was a freak because I was tall and freckly."

"You believed them?" His quiet voice dripped with anger.

"I did then, because at that age, you start to believe the bad things." Her own parents had left her, and it was therefore easier to believe the bad things.

Gently framing her face with his hands, he angled her head so that she looked up at him. "I love your freckles. What those kids said isn't true."

"I don't believe them now," she countered hastily. Yet she was still fearful of what others, those who hid behind IP addresses, might say, as only anonymous cowards could.

"You look like a TV presenter, Mackenzie. You are breathtakingly beautiful. There, I said it. What those kids did to you, how they hurt you, was unforgiveable. It was cruel. It couldn't have been easy dealing with that on top of what happened with your parents. I'm sorry you suffered."

She sucked in a breath, because Adam could get straight to the bullseye of her fears and put a salve on them.

"It's. Not. True. Do you hear me?"

"Yes."

"Then?" His eyes bore into hers, seemed to look deep inside her and find her fears. "You once told me that your grandma was your biggest champion. She told you to believe in yourself, she told you to be like the one and only Mackenzie. Didn't she?"

"Yes."

"Then be *you,* Mackenzie. Don't let anyone else's ugly labels define you." He curved his hand around her neck, a move that hinted at possession, and which sucked the breath right out of her lungs. Before she could think or breathe, or say a word, he kissed her, exploring her mouth gently as their bodies melded. She shuddered, excitement sparking in her heart. She needed this man, as surely as she needed the air to breathe.

She was sweet, and soft, and yielding.

After all the time they had spent unsure and hesitant, that he now had her in his arms was nothing short of a miracle.

"I was never sure of how you felt," he whispered, tucking an errant curl away from her face and gently behind her ear. She placed her hand over his, the touch new and unexpected.

"I worried that I'd pushed you away."

His hands skirted around her waist even more tightly, bringing her closer to him so that she was almost flush with his chest. Bending down so that their foreheads touched, he rubbed her nose with his gently. "Do we have a deal then? You're going to show your face?"

"I'm going to take the plunge and do it."

"And so you should."

They kissed again, his heart ballooning with joy at this sudden and new change in her. It had been bad enough, knowing how her parents had treated her, but to then discover the cruelty of teens. His heart ached for Mackenzie, for the broken teenager who had hurt so much.

Unable to resist, he hugged her closer. A sigh escaped her lips and she fell closer into the embrace, holding onto him as if she needed him.

"We could shoot all the videos again, with you showing your face."

"All over again?" She leaned away.

"We could do that."

"It would take too long." She nestled her face into the crook of his neck and he, enjoying the feel of her snuggled against him, kissed the top of her head again.

"It wouldn't be a problem. What's the rush?" Now that they weren't trying to determine one another's feelings, there was no guessing, no wrong intentions, or miscommunicated feelings. She liked him, he liked her, and now here they were with their arms wrapped around each other.

"Adam." She stared up at him. "There's no point in going back and redoing the videos. I want to look forward. We'll do the new videos, for the paid site, and we'll do those the proper way."

He sighed. Nothing was too much trouble for him to do. "If that's what you want."

"That's what I want."

"Why the change? Why now?"

"I was thinking of the Love Doctor, you know, the guy Leigh was talking about the other day?"

He braced himself for the bullet she was about to deliver. "I don't know what he's hiding," she continued, "I don't know *why* he's hiding, but it got me thinking that I didn't want to be like that. We all think he's a creep—"

"We?"

"We were talking about him at the women in business meeting I was telling you about. At the end, we all got talking about the Love Doctor."

The color drained from his face. Hearing this was like having a gut punch soon after a caress. He'd tasted Mackenzie's lips, and her soft, sweet mouth. But just as he found himself falling deeper for her, his heart booming loudly, announcing to the world that they were together, she slapped him with this news.

"Why do you all hate him?"

"He refuses to reveal who he is, so that tells me he's hiding something. What if he's really a creep? He doesn't seem like a nice, normal person, otherwise he wouldn't have anything to hide. I got to thinking that that's what people might think of me."

"What if he's not?" he asked as she stared up at him with her big shiny eyes, as if seeking assurance. He wanted to reassure her, but he was filled with worry himself. His secret was at risk of coming out. These women at the meeting, who didn't even know him, already hated him.

"We'll find out soon enough."

"Pardon me?"

"Lisa's going to track him down. She says she's—"

"Who?" The hairs on the back of his neck stood to attention.

"She's a journalist with the local paper."

"I thought the meeting was for business owners?" He was having a hard time keeping his anger in check.

"And successful women. Anyone can come, anyone who wants to talk about business and needs inspiration."

"Anyone but men," he commented, his mind uneasy knowing that someone was on his tail.

Mackenzie touched his lower lip and smiled. Standing this close to her, he'd barely had time to get used to this new shift in their relationship. He could smell her familiar perfume, and he rubbed noses with her playfully, loving the feel of her hands around his neck, their lips touching as they goofed around.

He needed to get back home and think about this. If things got any more complicated, he'd have to move.

Or reveal his identity.

The right thing to do was to tell Mackenzie. He wanted to, but with her opinion of the man so low, it would be risky. He couldn't tell her anything just yet, not while their romance was so new.

CHAPTER 20

She couldn't sit still when she got back home. Even when she got changed into her PJs, and curled up on her sofa, she couldn't focus on the TV.

With her belly trembling with excitement, she knocked on Leigh's door and was relieved to find her friend alone. No sign of Rourke.

Leigh only had to take one look at her to know. She pulled her into her apartment and then onto her sofa, where, in typical girlie fashion, they dissected the night's events and analyzed them in mind-numbing detail.

"I told you he was good for you!"

"You're only saying that with hindsight. How can you say that you know what he's like just because of the books he reads? And don't say because you could tell. You can't."

"I can," Leigh insisted, folding her legs so that she was sitting cross-legged. "I can judge a book by its cover."

"This man—" Mackenzie made a swooning gesture, something she would never have done before, causing Leigh to observe her with a concerned look on her face.

129

"One kiss and he reduced you to this?"

Mackenzie grinned, unable to contain her happiness. "Who said it was just one kiss?"

They had kissed again, and then some more. What had been a tentative touching of lips had turned into something deeper and more meaningful.

"I knew he would be the right man for you. He reads deep books, psychology books. The guy is smart and handsome. He's not the type of loser who would need the Love Doc's services."

They burst out laughing.

Mackenzie couldn't contain her happiness. Even now, she was floating on air. "He sees me, Leigh. He's sees the real me, and he understands me. To be understood is a magnificent thing."

"Oh, Mackenzie." Leigh clapped her hands together in delight. "I am *so* happy for you. Look at you!"

Mackenzie buried her face in her hands. "I feel like a dippy teenager in love."

"You look like one."

"Is it wrong to feel so happy? I feel as if my heart would burst. Is it crazy to feel all this after one kiss?"

"I thought you said it wasn't just one kiss?"

She shook her head, reminders of Adam's kiss, his touch, his arms around her, heating her body.

"We should go to dinner or something," Leigh suggested. "The four of us, or maybe he can come to—"

Mackenzie grimaced, interrupting her friend before she came up with any crazy notions. The relationship was too new. She didn't want anything to ruin it for them. "Let me enjoy him and have him to myself for a while first, please."

The email was sitting in his inbox, the headline in bold indicating that he hadn't yet opened it.

It was from a Lisa Kramer. This had to be the same woman Mackenzie had told him about. She had reached him via the email address at the back of his book. She wanted to do an interview with him:

Dear Love Doctor,

I would love to conduct an interview with you. The success of your book, The Love Doctor's Ten Rules for Dating: How to Find the Woman of Your Dreams without Swiping Left or Right, *has generated huge interest and I'd like to talk to you about it.*

Please get in touch as soon as possible.

Lisa Kramer
The Starling Bay Daily

He wiped his brow as if the creases of his worry would smooth away. And then he closed the email, almost deleted it but stopped himself.

He wasn't going to reply, but the sight of this in his email inbox would be like a ticking time bomb reminding him that there was a real danger of his secret being leaked. He needed to find a way to explain to Mackenzie. For all her loathing of the Love Doctor, she had no idea that she had kissed him. The problem was, she hated him with such intensity that he was starting to wonder how he could ever confess. There would be consequences.

Having just found her, he wasn't ready to let her go. Mackenzie would drop him like a hot coal. He couldn't just up and leave either, not now that he and Mackenzie were together. This was the start of something special, he could feel it in his bones, and he wasn't about to throw it away.

He wouldn't think about that yet. He'd worry about it later.

CHAPTER 21

"And another thing," Mackenzie had her laptop open and navigated the mouse. She and Adam were in the room at the back just after she had closed the shop.

They spent most evenings together, and most weekends, too. At her shop, they talked long into the evening, always after hours. She would light the candles, they'd get takeout, talk about business, about life, about them. For the past ten minutes, she'd been trying to ask Adam a few things about the software that ran the subscription site which they were now working on getting set up. But he was otherwise distracted, and the importance of the task at hand diminished with every kiss he rained down along her neck.

He had created a page on her website so that interested customers could sign up for her newsletter—another tip from Adam. Having him shoot the first video of her with her face in it hadn't been as daunting as she'd feared. Watching the replay hadn't been too bad either, and she was super motivated to check daily and see if any customers had signed up for the online class, the lessons for which she was slowly starting to put together.

Her free videos were getting some wonderful comments. She

couldn't have been happier because her business was starting to grow new green shoots. Her gift corner paled in comparison. Now, more than ever, she felt in charge or her destiny, as if she had a hand in her success, rather than allowing it to be driven by the number of customers walking into her shop. It was all because of Adam, because she'd taken a chance on him and let him into her life.

"This is confusing. This part here." She was trying to show him the part of the subscription site program she was having problems with but, unfortunately, he wasn't in a very helpful mood. If anything, he often made it difficult for her to focus.

"You're always working." He dropped a kiss on her back of her neck and ripples of tiny goosebumps skittered across her skin.

She giggled. "I want to take advantage of all these shiny new objects." He placed another kiss on the other side of her neck. He stood so close behind her that she could smell his aftershave. It was a familiar scent now, an exciting scent, one that caused her body to react, every cell jiggling for joy when he was near.

She let go of the mousepad and let her head flop back against Adam's shoulder. His hands slipped around her stomach, eliciting a moan from her. She loved being in his arms, loved being wanted and adored. Loved how Adam made her feel.

"Don't you ever stop working?" he asked. At this she turned around on her stool, facing him.

"You're making it impossible for me to focus."

"I can't help it." He dropped a kiss on her lips. The novelty and newness, the shiny sparkle of the first throes of being together, was like being in a dream she didn't want to wake up from.

They kissed again, this time he lifted her up onto her toes, and her hands instinctively went around his neck.

"Did you hear that?" Her heightened senses made everything brighter, louder, clearer.

"I didn't hear a thing," he murmured, nibbling her earlobe. She squirmed at the ticklishness.

"I take it we're not doing any more on the site tonight?" Her fingers traced along the pointed end of his shirt collar. She tilted her face, waiting for the prize, anticipating the touch of his velvety lips against hers.

He brushed his lips against her. "I'm not feeling in the mood for work."

"We can pick the work up another time, *guru*," she teased.

"Are you ever going to let me forget that?" He buried his face on her shoulder in shame. She laughed, bathed in happiness, which lit up her uneventful daily existence. Her world had turned brighter, better, filled with wonder. She had an appreciation for things she'd never thought about. A cup of coffee shared with Adam at the bookshop, a walk along the beach, feeling grains of sand under her feet, listening to the sound of seagulls squawking as they watched the sun dip into the ocean.

"Mackenzie?" Her eyes popped wide open.

"It *was* someone at the door." In her hazy dreamy state, she couldn't place the voice immediately. But then she did.

"It's my grandma." She rushed out of the room. "Grandma! What are you doing here?"

"Thank goodness. You're alive!" Her grandma put a hand to her chest in relief.

"Grandma!" Mackenzie swooped over to her side and gave her a huge hug. She hadn't been over to see her in a while and, worse, she hadn't called as often as she used to. She'd hardly called her for the past few weeks and it shouldn't have surprised her that her grandma had come over to check on her.

"Hey." Adam had walked out behind her, and the appearance of this man, coming out of the room, made her grandmother's eyes light up like streetlamps.

"I heard you laughing. I wondered who else was in there."

Her grandma was often direct, but the twinkle in her eyes told Mackenzie she knew Adam wasn't just an average customer.

"Grandma, this is Adam."

Adam stepped closer. "Nice to meet you, ma'am."

"You're the reason I haven't heard from my granddaughter."

Mackenzie cringed inwardly as Adam replied. "I wasn't aware of that, ma'am."

"I'm sorry I've been lousy keeping in touch, Grandma." Mackenzie wrung her hands together. She'd been caught red-handed. She'd wanted to tell her grandma in her own way, not have her find out in this way. "I've been so busy."

Grandma chuckled. "I can see."

"No, I really have."

"I don't doubt that." Her grandma winked at Adam.

"We've been working really hard. Adam's been advising me."

"I'm sure he has."

"Grandma!" Mackenzie winced. "We've been recording the videos for my new project."

"I know. We've seen them. They are good—"

"You've seen them? I haven't even told you about them yet. How did you—"

"Your mom keeps an eye on your website. She's proud of you, Mackenzie. She was recommending Bloom to one of her friends, and you have a link on there to the videos."

That's how her mother had found out. "You look so pretty, Mackenzie, and you sound so good."

"She is good, isn't she?" Adam agreed. "She's really easy on the eyes, and she's an expert at what she does."

"Oh, that she is. That's my Mackenzie. Mind you, she doesn't think she's easy on the eyes, but ..."

"Grandma!"

"Well, you don't. I'm not lying, and now this young man agrees with me. Isn't that right?" She shot a look at Adam.

"Yes, ma'am. I agree. One hundred percent. But, you know, the reason she's getting so much traction, and why so many people are watching and sharing those videos, and why she's building a list of people who want to pay her for more of this information, is because she's good at teaching and showing people. That's a skill that not many have. It's one thing to be able to do something yourself, but to be able to teach others, that's the real test of a teacher."

Her grandma beamed at her as if Mackenzie had won the Pulitzer Prize for flower arranging. "I always knew my Mackenzie would do well. But what's this about people paying you? For what?"

Mackenzie suppressed a giggle. "It's a new thing, Grandma. A subscription site. It's an idea Adam gave me."

Grandma looked at Adam as if he'd moved up to pole position in her estimation. "I like that you have her best interests at heart."

"How could I not, ma'am? Mackenzie means a lot to me."

Hearing Adam say that made her breath catch. "I'll tell you all about it another time, Grandma." She looked out of the huge window, into the street outside. "Did you come alone?" She'd half expected her mother to walk through the door, but there was still no sign of her.

"Alone? Heavens, no. I don't drive. Your mother brought me."

"Where is she?"

"Outside, waiting. Probably further up the street."

Mackenzie chewed her lip, feeling guilty. A silence stretched over the air like a vise. "Doesn't she want to come inside?"

"It depends," replied Grandma, looking thoughtful. "Do you mind her coming inside?" Grandma's eyes darted over to Adam, as if she wasn't sure of how much he knew.

Mackenzie walked to the door and pulled it open then looked outside. Sure enough, her mother was standing a few shops further along, peering through the windows. Mackenzie didn't know how to attract her attention. "Mom" still sounded like an alien word. Unused and unfamiliar.

The easy thing to do would be to go back into her shop and forget about her, but something inside her had softened. She walked out and went over to her mom. Her mother's nose was almost touching the glass of the shop window.

"You don't have to wait out here."

Her mother turned instantly, then blinked, her wrinkled features crinkling even more as she squinted at Mackenzie. "I was looking at a painting."

Mackenzie peered in. "Which one?"

"The one with the red poppies. They remind me of a dress I made for you. You looked real pretty in it."

"You made me a dress?"

"I could sew. Not very well, but I could follow a simple dress pattern."

Mackenzie rubbed her arms together, finding this meeting on the street strange and unfamiliar for so many long-lost reasons. "You can come into the shop. I won't bite."

"Are you sure?"

Mackenzie turned to leave. "That I don't bite? I'm sure." She walked back into Bloom, with her mother in tow. As she walked in, Adam's eyes grew, as did her grandma's. Before an embarrassing pause could grow, its gnarly roots taking an awkward hold on the mood in the air, Mackenzie forced herself to make introductions.

"Adam, this is my … my …" She couldn't say it.

"I'm Mackenzie's mother." Her mother beat her to it.

"This is Adam." Grandma announced proudly.

"Hello, Adam." Her mother's voice was tiny and polite, almost as if she wanted to make a good first impression.

"He's helping Mackenzie with the videos," Grandma explained, and Mackenzie was glad that her wise grandmother was doing all the talking. Fearful of being rude and cold, because this was her default state of being around her mother, Mackenzie kept her mouth shut, not wanting Adam to see her at her worst.

"*You're* making the videos?" her mother asked, and before he could reply, "We've watched all of them. They're *so good*. Mackenzie is amazing."

"Yes, she is. She is," Adam agreed, holding her gaze, his eyes full of admiration. Mackenzie walked away, leaving them to talk while she started to clean up. Grandma came over to her and put her hand on Mackenzie's shoulder. The touch, warm and comforting, made her stop.

"I see there was nothing for me to be worried about."

"You were worried about me?" Mackenzie asked.

"Wouldn't you be worried about me if you didn't hear from me for weeks?" Grandma's white brows pushed together.

"It hasn't been weeks, has it?" She was shocked. Surely it couldn't have been, but as she quickly and mentally calculated the time since her last visit, her grandma was right.

It had been weeks. Many weeks.

"I've been … busy."

"Distracted, too." Grandma gave her another one of her mischievous winks. "But you look happy, my girl. That's what I like to see the most."

*a*dam had just arrived back from his morning run when he saw Patrick waiting for him outside the door.

"What in the world ..." he muttered to himself. Patrick had left numerous messages via email and on his cell phone but Adam had been so busy with Mackenzie that he'd neglected the guy. He hadn't seen him since he'd seen the movie star.

The movie star.

Guilt melted his irritation. Patrick was a nice guy. He was also humble and lonely. Adam needed to help him, but the guy showing up like this was just plain bad timing.

He had plans for later. Mackenzie was coming over. He wanted to pick up a few things from the grocery store and then he was going to cook a nice meal for her. She had a party to deliver her arrangements to after work and he wanted to cook something special for her at his home.

She often came home late and tired on those evenings when she had a delivery to make. He'd seen it with his own eyes once when she'd come back from setting up flowers for a wedding reception and had been about to eat a leftover salad until he'd rustled her up some eggs and toast quickly, in her kitchen, while she'd sat at the table and watched him.

Today, he was going to do one better and she was finally going to come over to his place.

"Hey, dude." Patrick slapped him on the back by way of a greeting. "I almost didn't come."

"Yeah?" Adam wished he hadn't.

"I'm glad I took a chance." Patrick shifted out of the way, letting Adam open the door.

"I'm busy today, Patrick. You should have checked."

"I've called and left plenty of messages but you never got back to me." Patrick bustled in after him.

"Sorry about that." He owed Patrick. "I need to take a shower, buddy, but then I have things to do."

Patrick was already sitting on Adam's couch. He looked disappointed. "You still can't fit me in?"

"I'm kinda busy."

"But I haven't seen you for weeks." Patrick looked at him like an abandoned puppy, making Adam feel even worse. He'd been a lousy coach and none of this was Patrick's fault.

Relenting, "Can we do half an hour today? I promise to make it up to you the next time we meet."

"Will there be a next time?"

"Yes, there will. Sorry I haven't returned your calls."

"Half an hour will do. Mind if I drink this here?" Patrick took out a can of soda from his backpack. He seemed to have made himself at home, one leg bent at the knee and casually swung over the top of his other knee.

Startled, Adam had no choice but to let him. "Go ahead. What's up? You said there were developments last time we met." He hoped Patrick was making good progress. He sat down, his hands on his thighs as he willed Patrick to hurry this along. "Let's hear it then. What's going on?"

"She was crying, really loud, in her office, and I found out it was because she'd had an argument with her boyfrie—"

"Who are we talking about here?"

"My boss."

Adam whistled. Just when he didn't think things could get any more complicated for this guy, Patrick would always shock him. "You're after a woman who's already dating someone?"

"I didn't know that until a few days ago."

Adam huffed out a long-held breath. "Go on."

"So, we got talking, and she told me that they argue a lot, which is why she doesn't talk about him much, which is why I didn't know she had someone."

"Sounds like a messed-up relationship, if you ask me."

"Right, and a few weeks ago she came to work in tears. She tells me about this guy; she says he broke up with her. She was devastated. I think she wanted to confide in someone, and I think she found me easy to talk to."

"Right."

"He treats her bad and she deserves better—"

"Oh, boy." Adam swiped a hand over his sweaty brow, his need to shower becoming suddenly urgent. "She doesn't even see you, Patrick. It doesn't matter how much she and her boyfriend argue. She doesn't see you like that."

"But we were talking and she was opening up to me, and I was thinking that I'd treat her right, that all I had to do was be there for her."

Adam shook his head. He already knew how this was going to end. "No."

"I thought I had a chance."

"By listening to her breakup? You really are thinking about her best interests there, buddy." Adam didn't rein in the sarcasm.

"They made up. Just like that." Patrick clicked his fingers for effect. "They're back together, so all that talking, and me being there for her didn't help at all. He called and she went running."

"Well, there's a surprise. You don't exist for her, not in potential boyfriend territory. She doesn't know you, Patrick. She never could."

"B-but we were talking. It was deep stuff. I was dealing with her Achilles heel. I was concerned."

Adam got up to reach for his whiteboard so that he could quickly illustrate the problem here, since it was obvious that Patrick was having difficulty seeing it. But he was running out of time and exasperated, he picked up a pen and pointed to the notecards on the corkboard.

He went through the rules, tapping them with his pen as he discussed them. "You did number one, you were nice. You did this and this," he tapped the other rules in turn. "You didn't rush into things. Good." He tapped his pen on the sixth rule but before he could speak about that, he paced around the room thinking of how to explain this. "You can't go after women who are in relationships, Patrick. That's kind of like an unspoken rule."

"I didn't know that until she started confiding in me when he upset her."

"Right." Adam went back to the board and tapped Rule Six again. "Number six. Connect. Find her Achilles heel. You also don't want to become her therapist. Which is what I fear you were for her. She let of her steam, got it out of her system, you listened—"

"But I'd found her point of pain."

"She's already in a relationship. The Achilles heel is never about their boyfriends. I'd assumed that was obvious."

"I wasted my time on her."

"You were there for her, but as a friend, Patrick. She needed you as a friend."

"She doesn't even know that I like her. *Liked* her." Patrick took a swig from his can, before wiping his mouth with the back of his hand. "The sales assistant in the stationery shop seems friendlier."

"Is this the fancy notebook lady?"

Patrick pointed a finger at him. "That's the one."

"We can pick this up another time, buddy. I've got things to do, but we need to talk in more detail." He scratched his chin. The five o'clock shadow was starting to itch, and he was conscious that he needed to shave, as well as shower, and clean up the place. He'd started on it already, but he needed to triple-check that all traces of the Love Doctor had been removed.

"This is it?" Patrick asked.

"For now, buddy. I'll give you a longer session next time."

He felt guilty after he had quickly ushered Patrick out of the door, but this was Mackenzie's first visit to his apartment and he wanted to make sure everything was perfect.

CHAPTER 23

Twirling the spaghetti carbonara carefully, aiming to get a bite-sized amount on her fork, Mackenzie plopped it into her mouth, her eyes closing as she enjoyed the meal Adam had cooked for her.

She hadn't even eaten lunch today. "This is so good. *Soooo* good." She loved rich sauces. They were bad for her waistline, and her arteries, but there was something deeply satisfying about eating spaghetti slathered in a creamy, cheesy sauce.

"I'm glad you like it."

"Where did you learn to cook like that?" she asked.

"My mom. Were it not for her, I'd have lived my college years on ramen noodles. I would have probably ended up looking like a noodle, tall and thin."

She erupted into laughter. Adam was anything but noodle-shaped. Putting her arms around this man, she felt the hard-as-steel muscles, the taut chest and stomach. There was nothing noodle-ish about him.

"Your mom must have been an excellent cook. This is *soooo* delicious!"

"I'm glad you liked it. I have lots left over, and you're welcome to take some back with you."

"Thank you."

"You don't have to keep thanking me, Mackenzie. I love that you're here, having dinner with me. You work so hard, and you've been on your feet all day."

That Adam had done this for her meant a lot. For too long, she'd soldiered on alone, but this man clearly cared for her and he showed it to her in every little act he did. Her heart blossomed like the flower buds she often handled, opening slowly, then all at once.

"You have ..." Adam touched his own mouth. "A bit of sauce on your ..."

This was the look she had been hoping to avoid. She hastily wiped it away with her napkin. "Gone?"

Adam shook his head, then touched the corner of his lip. "To the right a little."

She dabbed at the corner of her mouth. "Now?"

He shook his head, and this time, picked up a clean napkin and wiped the corner of her mouth for her, prompting her body to break out into a rash of shivers. Any embarrassment she might have felt about having carbonara sauce on her face was quickly erased by Adam's touch. His soft eyes and sexy smile made her pulse race, her insides turn giddy. She'd been so used to being alone, eating alone, watching TV alone, that this was heaven.

"You make me feel so well taken care of, Adam. This is ... this is ..."

"This is what I could get used to," he said, finishing her sentence.

He understood her, and that was priceless. She leaned across the table and kissed him on the lips.

He was still smiling when they pulled apart. "I could definitely get used to this." She sat back in the chair and resting her entwined fingers over her stomach. A picture of complete satisfaction. How was it possible that this man was not only so good with marketing and business, but he was also great at cooking?

To have someone who fed her, and made her feel special, as if she mattered, was a feeling she'd only experienced with her grandmother. Now this man was offering to step in and show her another way. She leaned forward, both elbows propped on the table. He was hard to resist. He mirrored her move and soon they were gazing at one another, faces inches away. The intimate scene was dimly lit with the lighting from the wall sconces turned down. Flickering flames from the candles she'd brought with her added to the ambiance.

Adam's help had given her real, tangible results, and faster than she'd believed possible. Her website now had an influx of visitors all from the new pages and links to videos Adam had put up for her.

It was almost instantaneous to see the effect each time she put out a new video. It was mind-blowing to see the lift in sales and people coming to her website, just from her uploading a new video.

Over thirty people had signed up for her class which wasn't even ready yet. Thirty paying customers who were going to give her a thousand dollars apiece for her online floristry classes.

Thirty thousand dollars.

It blew her mind.

If it weren't for Adam, she wouldn't have ever been at this stage, creating and uploading videos, and being so self-assured in her demonstrations. There had always been that person inside her, but Adam had slowly coaxed her out from behind her toughened armor.

She no longer just lived to work, but lived to laugh, and spend time with a man who was quickly stealing her heart.

"Leigh says you're always ordering books."

"I am."

"She thinks you're a genius."

"I am." Adam laughed but she was beginning to think of him as a genius because he had done wonders for her.

"She was sure that you were a psychologist before she found out what you did for a living. She said you're always getting books on psychology."

"You'd be surprised how the two are connected. How we sell depends a lot on the psychology of people."

"But they are completely different things," she retorted. "One has to do with selling things to customers and convincing them to buy something, and the other is dealing with how people think and behave. What do they have to do with each other?"

He set down his silverware and watched her with amusement. "Everything."

"How?"

"When you sell, you sell not only your services but *you*. When, say, a customer casually comes across your website, you need to show them, convince them, that you are a nice, normal person, and someone who knows her stuff. You want them to believe that you are good at what you do. How do you convince them? You show them what you're making, because you want to earn their trust."

She tilted her head to the side, questioning his words. He spoke as if this made all the sense in the world. "What does selling have to do with psychology?"

"Being successful at sales and marketing means having to understand human behaviors well. Your job—because you need to sell—is to get your customer to take action every time. You want them to buy what you are offering, so you need to get to the core of what makes a person tick, what drives them, what makes them react a certain way, and then you use that knowledge to persuade them to buy."

"Hmmm." She twirled a finger around a hair, thinking over his words. "It still doesn't make sense to me. Can I see some of these books that have convinced Leigh that you're a genius?"

He laughed. "Sure. The new batch of books I picked up are on my desk. Excuse the mess but I'm working on a presentation for next week."

"Anything exciting?"

"Nothing exciting. I want to make an impression on the CEO of a company that I'd love to work for. I think I could help them get their marketing to another level. They're struggling at the moment, and I feel I can make an impact."

"Struggling like I was."

"You were doing just fine." He leaned towards her and kissed her.

"Thanks to you I'm doing so much better."

"It's all you, Mackenzie. You're the one with the knowledge. I just had a hand in pointing you in the right direction."

"I'm lucky you pulled me out of the flower pot." She dropped a kiss on his lips. "Good luck with your presentation."

"Thank you." He stood up and started piling the dirty plates on top of each other. "I'll put some coffee on. Why don't you check out those new books, they're on my desk in a box. The older ones are on the bookshelf."

"I shall investigate."

Psychology and advertising were the same? She didn't believe it, even though Adam had explained it to her in a way that made complete sense. She needed to see the types of books he was reading, the ones that had impressed Leigh so much.

Maybe she could borrow one or two of them and read them herself? Adam had opened her eyes to things she had never considered before; the behavior of people, customers, specifically, and how she might better entice them to be interested in what she had. It was all so interesting and a new way of looking at things which she had never before considered.

Not only was Adam a great partner, sexy, good-looking, and kind, and wonderful, but he was smart and knowledgeable and this was something she found irresistible about him.

There were many reasons why she was smitten with this man, but most of all it was because of how he made her *feel*.

She walked over to his desk, noting that it was clean and tidy with everything tucked away neatly in place. An empty corkboard hung from the wall. There was only one box on the table. She gently lifted out the books one by one, thumbing through them, quickly casting her eyes over the first few pages and the foreword, before reading the back cover, trying to decide which one to borrow first.

"This looks interesting," she murmured. When she flicked through a few pages, something slipped and fell to the floor. It looked like a bookmark, a clever marketing ploy, no doubt. She bent down to retrieve it, and as she did so, she saw a card on the floor. It was bright green. She picked it up and slipped the bookmark back into the book, then put the books back into the box, keeping the one which had caught her interest, so that she could ask Adam if she could borrow it.

As she placed the bright green postcard on the desk, she turned it over. In thick black marker pen was written:

6. Find her Achilles heel.

She frowned, not understanding what it meant. Adam rushed into the room, "Coffee's ready."

She turned around. "That was fast. I would have helped you." She stared at the green card again.

"No need to. It's all taken care of. Find anything?" He moved towards her.

"I found this on the floor." She waved the postcard at him.

"That," he said, smiling and plucking it from her hands.

"What does it mean?"

"That's … that's something for one of my clients. Did you find a book?"

"This one." She placed it facing him so that he could read the title.

"That's a good one. It's a bestseller. I think you'll like it. Read it and let me know what you think."

"I will." She was about to ask him about the postcard when he reminded her that the coffee was ready and would get cold if she didn't come now.

But before she could move, he reeled her in with his arms around her waist and kissed her. She moaned in approval, and set the book on the table, before sliding her arms up and around his neck. "I don't care for coffee just yet," she murmured, her lips pressed against his.

"Me neither." His breath was hot and sweet, his hands big and strong, holding her. He kissed her again, causing a ripple through her core. Everything in her life was starting to turn for the better. Her love life, her business, even her relationship with her mom held a tiny sliver of promise.

He fed the notecard to the paper shredder. The pesky little note had fallen down and he hadn't realized.

One notecard, listing one of the dating rules. It had been a careless mistake. He'd been in such a rush to clean up after Patrick had left. The question was, had Mackenzie suspected?

How could she possibly?

He was being paranoid. He'd come up with a good enough answer. But it still didn't sit well with him. Each time he'd been with her, each time he'd held her in his arms, or placed a kiss on her lips, he cringed at the idea of his Love Doctor role.

She would understand once he explained it to her.

The rules weren't rules. They were common sense packaged up into a handy little book of solutions for something that was the cause of pain for many men. He wasn't doing anything new or radical. He'd simply taken his father's good old-fashioned advice, added in a few nuggets of his own to make them sound more sexy and relevant, and then sold it as a solution that many were willing to eat up.

He winced.

Even he wasn't naïve enough to not know that these rules might be construed differently if some radical feminist, say, were to come upon them.

He'd received occasional hate mail from women who castigated him for the book and for his way of thinking. It was still a relatively small number compared to the enthusiastic fan mail.

But still, he could have done without Mackenzie finding it.

CHAPTER 24

They were sharing a huge slice of lemon drizzle cake.

"Another pile of books arrived for Adam," Leigh announced matter-of-factly, a sugary crumb from the cake resting on her lower lip. "I should give them to you."

"Crumb," said Mackenzie nodding to alert her friend. "I don't see him *every* day."

"No?" Sarcasm rolled off Leigh's tongue as she dabbed her lips with a napkin, then proceeded to reel off all the days that Mackenzie had been 'busy'. "And you went to his place after work on Saturday, and you haven't been free to meet me for brunch for weeks."

Mackenzie broke off another piece of cake and lifted the fork to her lips, inhaling the delectable lemony buttery aroma. "I'm in the middle of transforming my business."

Three women on a table near them erupted into a peal of laughter. At times their voices turned loud, a distraction even in the coffee shop, which was quite busy.

"But I hardly see you!" Leigh complained, glancing over her shoulder as the women burst into laughter again. "I'm not complaining. I'm just so happy you met your Mr. Perfect."

Mackenzie couldn't dispute that. Adam was some kind of wonderful. She'd turned all soft and mushy and she hadn't been that type of person. Ever. She grinned in response.

"You're not even disputing that," Leigh cried. "The old you would have denied it. You've gone all soft, Mackenzie."

"Maybe I have." This was exactly the same conclusion she had come to, especially given her recent experience with her mom.

"Before I forget, we're having a baby shower for Merry next month."

"It's that time already?"

"You have to come, you're invited. It's just a small get-together, but we also want you to make some pretty floral arrangements. Obviously, we'll pay for them."

"Don't worry about that. I can put something together, no charge. I could make that for one of my videos." But her attention had moved from Leigh to the noisy women nearby. She forced her head back to Leigh who was rambling on about Reed and Rourke. "What does the guy do that he needs to be pampered and have a baby shower for—"

Achilles heel?

Had the women said that, or was she hearing things? Mackenzie put her finger to her lips.

"Why are you shushing me?" Leigh asked, her face a portrait of indignation. Mackenzie strained her ears. The women were talking about the Love Doctor. She got up.

"What are you doing?" Leigh looked up at her. Mackenzie strode over to where the women were sitting.

"Excuse me, but I couldn't help but overhear your conversation. Did you say something about a Love Doctor?"

"You've heard of him too?" One of the women squealed, dropping her fork so that it crashed onto her plate.

"My boyfriend works with someone whose brother used him,"

another woman with a ponytail answered.

"Do you know who he is?" Mackenzie asked.

The women shook their heads. "No one does."

Mackenzie was about to leave, but something pinched her insides and she couldn't let it go. "I'm really sorry to interrupt like this, but did you say something about an Achilles heel?"

"It's one of the rules for dating," the other woman said, rolling her eyes. "Some said there are ten rules."

"Ten rules? As many as that?" one of the women exclaimed.

Mackenzie tried to look unconcerned, even though her insides were in turmoil. "Who would have thought men needed rules?" She choked out a laugh she didn't feel.

"Right?" the woman with her hair slicked back into a ponytail said. "But I'm not surprised men need rules and a coach."

They all laughed as if this was hilarious and relatable.

"I don't understand what the Achilles heel has to do with anything," Mackenzie prompted, hoping to squeeze some information out. She tried to suppress the urge to run away—from them, from here, from what this could mean.

The woman shook her head, as if doing so might loosen a fragment of information pertaining to what Mackenzie had asked. "I think it's something to do with a guy needing to figure out a woman's soft spot, something she's sad about, or that's causing her pain, her Achilles heel, if you will. And the advice is for the guy to fixate on that so he's seen as caring." She put a finger in her mouth like a gagging motion.

"And the other rules?" Mackenzie asked, feeling faint.

"I can't remember, but they're all pretty stupid. Why?"

Heaviness churned in her stomach. She'd heard all she needed to. "I was curious, that's all. There seem to be lots of rumors running around about this guy. I'm sorry for disturbing you."

"Don't worry, hon. It's good to be aware of scams like this."

Mackenzie slipped back to her seat. It added up. Adam and

his books, his desire to understand people, the interest in psychology. Finding that note under his desk was proof enough. She knew now why the corkboard had been blank. He'd probably had all ten rules pinned up on it as a daily reminder.

"What was that all about?" Leigh asked.

The nice and light feeling of having a catch-up with her friend now disintegrated into sawdust. "I think Adam has been coached by the Love Doctor."

"What? No!" Leigh's horrified expression reflected her own inner turmoil. The man had lied to her, and not only had he lied, but he'd used her pain and her past to ingratiate himself to her. Masquerading as a man who cared, he'd sought only to get closer.

He'd worked her. Played her. Found her Achilles heel. He'd used the teachings of a questionable leader to get her to fall in love with him.

For a smart man, he really wasn't all that smart.

CHAPTER 25

*H*is eyes were glued to his computer screen as he worked on perfecting the presentation. He needed this to be perfect. He needed it to impress. He wanted the contract because this company had deep pockets, and he wanted to put himself in a position where he would benefit.

When there was a knock at his door, he didn't rush to answer it. But when it became louder, harder, more insistent, he slowly got up, resenting the interruption.

He hoped it wasn't Patrick. His jaw clenching in preparation, he opened the door to find an unexpected and nice surprise. "Mackenzie?" Her unsmiling face stared back at him. This was a surprise; they hadn't arranged to meet this evening because of their hectic work schedules.

"I need to ask you something, and I want an honest answer."

His body tensed, braced on high alert.

She knew.

"You can ask me anything." He swallowed, steeling himself for a confrontation he didn't want. He'd tried to find a way to tell her, an opening in their cozy, curled-up-on-the-sofa conversations, but the perfect timing had eluded him.

"The Love Doctor," her angry eyes were flecked with distrust. "Have you used his services?"

"What?" He couldn't believe her words. Her question took him so much by surprise that he half-laughed, half-snorted in shock. "What did you say?"

"You're stalling for time," she cried, marching inside, her chin tilted up, her arms folded.

"What? No. I'm not. I'm shocked by your accusation." She didn't know the exact truth, but she was close, and yet her accusation had given him an out.

But—now was the perfect time to come clean or be saved. The choice was his.

"It's not an accusation, Adam. I want you to be honest with me."

Her anger burned like a wildfire and he couldn't believe her reaction, that she hated the Love Doctor so much. It was something he needed to understand more, so that he could defend himself in the future.

"Why do you doubt me? Why would you think I had?" But he had an inkling as to what had brought this about. The notecard, even though, in and of itself, her finding that one piece of paper didn't mean a thing.

"For the last time, Adam, did you use the Love Doctor to pursue me?"

The words were tempting. He'd get his ass kicked, metaphorically, if he told her the truth. Mackenzie wouldn't be happy, but he would feel so much better if he did.

She might dump him.

The jarring thought prevented him from telling the truth. "No. Never. Of course not. But remember, Mackenzie, I didn't pursue you. You're the one who came to me for help with your business."

"I came to you," she murmured.

"I liked you, I don't deny that. I was interested in the

beginning, but I sensed you didn't like me, so I kept my distance and made it be about the business, because I believe in you and I know you could do so much better from it."

"Why did you have that?" she asked. "That note with the Achilles heel phrase on it? That's a rule, right?" Her lips set into a firm line.

He had another chance to confess. To own up and to set the record straight. Better to do it now than wait for later, his heart whispered but his brain forced him to save himself.

"I was discussing it with a friend… and he didn't understand the concept."

"A friend? You said it was something for one of your clients." She turned her head as if trying to test the validity of his answer.

He stared at the floor, trying to dig himself out of the hole he'd dug for himself. Every white lie led to another white lie. But this, thankfully was the truth. "It was a client, but he's also a friend. A lot of my clients become my friends. Like you." He smiled, hoping to soften her mood, but it didn't seem to be working.

"What do you mean you were discussing it?"

"Guys discuss this sort of thing, you have to remember, Mackenzie, this is a hot book."

"You have the book?"

"It's a popular book," he exclaimed, as if she'd said something nonsensical. "It's gone viral on the internet. Every young, heterosexual man I know has a copy."

"If it's such a big bestseller, why isn't it in the bookshop? I checked in Leigh's shop and she said there was only an eBook version."

Because he hadn't been prepared for the phenomenal success of the book. He hadn't expected it to take off as it had. He didn't want to be known for something so … tacky? He shrugged. He didn't have an answer for her. Not a truthful one. "I don't know, but it's not a sin for me to be reading a book that a lot of guys are talking about."

Disapproval lined that lovely face he longed to frame in his hands and kiss. Knowing it would add fuel to the fire, he stayed where he was, even though it was a battle to not put his arms around her. "What's brought this on?" he asked, wondering how long he had before the truth caught up with him eventually.

It was bad enough having that journalist try to burrow her way to him, and now this with Mackenzie. He wasn't naive enough to think he could live here and not be found out. "Mackenzie?"

"I overheard some women talking at the bookshop. They talked about the Achilles heel and—"

"And you put two and two together."

"Hard not to."

He hung his head, so that he didn't have to face her and fight the temptation of taking her in his arms. "I'm sorry you thought that's what I did, but would it have been so wrong?"

Her brows pinched together, not unlike the pinch in his lungs right now. He shouldn't have said anything, and had only done so because of his desire to set the record straight, to find out why she hated the Love Doctor so much.

"To use someone to teach you how to get a date?" she snapped.

"That's not what he's about … I don't think …"

"You're defending him?"

He breathed out softly, hoping to diffuse the situation. "I don't think he's hell-bent on showing men how to get a date, from what I've read of the book. It seems to be he's just showing them a way to be more authentic, to be who they are when they meet someone. This book is for men who don't want to use social media to trap women, yes, trap, because I genuinely think a lot of guys alter their photos and make up lies about themselves to paint a picture of someone they think a woman will be attracted to, as opposed to painting a real picture of who they are. I think the Love Doctor is merely showing men how to be themselves."

"And the Achilles heel? The women I overheard talking said it was a way for the guy to find out what's causing a woman pain, so that he can pretend to care."

With this interpretation, one of manipulation, it was no wonder women hated him. "I don't think 'pretend' is the right word."

"Are you standing up for this guy?"

"I don't agree with what you're saying."

"This is a pretty big thing for us not to agree on."

He blinked, blindsided by her words and reaction. He didn't want to get into a fight with Mackenzie, but he also didn't understand her anger. The presentation he urgently needed to finish hung over his head like an axe waiting to fall, but he couldn't let her go until they had made up. This disagreement would weigh on his mind all day and night.

"Words matter, Adam. Actions matter, *why* people care for you matters. No one wants pity."

He lifted his head, saw the hurt, understood her. "You're right. Those things matter." He stepped towards her and enveloped her in his arms, not waiting for a signal. Mackenzie was hurting and she needed him. She had been let down by the people who should have always been there for her. The type of damage inflicted on the young Mackenzie had imprinted itself into her DNA. She doubted kind words and gestures, which was why she was so grateful for everything he did. Which was why she saw everything the Love Doctor did as manipulation.

Which was why he was a dead man walking the moment she found out the truth.

He held her tightly in his arms, then kissed the top of her head. "It's late," he said, "and I was about to eat." Even though he hadn't intended to eat. He'd planned on working on the presentation for as long as it took to make it shine. Mackenzie stared up at him.

"I should go. I hate that we had a fight over this."

He thumbed her lower lip. "It's not a fight, just a difference of opinion."

"You've got your presentation and I don't want to disturb you."

"That's in a few days. I have plenty of time, and you showing up here is the best thing that's happened to me all day. I love seeing you."

She moved her hands slowly up his chest and around his neck. "I love seeing you, too, but I should go. I didn't want to interrupt you."

He didn't want to let this hurting woman out of his sight. "I have takeout leftovers, and I'm starving." He heard a stomach rumble, but it wasn't his.

They ate, avoiding any Love Doctor talk, and he'd refused to let her leave, telling her he could work better with her around.

Bringing his laptop to the living room, he'd worked while she'd convinced him to let her clean up the dishes.

A few hours later, he finally extricated himself from a sleepy Mackenzie. She'd fallen asleep with her head on his lap. He rubbed her corkscrew curls between his fingers, the silky strands of hair soft to his touch. She murmured as he watched her sleeping. Not wanting to disturb her further, he decided to take his laptop to the bedroom and work in there, but Mackenzie stirred, flinging her arm over her head. In the next moment, her eyelids flew open, and she stared up at him.

"Hey, sleepyhead," he whispered. His and Mackenzie's lives were starting to become so inextricably connected now that it was hard to see where his life ended and where hers began. He liked her being here, sleeping on his couch, liked working knowing that she was nearby.

"I fell asleep," she groaned.

"It's okay. I was going to get you a blanket."

She bolted upright and her eyes went to his laptop. "You were working."

"I still need to prepare for that meeting."

"I'm so sorry I got in your way." She planted her feet on the floor and yawned, her sleep broken. "I messed up your presentation."

"You did not. It's not for a few days, so I have plenty of time." But he also had a full day of work for his other clients.

She rubbed her eyes. "I'm sorry I've taken up your evening, me charging in here and accusing you of so much nonsense."

He kissed the top of her head. "Hey, I love spending time with you."

"But you had work to do and I stopped you from—"

"You were upset."

She dipped her head back, her long-lashed eyes tempting him to move closer. He pressed his lips against her, forcing himself not to deepen the kiss, otherwise he would not want to get back to the work at hand.

"I overreacted. It's just that … I find it hard to put my trust in people. I felt you'd been dishonest. It's not your problem, it's mine. It's my own insecurity, not anything to do with you. I find it hard to trust people."

"I know." He crouched down so that his face was level with hers. "I understand that now." It hurt him to know that this woman who had so much to give had been abandoned by her parents from a young age and had then suffered bullying. These harsh blows life had dealt her had been softened by the love of her grandmother, and now he, too, never wanted to see her hurt as long as he could help it.

"I trust you, Adam. That's a big thing for me to say."

He rifled his fingers through her scalp. "I know. I understand how hard it is for you to let people in."

Her eyes bore into his face as if she were trying to read the code and decipher it. "You're the only person I've allowed in for a long time."

He stared at her, it was on his lips to confess. But it was also early on in their relationship and she had trusted him with her past. Did he want to risk throwing that all away now? "I think about you all the time, I know what you've been through, what you still go through, I don't want to be another person close to you who hurts you."

He'd taken the coward's way out.

Big coward.

He risked her walking away if he told her. Everything would take a huge setback, her business, the subscription site. All the things he was trying to put in place for her would fall apart. She'd avoid him like the plague.

He would tell her the truth one day. One day when things were much more solid between them. When they'd had more time together.

Right now wasn't the right moment.

He took her hands in his and held them gently. "You mean a lot to me, Mackenzie. I'm glad you let me in. I never want you to regret that." But even saying those words felt hollow. Being with her was a battle of truth versus his ugly lie. If he wasn't careful, he'd suffer for it soon enough.

"You say all the right things." She leaned towards him and pressed her lips against his, then, curling her arm around his neck, breathed into his ear. "I don't want to leave, but I have to. Let me go."

He pulled back, gazed into her eyes, saw that he had been forgiven. "I don't want to, but ..." They kissed again, stretching out their time together, tasting one another. So much for not deepening his kiss. This woman was hard to resist.

"I promise not to disturb you anymore."

"Maybe we can meet for dinner once my big day is over?" he suggested.

"Call me when you're done. Go now, and work on your presentation. Amaze the new client."

"I hope to."

"Hope to?" She asked, slowly raising herself to standing. "That doesn't sound like the suave advertising guru I know."

CHAPTER 26

She was paranoid. She was a worrier, too. It wasn't the best combination of feelings to have in a new relationship. She was better than that, she needed to be better than to let some random conversation plague her with doubt.

Adam's explanation made sense to her, and she was silly for doubting him in the first place. He was too confident, too charming, too wonderful, he was all the things, and a man like that didn't need help in pursuing women.

She hadn't been *worked* on. She was worthy, and deserving of love and happiness, and being with Adam was proof of that.

She'd slept on it all night, thinking these things over and over in her head. It was time for her to relax and enjoy this new phase in her life, especially now that things were going so much better than she could have ever hoped for. She was recording and uploading her videos to the internet. She was reaching a bigger audience and preparing her lessons and soon she would have an audience to sell to and her business would bring in another stream of income, a great stream of income, according to Adam.

In order to do this, she'd made herself vulnerable not only in her business life but in her personal life. When doubts reared their ugly heads, she needed to heed her grandma's wise words.

She could be, do and have anything, as long as she believed in herself enough.

She could be like the one and only Mackenzie.

Adam made her feel special, just like her grandma did. Now, she was better equipped to handle her mom reaching out to her. It was possible that people could change. That they made mistakes they lived to regret. Could she hold a grudge against her mother forever? The woman had hurt her gravely. But her mother had been hurting, too.

Maybe it was time she cut her some slack. That she was thinking of this at all was because of this new phase in her life and she owed it all to Adam.

She turned on her computer, rubbing her hands together as she got ready for another day at the shop. She logged on, her heart buoyed with excitement. Now that her videos were online, she received lots of emails and interest in her business. Her email inbox was flooded with people asking when the next video would be ready. Some people had suggestions for the different arrangements they wanted her to show them how to make.

Every single email put a smile on her face.

She had taken Adam's advice to only cultivate serious paying members for her subscription site, and had asked for a small deposit upfront to signal intent. She checked to see how many people had signed up now. Her heart almost leapt out of her mouth. Sixty-four people had signed up. She'd asked for a fifty-dollar deposit from each person to secure a seat in her online academy which was almost ready.

A quick round of mental math told her she already had just over three thousand dollars from this.

She wanted to jump up and dance, spin around. *Move*. Heat radiated from her chest, making her limbs light, almost weightless. She was no longer weighed down by a ton of bricks, layered with worry.

Her business was growing in ways she had never before imagined. Adam had not only transformed her personal life, he had transformed her business.

CHAPTER 27

*H*e was finalizing his presentation.

Because he hadn't been able to work on it last night, he'd had to work on it all day, in between doing the other client work. He didn't even have time to check anything about his Love Doctor business, no sales figures or emails.

The glowing reader emails would have to take a backseat. He couldn't work on anything but this.

The one thing that kept coming back to haunt him was Mackenzie. He hated that he'd hurt her, and even though he'd answered her as honestly as he could—he'd answered the specific question she'd asked him—he had still shied away from the truth.

While he hadn't taken any coaching from the Love Doctor, his sin was far, far worse and the day he owned up to her about who he was would be a day of reckoning for their relationship.

He started to type something out then decided to hell with it. He needed to speak to Mackenzie, to find out how she was this morning.

"You're supposed to be working," she cried.

"I wanted to hear your voice."

"You charmer."

"You sound a lot happier." She'd forgotten the drama.

"I have good reason to. I've had so many lovely emails about the videos, and I've had over sixty people sign up for the subscription site—"

"What? Over sixty?" *Heck.* That was amazing. Mackenzie was professional but also approachable. She came across as a 'nice' person, while also being so obviously talented. It wasn't surprising that the response to her subscription site would be so overwhelming.

"Sixty-four people, to be precise," she said, her excitement so vivid that it bounced across the airwaves.

"That's brilliant. This is going to take off for you. I can feel it in my bones." That many people signing up for something that hadn't yet been launched? And for someone who was establishing herself in that space, someone who was yet unknown? Simply fantastic. She'd only released five free videos. That this much interest had piqued and so quickly boded well for her, and he couldn't have been happier for someone who was so deserving of this success.

He didn't want Mackenzie to rely solely on her floristry business for income, a lot of which was dependent on the daily customers in the shop, as well as the additional extra work she did on the weekends or after work. He wanted her to see the value of passive income. By teaching a class, she was multiplying her income. Teach once to a class and reap the rewards. She could later sell those classes for less to new students, and update her course every year.

He was excited for her. "We need to get your lessons recorded as soon as possible."

"Yes, we do." She had the equipment, but now that they were dating, the recording was something they worked on together. He could help her get it done quicker, and with her creating the content and him recording meant they'd get the videos out of the way which would leave more time for them to spend together.

"Don't worry about my videos, you need to focus on your presentation. Good luck for tomorrow. How's it going?"

"It's going." He groaned. His momentum had been broken and it had been difficult for him to get his head back into the presentation when a part of him couldn't stop thinking about what Mackenzie would think when he told her the truth.

"How much of the way through are you?"

He sighed loudly. "About halfway."

"Halfway?" He could see it now, her guilty expression. "I'm hanging up. Go."

He chortled. "Okay, but only because you're telling me to." He hung up, found himself smiling, and felt buoyed up now that he'd spoken to her.

It was in that moment that he decided. He would tell Mackenzie his secret after the presentation was done, and he'd worry about the consequences later.

For now, he forced himself to get back to work. He worked tirelessly all day and into the early hours of the morning, stopping only to refuel with a few protein bars and shakes.

Outside, the sky turned from blue, to dusky peach and purple, until eventually night fell. And still he worked. When at last he finally lifted his head and stretched, the 3:00 a.m. in glaring red lights on his digital clock told him he needed to get to bed otherwise he would be late to the meeting tomorrow. Creating a bad first impression wasn't the thing to do. This was a contract he wanted.

On the side of his PC, an icon flashed. He clicked on it only to discover that it was a message from the town forum. He didn't have the time or mental bandwidth to deal with any business queries right now. He had a big day ahead of him and sleep beckoned. He turned his PC off and headed to bed.

"We've heard a lot about you." Sean McGregor, the owner of the company whose business he wanted, shook Adam's hand firmly and showed him into the conference room.

"All good things I hope." Adam surveyed the large wooden-paneled room with its antique style tables and chairs. It was in stark contrast to many contemporary rooms he'd been in for meetings. This family business was small but expanding quickly and they didn't have the experience to deal with their marketing needs.

"All good things. It's the reason you're here. We've seen a few marketing agencies. You're the only person on our list who is a one-man team."

Adam smoothed down his tie as he set his briefcase down. "I'm used to competing with small- to medium-sized companies. I'm sure I gave you a list of my existing clients?"

"You did. You were the only one to do so. It's mighty impressive." McGregor's eyebrow lifted ever so slightly.

Adam smiled at the compliment. "Thank you." He got out his slimline laptop. "Mind if I get set up?" He eyed the large smartboard display screen on the wall, shiny and sleek; it looked out of touch with the rest of the room.

"Go ahead."

Adam set up his laptop, making small talk, asking McGregor questions about his company and its origins. "Will anyone else be joining us?"

McGregor laughed. "No, it's just me. We're quickly expanding from the family business but I'm still the man at the top. I make all the decisions."

"Then you obviously hold all the keys to the kingdom, you must know everything about the business, and you've seen it grow."

"Absolutely, and my goal is to make it grow even more."

"I can help you with that." Adam smiled at the man as he smoothed down his tie.

"I'm looking forward to seeing what you've got."

"Shall we start?"

"Best get to it. I have four more people to interview after you, and then interviews for the next two weeks. It's hard finding good people."

Adam's smile slipped a little. The competition was steep. Four more interviewees after him and this was just today. But healthy competition wasn't necessarily a bad thing. All he had to do was convince this man that he was the only one for the job. He took in a deep breath and began his presentation.

Delivering his vision and his plans for what he could do for this company was easy, because he loved nothing more than presenting. Confidence poured from every cell in his body. Not a bad end result for a nerd who'd once been scared to put his hand up in class.

He settled quickly into a flow, and everything was going well until a cell phone rang. Adam panicked, praying it wasn't his phone. He was usually good about turning these things off.

McGregor got up, holding his phone up. "Sorry. This one's urgent. Mind if we take a short break?"

"Sure, that's fine."

McGregor left the room leaving Adam to bask in the good feeling he had about how this presentation had gone so far.

It had gone well. Exceedingly well.

He looked around the room, still waiting for McGregor to get back, but there was no sign of the man. So, he quickly checked through the presentation slides on his PC, even though he knew everything was perfect because he'd checked it all last night and then again this morning. His eyes caught on the blinking icon on the side of his screen.

The pesky little thing was an annoying distraction and one he didn't want to deal with now. But as it continued to blink, and with no sign of McGregor, he decided to deal with it now. He clicked on it and was taken to the Starling Bay forum where he had notifications for a dozen or so email messages. He blinked a few times. This wasn't normal. He usually received one or two queries every couple of days. This many was excessive. Curious, he clicked on one. His belly flopped.

It couldn't be.

He clicked on the next email, and the next and the next. The small bowl of oatmeal he'd had this morning churned inside him, threatening to eject from his mouth. As he frantically skimmed through them one by one, the emails didn't make sense. Requests for coaching intermingled with words in capital letters screaming at him. References to the Love Doctor were in emails addressed to Adam Hartman.

What the heck?

Alarm bells shrieked in his ears, warning lights flashing. He couldn't yet connect the dots. He'd worked hard to keep the two separate. No one knew he was the Love Doctor. And yet in the Starling Bay forum, somehow, his secret had been leaked.

His gaze fell on an email from a Lisa Kramer, a name which looked familiar. Then he remembered, she'd contacted him before, except that this time she knew who he was.

Adam,

I would love to interview you and find out more about the Love Doctor and your explosive growth and success.

Please reply back to this email or contact me in my office.

Lisa Kramer
The Starling Bay Daily

Rising numbness spiraled through his body and turned to full-blown hurricane-level panic.

What? How? When? He quickly clicked on the home page to check the posts. A headline from the top trending post screamed at him:

Meet Adam Hartman, the Love Doctor.

He stared at the name of the person who had made this post. R Yew Kidding. Panicked, he clicked the name for more details to find that this was an empty profile, with no details of the person other than the name and that they'd only joined the forum a few days ago.

R Yew Kidding.

His heart beat like a drum as he skimmed through the flurry of replies this post elicited. Most people were in disbelief, their outrage melding with hysteria. His mind raced and beads of sweat sprang up on the back of his neck. The ugly, unexpected, unbelievable truth began to emerge.

Someone he had trusted had revealed his identity, and in the worst possible way.

"Sorry about that." Sean McGregor walked back into the room. "I don't usually take any calls, but my wife … she's the exception to that rule. You know how that is, right?"

Adam stared at him blankly.

"Are you married, Adam?" McGregor asked, completely oblivious to the tsunami of emotions that had swallowed him up.

"Married? No." At this rate he wasn't even sure he'd have a girlfriend to go back to. He stared at his screen, quickly closing the emails before logging out of the forum. McGregor took a seat and stared up at him expectantly.

"I like what I've seen so far. Let's continue."

Adam opened his mouth, his fingers hovering over his mouse as he tried to regain his composure and remember where he was in the slideshow. McGregor folded his arms and settled back in his chair as if he was making himself comfortable for the next installment of the performance.

"So … uh … we were talking about …" But all he could think of was what Mackenzie would think. She would find out.

Maybe she already had?

What now?

And who the hell was hiding behind the name of R Yew Kidding?

Jake Parnell?

Someone else?

Another coaching client who hadn't gotten the results they'd wanted?

He tried to think. He hadn't dealt with anyone aside from Patrick. He'd declined requests for new coaching ever since he'd become busy with Mackenzie. It had to be someone he had coached in-person, someone who knew him. Someone who had signed the NDA.

Someone who was a disgruntled and bitter student.

Jake.

If it was him, the guy was in for a nasty shock. He'd signed an NDA prohibiting him from revealing Adam's identity, and he'd blatantly ignored it. Adam was going to examine all legal options and hit this man where it hurt the most—in his wallet.

"Something wrong, Adam?" McGregor squinted at him.

"No… no … no, sir. I was …" He couldn't think. He couldn't focus. He couldn't continue. He scratched his chin, laughing to ward off his unease. "Where was I?" He stared at his laptop screen, then stared at the smartboard even though it mirrored what was on his laptop.

"You seem lost, son." McGregor stated. "Are you?"

"We were talking about the performance indicators and, uh …"

McGregor chortled. "It seems as if my interruption made you lose your train of thought."

"Uh …" This time he felt the vibration of his phone which was snuggled away in his pocket. Someone had called him, or texted. Luckily, McGregor couldn't hear the vibration. "We were talking about …" The phone vibrated again.

Then again.

"Adam?" McGregor looked puzzled. "What's happened? You seem to have fallen flat and all I did was step out of the room for a few minutes."

His phone vibrated again. The blood in his veins froze.

Mackenzie.

She knew. She was calling to break up with him. His gut clenched. He wanted to wring Jake Parnell's neck.

He needed to know who was trying to contact him but McGregor's watchful eyes were on him.

"Would you mind if I check something on my phone, please? I'm sorry. It's important." He had never done this before, but this was a moment like no other.

"Go ahead."

He stepped out of the room, pulled out his cell phone and looked. A wave of relief swept over him.

Patrick had called.

And someone else, a number he didn't recognize.

But at least it wasn't Mackenzie. She didn't know, otherwise she would have confronted him—presentation withstanding or not.

He slipped the cell phone back into his pocket and took a big, long inhale. He would deal with the fallout when he returned home later this evening.

This was important. Sean McGregor's business was perfect for him, and Adam was the man to take it into the digital age. He needed this as much as the man needed him.

He walked back inside the conference room, trying to still his beating heart.

"Digital campaigns," he started, finding a new burst of energy. "This is where we can …"

Another vibration on his phone stole his attention. Why the heck was Patrick calling him again? Or that other number? In his rush not to mess up the presentation, he hadn't bothered calling back to see who it might have been. He glanced up to find McGregor staring at him as if he'd just escaped from an asylum.

Holding up his index finger to stave off any questions, Adam pulled his cell phone out again.

It was that same number he didn't recognize. But, again, at least it wasn't Mackenzie. He switched the phone off completely, shoved it back into his pocket and cleared his throat, determined to press on ahead.

"Digital campaigns are … uh … a way we can reach a larger audience of prospective … uh."

McGregor sat forward in his chair, his expression resigned. "Clearly, your mind is elsewhere. I don't know what's happened to you in the last ten minutes, but you're struggling to sound coherent."

"I can do this. Please." He needed this. He tried to push the personal matter to the back of his mind.

Act confident, and in time you will be.

One of his dating rules.

The goddamned dating rules.

The things that had gotten him in big, big trouble.

"Adam," McGregor shook his head. "This is your last chance."

"Yes, sir. Thank you."

McGregor sat back, an air of expectation on his face. Adam needed to make up for lost time and lost ground. His performance had started off well but had now nosedived like a fallen rocket. He was going to crash and fail spectacularly.

Desperate to salvage this, he opened his mouth to start again but an image of Jake Parnell flashed into his head, followed by an image of Mackenzie face down in the flower pot. His mind emptied.

"Adam. It's a shame." McGregor stood up decisively, spelling the end for Adam and his presentation. He seemed to know what Adam wasn't willing to own up to; that he couldn't save the day if he tried. "I really liked you, but I have other people to see."

"I'm sorry. I … I can try again tomorrow or …"

"We have four other people lined up today, and we're booked

with interviews for the rest of the week. I'm not sure if we'll be able to fit you in. I need to make a decision quickly and I'm pretty sure we'll have found someone in the mix of candidates we have."

Adam stepped towards the man, eager to salvage what he could. "I can help you in ways other companies can't." That was a bold statement. "I've worked with more than a handful of medium-sized companies all over the country. Nothing is too difficult now that we can do so much online. Even meetings. Could you fit me in for an online meeting?"

"You're asking a lot, young man."

"I want the contract, and I know I can do a lot for your business, sir."

"You haven't convinced me yet that you're the right man for the job," the older man countered.

Adam's insides sank. "I haven't. You're right. But I'm only human. Not a machine."

"I'll have my PA get in touch, but with all the people we have lined up, don't be upset if you don't hear back. Sometimes, son, you only get one shot to make an impression."

Another dating rule.

"I know, sir. I understand that one completely. But sometimes, *sometimes*, there are calls you have to take, like you did when your wife called."

"I thought you said you didn't have a wife."

"I don't, and at this rate I won't have a girlfriend either."

McGregor looked at him as if he'd looked right through him. "I don't know why I'm doing this. I really don't. But you remind me of myself when I first started out. Tenacious, not giving up, needing a break."

"I'm not des—" He wasn't thinking straight. He'd just been about to tell the man that he wasn't that desperate for business.

Shut up.

"I'd appreciate another chance, sir."

"My PA might get in touch with you, it depends on how we do. Time is of the essence these days."

"Yes, sir." Time was most definitely of the essence. He'd screwed up here and he needed to rush back to Starling Bay before he screwed up with Mackenzie forever. He quickly got his things together.

McGregor opened the door. "It's a shame. I liked what you were talking about. You were doing so well."

CHAPTER 29

"Adam's on his way from Philly," Mackenzie explained as she and Leigh stepped into the lobby of the Grand Hotel for another monthly SBWEB meeting.

She hoped tonight's meeting wouldn't go on too late to because she wanted to get back and see Adam and ask him all about his presentation. He'd called her earlier to tell her he was heading back.

"How about you and I get dinner after?" Leigh suggested. Sometimes the SBWEB meetings were held over dinner at one of the restaurants, but tonight the meeting was in one of the conference rooms at the hotel.

Mackenzie winced. "I wanted to see how Adam's presentation went." She already felt guilty for showing up at his place and disturbing him when he should have been working.

Leigh stopped and gaped at her. "I can't believe you're blowing me off again. The only way I have access to you is if Adam is out of town."

Mackenzie poked her lightly in the arm. "Don't say that."

"You've turned into one of those women. It's sad, but it's

true." Leigh turned her face in mock indignation, as if she was refusing to have anything to do with Mackenzie.

"That is so not true." She and Leigh had often talked about women who forgot about their friends and loved ones when they met a guy and fell head over heels in love. She wasn't head over heels in love. Not yet, not *really*, though she hadn't gone a day without seeing Adam, and she thought about him all the time. Happiness hugged her like a big, enveloping, all-encompassing embrace each time she thought of him and she now couldn't imagine her life without him.

Was that head over heels in love? *Almost?*

She braced herself to counter Leigh's reply but her friend seemed to be distracted. "Hmmm. I wonder what they're all huddled together for," Leigh remarked as they headed towards the meeting room and saw a group of women bunched together outside the door.

"What's going on?" Mackenzie asked.

Roxy turned around. "Haven't you heard? About the Love Doctor?"

"No. What about him?" Leigh's voice turned high-pitched. "Did Lisa get her scoop?" The journalist had intended to reach out to him at the last meeting.

"Oh, Lisa got much more than her scoop," Lisa replied, talking about herself in the third person, her face jubilant with smugness. Her wide and contented smile reminded Mackenzie of a cat who'd devoured a huge vat of cream.

"The suspense is killing me, who is it?" someone whisper-hissed as the ladies jostled even closer, Leigh bustling in for a place while Mackenzie stretched her neck, towering over most of the women.

"It's …" The sound of a virtual drum roll played in Mackenzie's head. "…Adam Hartman," Lisa announced, "the marketing guy."

"What?" Leigh cried, as the air emptied out of Mackenzie's lungs. It was as if someone had landed a Herculean punch to her solar plexus. She stumbled back a few steps, shock layered thick with confusion.

"It can't be." Her voice was so quiet, so breathless, no one heard her. The chatter of conversation continued as she took a step away from the group.

It couldn't be.

It couldn't.

"Can you believe my luck? The guy lives here. In *Starling Bay*. How's that for a shocker? Starling Bay? He was here all along, right under my nose. I was prepared to travel to Seattle for an interview. Starling Bay, ladies. The Love Doctor lives right here." Murmurs of shock flew around.

"But how did you find out that it was him?" someone asked.

"It was posted in the forum," Lisa announced proudly. "Most probably by someone with a grudge."

"I saw that post." Another woman joined in, and then they all started talking at once.

"How do you know for sure?" Leigh demanded, expertly placing herself between Mackenzie and the group, so as to protect her. The woman chattered, everyone having something to say.

Mackenzie's mind was a riot of disarray. How could it be Adam? He would have owned up to it when she'd accused him of using the man's services. But then another punch slammed her in the stomach, as sharp as a knife and as heavy as a brick. The notecard she'd found under his desk.

His explanation seemed weak now compared to this news.

This made sense.

"Who outed him?" someone asked.

"I've heard rumors that it might have been Jake Parnell. He used the guy's coaching services but things didn't work out between him and his fiancée. Someone said he demanded a refund from Adam which he refused to give."

"That's just dumb," a woman laughed. "That's just … that's guys for you." She shook her head. "Just because you break up with your fiancée doesn't mean it's anyone's fault but yours."

"It depends on what he taught them," retorted Lisa. "I'm curious to know what advice he gives."

"My brother's friend said he'd read the book," said Roxy, as if this might shed some light on the matter.

"Did he get any coaching?" Lisa asked. "I want to interview people who've taken his coaching."

Roxy shook her head. "Patrick isn't the type of guy who'd want to be coached. Did you ask the Love Doctor for an interview?"

"I've left messages and emails, and the guy isn't answering me back," Lisa replied.

"How did you get his number? There's no contact number on the website, there's only an email address," Roxy stated.

"As soon as I found out who it was, it was simple. Adam Hartman is quite a proactive, entrepreneurial type. He'd listed his marketing services on the forum and that's where I got all of his contact details from."

"No wonder you're a journalist." The women laughed and continued talking. Mackenzie felt hollow, as if all her bones and muscles had left her body. Leigh approached her, her brows a criss-cross of worry.

"It might not be true," she said, her voice low.

Leigh could sugarcoat this news all she wanted, it wasn't going to make it any more palatable. Mackenzie knew. She knew in her heart that it was true.

Dazed and hurt, shocked and humiliated, she stood broken, trying to make sense of the unexpected news which had trainwrecked her day. Numbness wrapped itself around her like a big, woolly cloud.

It wasn't public knowledge that she and Adam were dating, and after this, she didn't want anyone to know at all.

"Mackenzie." Leigh tried to reach out for her as she started to slip away, needing to put distance between her and the group of cackling women.

Adam?

The Love Doctor.

He'd made lying an art form.

She didn't want to have anything do with Adam.

Ever.

CHAPTER 30

He raced back, driving directly to Mackenzie's shop and was worried to see that the lights were off. Even though it was past closing time, Mackenzie would still be pottering inside for a while. He knocked on the glass window, peering inside to see if he could catch a glimpse of her.

"Mackenzie!" he shouted. But there was no reply. He'd called her as soon as he left McGregor's company, trying to gauge if she knew, but she'd sounded normal; still concerned about him and wanting to know how his presentation had gone. He'd lied and told her that it had gone well and that he'd be back soon.

But not seeing her here set off a riot of worry inside him. Reason battled with fear as he tried to figure out where she might be. "Mackenzie!" He knocked again, hoping that she might be in the back, in her work room, recording another video.

Or maybe she had now found out.

That would explain why she'd closed up early and vanished.

He pulled out his cell phone to call her, and that was when he remembered. He was sure that she'd previously talked about there being another SBWEB meeting this week.

Was it today?

He paused to think, his scrambled mind trying to remember what day she'd said it was. Maybe it was wishful thinking—the reason for her not being here—that he wanted to believe this instead of any other reason.

Leaving his car parked outside her shop, he ran to the hotel. From past experience, he knew these meetings were sometimes held at the restaurant there or in one of the conference rooms.

He rushed into the restaurant, frantically glancing inside and looking for a table of women, but there were only couples sitting together. He rushed down the hallway, towards the conference rooms, all the while berating himself for not telling her sooner.

He'd planned to tell her once this presentation was out of the way, but Jake Parnell, or some other lowlife like him, had put a wrench in that plan.

If she knew, then she had found out from someone else, and if that were the case, they were well and truly over. Mackenzie wouldn't allow him to explain his side of the story. She wouldn't want to hear what he had to say.

As he turned a corner, his heart leapt for joy when he saw her in the distance. But she stood away from a group of women. Fear kicked him in the gut and his nerves knotted. That wasn't the pose of a happy woman. Leigh was trying to talk to her, maybe even comfort her, judging from the way she was standing with her arm around Mackenzie.

This didn't bode well.

"Mackenzie." He called out to her, not daring to go right up to her, knowing from her closed body language that he couldn't invade her personal space. In this moment, he was less a concerned boyfriend and more a worried friend.

The women gossiped and laughed, the rumors flying around like missiles. Each comment, each peal of laughter, each exclamation of surprise firing deeper into her chest.

"Mackenzie?" Adam's voice sliced through the heavy fog that dulled and dimmed the deep recesses of her mind. Her heart sank. She had no desire to see him, much less talk to him.

She looked at him, and the raucous group of women fell silent as quickly as if a scythe had cut through the air. He stared at her warily, his feet planted a few steps away as if he was too scared to come closer.

"You know."

It suddenly became harder to breathe, as if a blockage constricted her windpipe. She was conscious that Leigh had moved to her side, had hooked her arm in hers, but his words sealed the truth she had been trying to deny.

"Mackenzie, say something." Adam peered at her, his eyes narrowed with guilt.

"Do *you* want to say something?" Leigh asked her softly. She needed to, but her mouth turned desert-dry, and all she could do was think back to the times she had asked him about the Love Doctor. She'd been so worried that he might have taken coaching lessons from the vile man, that it had never in a million years crossed her mind that he might have *been* the Love Doctor. The inane thought bubbled up, causing her to erupt into laughter.

"Mackenzie?" Leigh's worried voice whispered close to her ear, but all she could think about was the Achilles heel and how Adam had worked it to his advantage. How he had scooped up all the news about her mother, and the bullies, her childhood without parents, all of it, and used it to snake his way into her life.

"You lied to me." Her voice, hard and brittle, didn't sound like her. From the corners of her field of vision, she could see that the other women had formed a line on either side of her, a protective riot shield that would not let this man pass.

He stepped closer, held out his hand to her in a placating gesture. But it was wasted. "I was going to tell you," he whispered, his expression the most somber she had ever seen it.

"What stopped you? Or don't you have a rule for something like that?"

He took another daring step closer. "I can explain—"

"I don't want you to." She stepped back, recoiling from him.

"Now that you're here, Adam. Shall we set up a meeting?" Lisa, not one to miss an opportunity, stepped out of her shield line and got out her phone. "How about we set a time for tomorrow?"

His face twisted.

"Or you could suggest a time to talk to me?" Lisa was persistent, if nothing else. "I never for a moment pegged you as being a local. This is the best scoop I've ever had."

"No interview. Please, back off." His gaze never wavered from Mackenzie.

Leigh squeezed Mackenzie's arm. "Do you want to go home? I can take you home."

"I can take care of myself," Mackenzie replied unconvincingly.

Adam looked distraught. "Give me a chance to explain, Mackenzie. Please."

"Are you two together?" Lisa's voice grated on her nerves like sharp fingernails on a blackboard.

A babble of gasps filled the air. "Are you together?" someone cried out. Another roar of knowing was followed by cries of, "You never said!" and "You quiet little vixen." And "You and the Love Doctor?"

It was humiliating.

Leigh tried to pull her away, but she was suddenly reinvigorated by a fresh bout of energy. She met Adam's gaze hard. "You lied to me. I asked you for the truth. I gave you many chances, and still you lied."

"I answered the question you asked."

She remembered. What a snake, using *that* as his defense. "So you did. Sneaky. I was so wrong about you. You're nothing but a slimy salesman."

"Who have you coached?" one of the women asked. "Do you have a list of names?"

The look he gave her could have caused a flower to wilt.

"Adam," another woman called out, "did my boyfriend ever come to you?"

The next thing she knew, the women broke rank and huddled around Adam, throwing a hundred questions at him.

It was the perfect moment for escape. "I need to get out of here."

Leigh grabbed her hand and pulled her away. Soon they were in the car and all she wanted was to put a million miles between her and the man she had once trusted.

CHAPTER 31

The women were in his face, suffocating him like a swarm of busy worker bees, deadly and loud. Questions and accusations were hurled at him like stings. They blocked his view so that he could no longer see Mackenzie.

"You haven't denied it," said the woman he'd come to know as the journalist. At last he was able to put a face to the name. Now that she knew who he was, she circled around him like a bloodthirsty piranha.

He tried to back away, but each time he took a few steps backwards, trying to get away, the women advanced and before he knew it, he was backed up against a wall.

"Can you all please leave me alone?" he cried, when he saw that Mackenzie and her friend had gone and that he was now left with these vultures.

"Give me one interview and I will." The journalist was relentless.

"Leave the poor man alone, Lisa."

"Poor man?" someone cried. "He's the Love Doctor. This guy's made a fortune. There's nothing poor about him."

Another woman raised her voice and announced that they

needed to get started with their meeting. One by one, they started to walk away except for Lisa who stared at him like an angry bulldog.

"You're not making this easy Adam. This could be a chance for you to tell your story." She pulled out a business card and thrust it into his hand with a wink. "You never know, I could do some good marketing for you."

He ground down hard on his molars, determined to keep his mouth shut for fear of saying something that this woman might twist for her own benefit. He hated that these women had let Mackenzie—the only one who mattered, the only one he needed to explain to—get away.

At last, the journalist walked away, leaving him plastered against the wall. He shoved the business card into his suit pocket and smoothed out his shirt.

He'd never before been surrounded by a group of angry females. What he didn't understand was their abject resentment. Why did they care so much about what the Love Doctor stood for?

Surely, they couldn't have been angry that *he* was the Love Doctor—it was Mackenzie's right to be angry about that. He was coaching men on how to pursue women in a gentlemanly way.

What was wrong with that?

"I trusted him. For once, I let my guard down and I trusted him." The numbness had engulfed her body. Even her thoughts were mired in glue. It was hazy, trying to remember the past, and the good times with Adam. There were many. She had been happy. She had allowed him into her world.

She lay on the couch hugging a cushion while Leigh sat on an ottoman facing her.

"I liked Adam," Leigh announced. "I thought he was good for you."

"Are any of them good for us?"

"Who? Men? Yes. Once you find the right one. I thought Adam might be the right one for you."

"Turns out we were both wrong."

Leigh slid off the ottoman and squatted on the floor so that her head was level with Mackenzie's. "I've known the assholes, but I have also come to see that not all men are like that. My hope has been renewed, thanks to Rourke, and one day, just you wait and see, you'll find a precious diamond in the rough."

Mackenzie moved her head and focussed her gaze on the ceiling. Things had moved so slowly at first with Adam, but once she had seen—or thought she had seen—that he had her best interests at heart, she had given in to the attraction she'd been trying to resist.

Their getting together had flowed so seamlessly. They'd slipped into a little twosome, connecting and bonding as if they were fated to be together. Letting him in on her wounds and worries, allowing him to comfort her, make her forget, make her feel special—she'd been sucked into thinking he cared.

He'd been the perfect charmer and now she couldn't let go of the fact that he had lied so blatantly. He'd lied to cover up who he really was.

"You should eat." Leigh got up and stared down at her.

"I'm not hungry." Food was the last thing on her mind. She replayed all the conversations she'd had with Adam, all the intimate details of her life that she had shared, and she now hated herself for being conned by this marketing guru.

"You have to eat," Leigh insisted. "I know how you feel, Mackenzie, but there's no point dwelling over what's happened. He lied, I don't know why, but there's no point in thinking of all the ways you can get back at him. Not now. Besides, I need to eat."

"What time is it?"

"Almost midnight."

"Almost midnight!" she screamed, bolting upright. "You go on home, Leigh. I'll be fine. Don't worry about me." She had lost track of time, of thought, of the fact that Leigh hadn't left her side ever since they'd come home. She didn't want to think about the table conversation at the SBWEB meeting. She didn't know how she was going to face those women the next time.

"But I do worry about you. You're upset, and you feel humiliated. Finding out the way you did must sting, and Adam coming to the hotel didn't help."

"If I'm upset, it's my own fault. Falling for a salesman, a conman, a marketing man. *A guru.*"

"Don't keep thinking about him."

"How can I not? He's the Love Doctor. He's the man who teaches other men how to win women."

Leigh paused, cupping her chin thoughtfully. "Is that such a bad thing?"

"What?" Shock torpedoed through Mackenzie. "We both agreed it was. Whose side are you on?"

"I've been looking at his website, while you were wallowing in revenge," said Leigh. "He says on there that he's teaching men to woo women without using dating apps." She faced her cell phone so that Mackenzie could see it. "Look, he even says, no need to swipe left or right, no need to use fake photos, or be someone you're not. No need to post lies about who you are, no making yourself out to be someone you're not. Here, look at what he says here, 'You can find the right woman for you by being *you.* I will show you how.' He doesn't sound like he's giving men the wrong approach."

Mackenzie's lips turned up at the corners. She didn't know

whether to laugh or cry as she looked at her friend in disbelief. "You're the one who hated the idea of the Love Doctor more than I did."

"I did, because I assumed he was doing things a certain way, you know, like teaching men cheesy pick-up lines, and telling men to do whatever it took to pick up women, but the more I'm reading this—"

"I don't want to know, Leigh. Stop trying to convince me. It's simple. He lied to me. He could have told me who he was and what he did. I gave him plenty of opportunities. I even asked him outright when I found that note, and when I overheard those women at your shop talking about the Achilles heel, I asked him."

"I remember." Leigh fiddled around on her phone. "It's a dating rule. Here." She shoved the phone in Mackenzie's face. "These are the rules."

"He used his rules to win me over." The man was a sleazeball. He'd betrayed her trust even though she had told him how hard it was for her to get close to someone. Knowing everything about her, he still couldn't find it in him to come clean, and that had hurt her the most.

How could she ever trust him again? What future lay ahead for them after this?

None.

She managed to convince Leigh that she was fine, and that she needed to get some sleep.

When her friend left, she lay back on the couch and thumbed through her cell phone looking at the Love Doctor's website. Curiosity goaded her. She wanted to know what those rules were. She needed to know how Adam had worked on her.

She hit the buy button and bought the book, and for the next few hours, she devoured it all, understanding the man better than she had before.

~

He rapped his knuckles hard on the door. It had been a gamble coming here, but the guy wasn't answering his phone calls and Adam had no choice. Resentment simmered under his skin, but to his utter surprise, Jake Parnell opened the door, his expression turning stone cold when he saw Adam's face.

"You look worried, Parnell. Any reason why?"

"What do you want?" Jake barked.

"I know it was you. We signed an NDA. You broke our agreement."

"I don't know what you're talking about."

"R Yew Kidding," Adam roared. "That's you?"

Jake's expression sobered.

"That's what I thought. You've caused me and my business considerable damage—"

"I don't know what you're talking about."

"You posted in the forum." He fisted his hands by his sides, all his pent-up anger now directed to the man who had set out to ruin him. He wasn't here to listen to anything Jake had to say. He only wanted him to know that he was on to him, and that there would be consequences, exactly what those would be he didn't yet know. "You revealed who I was, despite signing an agreement to keep my identity private when I took you on for coaching—"

"As if that helped," Jake snarled.

"My coaching is supposed to advise and encourage. I'm not a miracle worker."

Jake punched the door. "Get lost."

"You'll be hearing from my lawyer in due course." Adam turned to leave. He was done with this man.

"Bring it on." Jake growled behind him.

How enforceable was an NDA? He didn't know. Nor was he

sure if the time and money in trying to sue this man would amount to anything.

Probably not.

It was likely he wouldn't be able to do a thing. He'd taken a huge risk with the Love Doctor business. The only reason he'd persisted with it was because the damned thing had taken off and he'd been so unprepared for its success. It had seemed so easy, compared to dealing with clients and working on their businesses.

The way he did with Mackenzie.

But he had so enjoyed doing that. Working with her had meant something. Watching her business grow green shoots of possibility, seeing her eyes fill with hope, these things had brought him a sense of achievement.

He had so enjoyed working with her and helping her. But now he'd lost her.

Not forever.

He was determined that it wouldn't be forever. She was upset and he understood why. She'd disappeared before he'd had a chance to try to put things right. It hadn't been the right time or the right place.

He was going to fix this even though, knowing Mackenzie, he had a battle ahead of him.

CHAPTER 32

When she arrived at her shop the next day, the last person on earth she ever wanted to see was waiting for her outside.

Reaching deep into her mind and body, she reverted to her former ways, blanking her expression and erecting a guard around her emotions. Having read his book, she now had a better insight into the man and his tactics, and she didn't want him within earshot of her.

"Please leave." She turned the key to open the lock.

"Please hear me out," he begged. "I know you hate me, and you have every right to but—"

She stood in the doorway, barring him from entry, and forced herself to look at him, no easy feat given the way she felt.

"Please, Mackenzie."

"I don't want to see you, Adam. Don't be selfish, coming here needing to explain things to me now. I gave you plenty of chances. You could have told the truth, but you chose not to."

"I hated keeping it from you, and I was going to tell you. You have to believe me."

"Believe you?" she snorted. "I'll never believe another word you say."

He shook his head, as if he refused to accept this. "I would have told you sooner, but you and Leigh were so against me, against the Love Doctor, and you made him sound like a misogynist. You never saw him for who he really was."

"I see him for what he is now, a liar, someone never to be trusted."

"I lied because I didn't want to lose you, but I hated carrying that with me. I didn't want to keep secrets between us, Mackenzie. I was going to tell you."

"I don't believe you. I don't want to see you again. You took what I said about my past and used it against me. I can't trust you."

"How did I use it against you?" He looked genuinely perplexed.

"Me telling you about my parents, about my school days … you found out what hurt me and made me think you cared."

"No, I didn't. I cared. I really cared. I never 'worked on you'. I saw you for who you were, a strong woman, determined to get ahead no matter what card life had dealt you. I wanted to help your business grow because I saw that you had so much potential."

She didn't believe liars, and she wasn't about to now.

He looked distraught. "I never intended for you to find out the way you did. I was going to tell you after the presentation."

She gave a hollow laugh. "You expect me to believe that?"

"My book, and the coaching, what I did, it was never meant to be serious, not for the long haul—"

"More lies. Don't you ever stop?" Did he expect her to believe that he was going to discard this new business opportunity when he was making so much money from it?

"I wrote it never thinking it would take off the way it did. I wrote it because once upon a time, a guy like me could have benefited from reading something like—"

She put her hand up in the air, halting him. "I don't want your sob story. I have to open the shop. I don't have time for –"

"You women don't know how hard it is for men to ask a woman out, you only have to say yes or no, and for some men, I was one of them, that rejection can scar. It leaves us feeling we aren't enough. Some men give up, and they think they're never going to find anyone. I wrote the book for those men. To help them."

She lowered her hand, found herself listening in spite of her mood. This information was enlightening, but as genuine as he seemed, she couldn't imagine Adam being someone who didn't have the confidence and charisma that seemed ingrained in him.

"That's why I did this, Mackenzie. It's not even my main business. It's a side job, something I did for fun. I'm still trying to come to grips with its success. There's nothing eye-opening in it. No new secrets or tips, or hacks. There's nothing new here but good old-fashioned courting."

He was doing it again. Working his charm on her, getting her to see the good in what he did.

She would be a fool to fall for it again. "I don't want to talk to you, Adam, and I don't want to listen to what you've got to say."

"That's not fair."

"Fair? Don't you talk to me about fair." She turned on him, irritation stoking the flames of fire that were already kindling in her stomach. The audacity of this man to complain about her not being fair.

His mouth opened, but she wasn't interested in anything he had to say.

"Find her Achilles heel, her soft spot," she snapped, quoting from his book as her anger melded with bitterness at the way this man had used his rules on her. It struck her as soon as she read that in the book. The short book hadn't taken long to read at all. It didn't need to be a *War and Peace*-sized tome, after all, what was there to say about how to pursue women? Within less than an hour, she'd come to know how this man's mind worked.

"I can explain—"

"You found mine, didn't you? You listened, and soothed, and made me feel important, digging deeper into my wounds and fears, telling me it was okay to feel the way I did, telling me I was so amazing. You got under my skin, you became my friend, my confidante. You charmed me and made me believe you cared about me, that you had my best interests at heart. Now I see what it was all for. It was a revelation getting inside your mind and seeing first-hand how you *wooed* me."

"I didn't use any of those rules on you. I didn't play by any of them. I didn't need—"

"Shush." She put a finger to her lips. "You've said enough. You won't convince me."

"You're accusing me of something, and it's not how it was."

"You're a shameless snake oil salesman and you're wasting your time and mine." She tried to close the door, but he held his arm out, preventing it.

"But now that you've read the book, surely you can see that the rules are nothing but harmless, basic facts? Think about it, what advice am I giving? What message am I trying to impart? There are men out there who don't want to download dating apps, who don't have the confidence to show their pictures because, oh, I don't know, maybe because they're not muscular and jaw-droppingly handsome, and they don't look like some hot movie star—"

He'd done it again, made her listen. She seemed to have no defense against him. How did he do it, manage to hold her attention even though she hated everything about him?

"I hear from men daily, and they thank me for the book. They tell me they needed guidance because so many don't know what to say to women when they have to talk face to face. In this digital social media driven world, where you can't even be sure of who you're really talking to, is that such a bad thing—trying to get people to connect in person? If a man who's had no success, who lacks confidence, who has been rejected so many times, needs support, needs someone to show him the way, is that so wrong of me to help him?"

"If you consider this to be something noble, something you were proud of, then what stopped you from telling me? Why didn't you say something when I asked you about the notecard?"

"Because … because you would have hated me. I've heard you dismiss the Love Doctor as some sleazy guy. Leigh hates him."

"Leigh has a reason to."

An unasked question formed in his eyes. "I don't teach men to be something they're not. I don't teach them to pursue women as if they are prey."

This had to stop. She'd been trying unsuccessfully to close the door on him for a while "I'm done, Adam. I don't want to discuss this. You lied to me, and I can't trust you. All of your explanations mean nothing after the fact."

"I hate that I hurt you, but I am not the monster or sleazy douchebag you make me out to be. I can see that you need more time."

"It's not more time that I need, Adam, it's that I've lost all trust in you."

"I've tried to tell you why that was—"

"For the love of all things, please leave me alone. I have a business to run."

She looked away, not wanting to see the desperate look in his eyes. Heeding her wishes, he left her alone.

For the rest of the day, she kept herself busy. Leigh helped by popping in to see her throughout the day, bringing a boatload of calories in the form of comfort food. She was inundated with cakes, muffins and all sorts of delicious pastries.

But underneath her poised demeanor, restlessness pricked and poked at her bones. As hard as she tried not to, she couldn't help but think about Adam and what had happened.

Not wanting to go home, she drove to the one place that was familiar and comforting, into the arms of the one person who had the power to make her feel whole again.

CHAPTER 33

She had the key to the house, but she rang the doorbell anyway. When her grandma opened the door, Mackenzie fell into her arms, prompting her grandma to worry and wonder what had happened.

Over her grandmother's shoulder, she saw her mother in the kitchen, cooking something over the burner, a look of quiet surprise on her face.

Mackenzie didn't usually show up at her grandma's unannounced, and she could tell that they sensed something was wrong. Not wanting to worry her grandma too much, Mackenzie told her that she was fine, and that she was tired and needed a break. But as she spoke, unable to put on a happy face and spin on things, her eyes began to well up, and there wasn't a thing she could do to stop it.

"This wouldn't be anything to do with that fine young man, would it?" her grandmother asked. That was all it took. A fat tear drop rolled down her cheek. She couldn't hide anything from this woman.

"Come in here and set yourself down. I want to hear everything." Her grandma ushered her into the living room and

Mackenzie sank onto the soft, squishy couch, memories of her childhood life rushing back to her. She'd finally come home.

She started to talk, at first unsure of where to start, glancing at the door each time she thought she heard something.

"Don't worry about your mom. She won't come in. She wouldn't think of intruding."

Feeling relieved, Mackenzie told her grandma everything, about her and Adam getting together, about how helpful he had been, about how he'd done so much for her. Her grandmother's eyes glistened with joy, until Mackenzie told her about Adam's side business, about his infamous book, and how he coached men and had hidden this from her. How he lied to her face.

She waited for solidarity, for support, for Grandma to take her side. "A *Love* coach? My, my. That's an interesting career choice if ever I heard one."

Mackenzie's mouth fell open. "Is that all you have to say, Grandma?"

"It's interesting, no?"

"Grandma! He *lied* to me. Haven't you been listening?"

"I hear you, Mackenzie. That I do."

"He hurt me."

"I can see it on your face. I could tell as soon as I saw you."

"I just wanted a break. I just wanted to come here."

"You can always come here. Now, slip off your shoes, and lay yourself down." Feeling worn out, Mackenzie slipped off her shoes and lay down on the couch, yawning. Her grandmother slowly walked over to her with a blanket.

"You look tired."

"I haven't been able to sleep."

Her grandmother sighed loudly. "I expect you haven't." She laid the blanket over Mackenzie. "Why don't you stay here for a few days? You can travel to work from here. I don't want you on your own, not when you're looking as if you've given up."

She tilted her head towards her grandmother. She had given up. How astute of her grandmother to notice.

Her mood had simmered in anger, then sadness followed, and now the weight of defeat bore down on her. She lacked energy and willpower, wanting only to be left alone with her thoughts.

Grandma was right. She had given up.

"We can take care of you. It would be so lovely having you here again, Mackenzie."

She had already closed her eyes. For some reason, merely telling her grandma had shifted a huge weight off her chest. She'd expected more support in her favor, instead of the reaction her grandma gave, but it didn't matter. Nothing mattered right now because her tired body wanted sleep, nothing more. There was something comforting about being taken care of. She still had some clothes in her closet here and she could manage for a few days.

"I'll stay for a few days," she said, nestling further into the soft cushions, but then her eyelids flew open. "Doesn't m—mom sleep in my room?"

Grandma chortled. "Your mother has never used your room. She's always slept on the couch."

Mackenzie sat up. That was insanity. "Why?"

"She didn't want you to get mad at her for taking your room."

"But ..." Words failed her. She was overcome by guilt knowing that her mother had slept on the couch for so long when there had been a spare bed, *her* bed, all along. And that she'd done so because she hadn't wanted more bad feelings between her and Mackenzie.

"I've been such a brat," Mackenzie said slowly. "Why didn't you ever tell me?"

"You haven't been a brat. But had I told you, would it have made any difference then?" Grandma asked, slowly getting up from the couch. "You rest up, and I'll see what your mother is up to in the kitchen."

But Mackenzie couldn't rest up. She was haunted by the idea of her mother sleeping here all this time. If she had known, she would have fixed it. She would have said something. She would have told her mother to take her room because she no longer needed it.

A heavy feeling settled in her stomach. When people hurt her, she blocked them out of her life, never giving them a second chance.

"Mackenzie ..." Her grandmother had walked back in. "It will be dinnertime soon. I hope you're hungry because you mother is making your favorite dish, macaroni and cheese."

CHAPTER 34

It was difficult to do, letting the days pass without him seeing her, but when his phone and text messages to Mackenzie still went ignored, Adam decided that he had no choice but to try again.

Bracing himself for more knockbacks, he returned to her place, anxiety flushing through his veins when he knocked on the door and heard footsteps on the other side.

He took a deep breath. This wasn't going to be easy, but he'd be damned if he wasn't going to chisel away Mackenzie's hatred of him bit by bit until he got through to her.

In the broader picture, he hadn't cheated on her, he hadn't done anything as unforgiveable as that. He'd done nothing too wrong.

Except lie to her and hide who he was.

But in his defense, he had done this to help people. If only he could get Mackenzie to see that.

When she didn't open the door, he knocked again, preparing himself for the dour mood he would no doubt find her in. But there was still no reply. He tried again, knocking harder, and this time the door opened just an inch. His heart leapt inside his rib cage and when the door fully opened, his forced cheeriness deflated like a pin-pricked balloon.

"You?" he cried.

Leigh was the last person he wanted to see. There was no way that this piranha was going to let him in. She had shredded his reputation before he'd had a chance to defend himself.

"You?" She parroted back, hands on hips, preparing for a standoff.

"I want to see Mackenzie."

"You can *want* all you like. You can't see her."

He sucked in an irritated breath. "Shouldn't you let Mackenzie be the judge of that?" He was sick of Leigh being the gatekeeper. "Mackenzie!" he shouted, hoping she would hear him.

There was no reply. The signs didn't look encouraging that she was anywhere near forgiving him.

Leigh placed her hand on the door, as if to delineate the invisible boundary beyond which he could not advance. Blocking her out, doing his best to, he looked over her shoulder and called for Mackenzie again. "I just need to talk to her, alone."

"You've done enough talking"

"Can you please ask Mackenzie to let me have a few minutes of her time?"

"She's not here."

Their eyes locked in an angry standoff. He didn't know whether to believe her or not.

"Where is she?" It was late, he realized, glancing at his watch. Time-to-go-to-bed late.

"She needed to get as far away from you as possible."

He tried to think where she would be at this time of night, if not here or at Leigh's place?

"She used to gush about how you lifted her, how you helped

her self-esteem. She thought she was lucky to have found you." If Leigh's expression could shoot bullets, he'd be a dead man now.

"I was lucky to have found her. You saw the change in her, I'm not saying it was because of me, but I like to think that I helped her with the business. That's what got her all excited. I want the best for Mackenzie. I'm not out to lie and cheat my way into her life."

Leigh nibbled her lower lip. "I've read your book."

This was a surprising admission, for such a self-confessed hater. "You have?"

Leigh nodded, and just then it came to him, the place where he could find Mackenzie. "She's at her grandma's, isn't she?" He was certain that that was where she would have gone to hide and heal.

Leigh shoved her hands into her sweatshirt pockets, her lips working as if she was mulling something over.

"What?" The idea that Mackenzie hated him so much that she'd had to leave her home and escape to her grandma's soured his mood further.

"Your book wasn't all that bad."

"No?" He waited for her to deliver the punchline, the one where she trashed him completely.

"I've known some real douchebags in my life, and I didn't have such great expectations for the book, but you surprised me."

Her sincere tone made him stand straighter and hold his attention. "I didn't set out to trick men or give them dishonest ways of attracting women. I wanted to help the guys who struggle to make connections."

"I know. I've read the book. You don't need to sell it to me again."

"I was hoping that Mackenzie would come to the same conclusion you did."

"You were dishonest with her. It's not a great basis for a relationship. You lied."

"I was going to tell her."

"She has trust issues. I believe you know all about that."

He almost rolled his eyes. "I've tried to explain my actions and tell her why I wrote it, but I don't think I got through. I wasn't appealing to men's baser instincts."

"No?"

"No! You said you liked it and it wasn't what you expected. You expected something else, like a playboy's playbook, and it wasn't that at all, was it? Admit it." When she said nothing, he continued. "The ten rules? They're just basic, decent tips."

"Like finding a woman's Achilles heel? Mackenzie feels used by you."

He drew in a sharp breath. He could see why she would. Why she might interpret it a different way than he had intended. She and Leigh had probably discussed this in depth.

"Most people aren't accustomed to listening. Especially men." He hoped this would get her attention. "We're living in such a 'look at me' society, what with all the photos of happy times and vacation pics, buff body photos that everyone is desperate for their friends to see. At the other end of the spectrum are the awkward guys, the geeky nerds who want only to play their video games, and somewhere in the middle is a group of men for whom the idea of meeting a woman scares the bejesus out of them. These men might be shy, or unsure, or not confident, or a host of other things that keep them in limbo. They're good men who want to have a relationship, who want to get married someday maybe, and they break out into a cold sweat at the idea of putting themselves out there. They don't want to use a dating app or make small talk filled with innuendo. If I put out a book helping these men, is that such a bad thing?"

Leigh blinked, but she was listening, which gave him

encouragement. If he could only get the opportunity to explain this to Mackenzie. If only.

"But," he sighed loudly, hoping that Leigh might be able to convince her friend, "Mackenzie doesn't want to see me, or let me explain. I'm determined to make it up to her, so you can tell her that I won't give up. She needs to hear my side of things, and then whatever she decides—whether she still hates me, or even if she tells me to get lost—I'll honor her wishes. She just needs to give me a chance to talk to her."

"Mackenzie doesn't have to do anything she doesn't want to."

"You're her friend. You can get her to see."

"Not all men have good intentions, Adam, but like I've already said to you, in reading your book, I expected the worst, but I was pleasantly surprised."

"There, you see, you've said it. Can you tell Mackenzie?"

"I will, but she's hurt and upset because you lied. What a man says and does, it matters. How a man treats you is telling. After everything she told you, surely you should know that?" Leigh pressed her lips together as if she'd said all she needed to.

"I do know that. Why do you think I'm here?"

He returned home, feeling as if he hadn't achieved much. In a fit of anger, he logged onto his computer and removed his personal number from the Starling Bay forum. He was tempted to leave altogether but it had proved useful to him in the short time he'd been here and he'd managed to get a few clients from it. For now, he decided to stay a member, even if the disadvantages of being a part of this online community far outweighed the advantages.

In a way, it was cathartic knowing that his secret was out. He'd been so paranoid about revealing his identity, that now that it had been done for him, it suddenly felt liberating.

He had also received many more emails. Most were to do with his Love Doctor identity being revealed.

One email caught his attention, though. That journalist was still relentless in her pursuit of him. Not only had she left him a few voicemails asking him to call her, but she'd emailed him again.

He deleted all of her messages.

CHAPTER 35

"He deserves to be heard."

Leigh was changing her tune and this in itself had come as a shock to Mackenzie. They were catching up over a sandwich at Roxy's diner at lunchtime, with Leigh telling her that Adam had come looking for her last night when she'd checked in on Mackenzie's plants and watered them.

"I'm not ready."

"It's been a week!"

Mackenzie's eyes widened. A week? Which meant she'd been at her grandmother's place for a little less than that. She couldn't stay there too long. The idea of depriving her mother of a bed riddled her in guilt. Not that she'd made a move to talk to her about it.

"Hey!" Leigh clicked her fingers together. "Where have you gone? I've lost you."

Mackenzie shifted her attention back to her friend. Leigh wanted her to hear Adam out. She had also read the book, and she was raving about it. All of a sudden, she seemed to be Adam's new friend. "I'm listening."

"I underestimated him," said Leigh, taking a bite of her bagel. "And I think you're doing the same."

"Please, give me a break." But knowing that he'd come to her place last night wanting to talk made her feel good. It meant that he'd been giving her space. She had half expected Adam to show up at her shop, but when days passed by and he hadn't, sadness enveloped her like a thick heavy blanket.

It was impossible to erase their time together, making recordings, sitting side by side staring at his computer screen as he explained technical issues to her. He'd done a lot to help her, she couldn't deny that.

Staying at her grandma's house had been the best thing for her. Being fed, and cared for, having to do nothing once she got home from work, gave her time to think. But it had also left her swimming in her own pool of sadness. She missed Adam. The Adam she *thought* she knew. What she couldn't reconcile with was the fact that he was the Love Doctor.

Her mother had also been trying to make amends and do what she could to lift Mackenzie's spirits. Guilt sliced through Mackenzie at the way she had treated this woman who had given birth to her.

But then left her.

Her mother had been making all of Mackenzie's favorite dishes, but mostly kept out of the way.

"Why don't you sit with us and eat ... M... Mom?" she suggested one evening. As soon as she came in from work, the table was always set for dinner. This was her mother's doing, because Grandma didn't have dinners timed to military perfection.

Her grandmother waved for her mother to join them. "Sit with us, Mandy."

"But I've already eaten." Her mother glanced at Mackenzie then looked away quickly.

"Sit with us anyway. Mackenzie's asking you to."

"Are you sure?" her mother asked.

"I don't bite, Mom."

Her mother sat down, toying with a small plate of salad. Dinner was quieter than usual, but they managed to get through it by making small talk, and with her mom and Grandma asking her all sorts of questions about the shop and the videos.

The videos.

Mackenzie had pushed all thought of those to the back of her mind. She could record them now that she had bought her own camera, the same as Adam's, and knew how to use it, but what she didn't know was how to edit them or upload them to the internet.

"Seems like having time away from your beau isn't such a bad thing," her grandma whispered to her, when Mackenzie went to check on her before bedtime, like she did every night before she went to bed.

"He's not my beau." Mackenzie perched on the edge of the bed, reveling in these nuggets-before-bedtime talks that this time with her grandma afforded her. Her grandmother hadn't brought up the topic of Adam since that first night, but Mackenzie hadn't been able to stop thinking about him.

"I like him, Mackenzie. I really do."

"You don't really know him, Grandma. I was going to bring him over some time soon, but ..." her voice trailed away.

"Do you know how I can tell that this man has been a good influence on you?"

"He hasn't had any influence on me." Mackenzie frowned as her grandma's soft eyes looked through her, penetrating her soul, finding all her little secrets, her upsets, her triumphs and jubilations, all locked away in tiny little chambers of her heart.

"I wouldn't be so sure of that. You've changed. You're giving your mother a chance. Something has gone soft inside you,

Mackenzie. The hard edges—the things no one else can see—they're melting away."

This was not because of Adam. Mackenzie gave an imperceptible shake of the head. That man hadn't done anything like that. How could he have when she'd only known him a short while? A self-absorbed marketing guru like him wasn't capable of eliciting such change and she wasn't about to give him the benefit of the doubt.

She was merely taking pity on her mother and now that she had spent a few days with her, it was impossible to completely ignore the woman who cooked her meals.

"You closed up when those nasty girls said such terrible things to you. I should have come down harder on the school. I wish I'd gone to their parents, each and every one of them, and given them a piece of my mind."

"Don't blame yourself for anything, Grandma. You made me feel loved. You made me believe in myself. You were enough. You did the best you could and I am so grateful to you."

"But I could have done more. I was so wrapped in worry about you. You believed everything they said, and I was trying to show you that their words were lies born and spun out of jealousy."

Mackenzie touched the old lady's face tenderly, feeling the same old kinship she always did. "I don't want you to feel bad. You've always been there for me, Grandma. Always. You made me believe in myself."

A tiny smile appeared on her grandma's lips. "I could see that they were jealous. You were so tall, so graceful, so beautiful. Strangers used to turn their heads in the street when you walked by. You couldn't see it because the poison had already buried deep. It made you loathe yourself. You were hunched, head down, not looking at anyone when you walked. Not daring to meet anyone's eyes. But I knew that there was more to my Mackenzie.

I didn't want other people—jealous, bitter, nasty people—to define who you were and who you could be."

Mackenzie reached down for her grandma's hand and stroked it. "You say the nicest things, Grandma. I'm the luckiest person in the world to have you."

"I'm the luckiest Grandma in the world to have someone like you. I know you've been through your hardship. I know your mom crushed you, but she's trying, Mackenzie. She's trying. She was broken like you once, too. She wanted to believe your father's words more than she did mine."

Her grandmother's wisdom floated over her like a patchwork quilt, warm, and comforting, made of kindness and love.

She bade her grandma goodnight and went to her room. Downstairs, she could hear her mother opening up the sofa and getting ready for bed. She took a deep uneasy breath, guilt choking her airways. Her mom could sleep with her. She was almost tempted to ask, but as she walked towards the door, she held back. She wasn't ready for that level of bonding. She couldn't stay here for much longer. She needed to tell her mother that she could start using her bedroom. It was only a small part of a more important conversation she needed to have.

She hopped on her bed, then lay on her stomach and switched on her laptop to check her emails. A gasp flew from her lips when she saw that over a hundred people had signed up for her floristry lessons. They weren't even ready yet. She still had to complete the course then edit it and upload it.

She still needed Adam.

CHAPTER 36

The clouds, dark and angry, glared down from the sky, which threatened to unleash its tears.

But Adam was a determined man, and it didn't stop him from driving to town. Catching Mackenzie in the middle of the workday would be a sure-fire way of getting her attention.

He slipped into Bloom during the lunch hour and was relieved to find another customer in the shop. Mackenzie wouldn't tell him to leave or create a scene in front of a customer. She glanced at him as he walked in, a cold, stony stare on her face, but after that she didn't look at him again.

He pretended to examine the bouquets on display, and couldn't help but overhear her conversation with the customer with whom she was all smiles and graciousness. The way she had been with him once.

When the customer left, clutching a huge bouquet of red roses, he wasn't prepared for Mackenzie to follow suit. She opened the door, waiting for him to leave. He hesitated, watching the rain lash down in heavy rivulets.

"I'm closing for lunch," she announced.

"It's raining." He hadn't been prepared for this move of hers and was suddenly blindsided.

"Yes, it is," she retorted in a condescending manner. Not waiting for him, she stepped out of the shop and waited for him. With no choice but to leave, he followed her out and watched her lock up.

"You don't usually close for lunch."

"I am today." She looked straight ahead, refusing to meet his gaze, and when he reached for her hand, she pulled hers away on contact.

Splat, splat, splat.

The blobs of rain grew bigger, falling thick and heavy.

"You're avoiding me," he stated, rushing to keep up with her as she sped off.

"If you've figured that out, then why can't you leave me alone?" She rushed through the heavy rain, and his frustration was growing in proportion to him getting very wet.

"Mackenzie, *please*." His outburst made her stop. "I'm not a bad person. Leigh understands what I was trying to do with the book. I didn't set out to deceive you. I didn't use any tricks to try to get your attention."

"You helped me, in my business, I'll give you that, but as for—"

"Because I wanted the best for you." He didn't want to hear the end of that sentence. Didn't want to give her the chance to break up without saying what he had to. She was angry and upset, and she had reason to be. He had lied, he deserved her wrath, but he deserved one conversation so that he could explain his side of things.

She started to walk off again.

"That's all I ever wanted," he cried, rushing to keep pace again. "Please. Have a cup of coffee with me. Just give me a chance."

She spun around, rivulets of rain bouncing off her skin, trailing down her cheeks and chin. "I still need your assistance, at least until I find someone else to take your place, with the subscription site, I mean."

It pained him that she'd thought so far ahead already, and had calmly found a way to cut him out of her life. He didn't want that. "You don't need to find anyone else. I can still help you."

"It would be better for me to find someone else, but until then …"

It wasn't fair. Not only was she not listening to him, but she was ditching him professionally. He didn't need her money, but he knew it wasn't going to be easy for her to find someone nearby who could help her as much. "Don't sabotage your business because you hate me."

She chortled. "I don't hate you—"

"You don't?"

"I just don't want to be near you." She ran to the coffee shop, with the rain pouring relentlessly and all he could do was watch her go.

He'd only just returned home and gotten out of his sopping wet clothes when there was a knock at his door.

Mackenzie?

Adam rushed to open the door and was immediately enveloped in a way-too-long bear hug by Patrick. "How are you holding up, dude?"

Adam stared at him blankly, shock and surprise rendering him speechless. Patrick had left messages of support for Adam ever since the story had broken in the forum, but Adam hadn't ever called him back.

"Do we have a meeting today?" He'd lost track of so many

things lately, especially everything to do with the Love Doctor. He hadn't checked his emails, or his daily book sales. He'd only kept a close eye on his marketing business, and had been disappointed that nobody from McGregor's office had been in touch.

"No, I was worried about you, dude." Patrick stepped inside and set down his backpack. "There are a lot of rumors and bad stuff flying around about you. I'm sorry someone ratted you out."

"So much for the power of a confidentiality agreement."

"Things are bad between you and Mackenzie, huh?"

Adam's brow furrowed. "Me and Mackenzie?" He hadn't ever mentioned to Patrick that there was anything going on between him and Mackenzie. He was sure he hadn't ever mentioned her name to him either.

"About what happened at the hotel, dude. The way that she found out."

A rush of adrenaline coursed through his veins. "How do you know about that?" How in the world did Patrick find that out? Did Starling Bay have a team of covert spies everywhere, reporting back on everyone's business?

"Roxy told me. She was at the women's meeting. She said you showed up and tried to defend yourself but Mackenzie was really mad. Roxy said the women were shocked because they didn't even know that the two of—"

Adam wiped his brow. "How do you know Roxy?"

"She's the sister of my best friend, Jax, the guy who's going out with Hailey Ross, the Hollywo—"

"Right, Right." Adam lifted a finger to his temple as if he was getting ready to massage away the tension headache that was building.

"How bad is it?" Patrick asked.

It seemed that Patrick had taken up a role as his best friend and confidante. "She doesn't want to know me. She thinks I used the rules to get close to her."

"Your rules are basic common sense," Patrick said. "Most people don't even think of them as rules."

Adam lifted his head, surprise quickly taking over his niggling worry. At least this guy understood. "You finally get it."

"Yeah, dude. It's just basic common sense. But the part about connecting, and having one chance to make a first impression, dressing to impress and being confident, that's stuff I hadn't really thought about much. So, I did find some of the stuff you told me helpful."

Adam smiled, feeling warm and hopeful. Patrick understanding this brightened his day a little. "That's great. I'm glad it helped, even if only a little."

"The fancy notebook girl and I, we're going to the movies on the weekend."

"You and the fancy notebook girl. For real?"

Patrick nodded, an uncontainable grin on his face. "She's great. She thinks I'm funny. She thinks I'm a great listener."

Even better. "That's the best news I've had for days. I'm happy for you. I really am." He gave Patrick a pat on the back.

"I'm sorry things aren't going so great for you."

Adam grasped the back of his neck and released a sigh. "It was my fault. I should have told her." He pointed a finger at Patrick. "New rule, don't have any secrets."

Some Love Doctor he was. A phony and a fake. He knew nothing about relationships. He'd quickly penned his book and thrown it out there, not even stopping to think about the fundamental tenets on which relationships should be based— truth, honesty and trust.

"Do you want to schedule the next meeting? I'm sorry I haven't replied to any of your messages."

"It's okay, dude. I don't need you," Patrick replied.

"You don't need me?"

"I might have at the beginning, but I think I'm good now. I've learned enough, so we're cool."

"Yeah?" He was being let go by so many people. First Mackenzie, now Patrick. He suddenly felt alone.

"I just wanted to see how you were."

"Thanks for stopping by. I appreciate that."

"The forum's buzzing with a ton of nasty posts. You know how people like to gossip. I see that journalist keeps asking you for an interview."

"She's a pain."

"Could you maybe use her in some way?"

Use Lisa Kramer? He wanted nothing more to do with her. "I'd rather stay out of her way."

"Don't blame you, dude."

CHAPTER 37

"Hi, can I help you?" Mackenzie asked the large man who was peering at the bouquets on display.

"I'm not sure."

"You're not sure what you want?" Mackenzie asked. "Or you're not sure you want my help?" She flashed the man a smile. It wasn't her way to approach her customer and be pushy, unless they asked for her help, but this particular man had been examining all of her flower displays, before going to her gift corner and looking at her candles and bath bombs, and then returning to the flowers again. She sensed that he was having a hard time making up his mind.

"I'm not sure what to get her."

"What's the occasion?" she asked.

"There's no occasion. I'm looking for some flowers to give to someone, just because."

"Just because?" Mackenzie laughed. "Is it a friend, a partner? A grandmother?"

The man bobbed his head as if he was weighing up the question.

"A friend."

"How about these?" She showed him a bouquet of lilies. "Or these?" She pointed to a bouquet of orchids. "These are good if you want to impress someone."

The man gave her a puzzled look. "I don't need to impress her. I just want her to know she's special."

Mackenzie nodded, liking his answer. She liked that; a man who didn't need to inflate his worth just to capture a woman's attention. "How about these?" She pulled out a bouquet of tulips.

The man nodded, reaching out for them. "I think she'd like those."

"You can't go wrong with tulips. They're simple but pretty. I love them."

"Nice colors too. Do you have them in purple?"

Mackenzie moved away to find a bouquet of purple tulips. "These ones?" She held up the bouquet for him to see.

"They look good. I'll take them."

She moved over to the counter to wrap them in paper. "That's a good choice."

"I think so." He handed her a few bills.

"I hope she likes them," Mackenzie said, slipping him the change. The man gave her a shy, uncertain smile before walking away. She looked around her shop and saw that two more customers had come in. She decided to let them peruse the displays themselves.

A short while later, the shop door opened again, and the man who'd bought the tulips had returned.

"Changed your mind?" she asked, guessing that he wanted a different color.

"He never used his rules on you."

She frowned, his words confusing her. He might as well have been talking in a foreign tongue.

"Adam, the Love Doctor," he said, and before she could utter a word, "he's not really a Love Doctor, he doesn't have a degree, and he's not trained, he's not a doctor like you would think—"

"You know Adam?" Why was Adam talking to a stranger about his personal affairs?

As if he'd read her mind and guessed her concerns, he said, "It's got nothing to do with me, and I'm sorry if you think I'm sticking my nose in your business, but I see this man getting slammed all over the place and I can't stand by and say nothing."

Slammed all over the place? "Who are you, and how do you know Adam?"

"He's more like a friend now, at least, I consider him as that because what he gave me was the confidence to be myself."

The man was talking in riddles. "What do you mean he's getting slammed all over the place? Slammed where?"

"In the Starling Bay online forum. People keep sticking their nose in his business and dissing him when they don't know the truth about things, or what he tried to do. He helped me, and I don't know exactly what beef everyone has with him, he didn't do nothing wrong, the way I see it. His rules aren't even rules, they're just things any decent person would do. Adam helped me, and knowing him the way I do, I know he didn't set out to hurt you or deceive you. He's not like that. I saw him a few days ago and the guy is low. It's not fair that people can attack him and he doesn't answer back. They're being nosy and making assumptions. Try asking the people who knew him better and who appreciated what he did for them."

His impassioned plea struck a chord. He seemed so sincere, as if he meant every word he said.

"Did you get coaching from Adam?" she asked.

"I can't answer that question." He started to walk away.

"Did he ask you to come here?" Mackenzie demanded.

The man stopped and turned around. "He would never do something like that. I just figured that you should know."

CHAPTER 38

"You're leaving already?" her mother asked.

Mackenzie stacked her belongings by the door. It was time to go. As much as she had loved being here, it was time to get back to her own place. As she walked past the living room, she saw Grandma starting to slowly raise herself from her armchair.

"Don't get up, Grandma. I'll come over to say bye in a minute."

She walked into the kitchen and grabbed an apple from the fruit basket.

"Are you leaving, Mackenzie?" her mother asked again. She had so gotten used to pushing her mom's voice to the background, that it had almost become like white noise, something that was unheard and ignored.

"Uh … yeah … I can't stay here all the time."

Tension crawled into the air as Mackenzie filled up a bottle of water. She no longer could cope with moments like these, and there had been plenty of them, prickly like barbed wire, uncomfortable and painful to be around.

"Why ever not?" her mother asked. "This is your home."

"It's not. It's Grandma's, and I've got my own place now."

"I'm looking into renting a small place around here. I've got an interview for a job in a warehouse, fingers crossed. I keep looking and applying, but this is the first time that I've gotten this far." There was a ring of pride in her mother's voice. "Once I get a job, I'll be able to help out more."

"An interview?" She'd seen her mother sitting at the kitchen table over an old laptop, and now knew why. The guilt lodged in her belly felt even heavier. Up until now, their conversations had always been stilted, even though her mother had started having dinner with them. It wasn't easy to fall into a 'happy family' mode when there had previously been only her and Grandma at the table. Her mother being there was like a wobbly leg on a three-legged stool.

She wanted to be better, but it wasn't easy to suddenly grow feelings for a woman she didn't see as a mother.

"I'm hoping something good will come of it," her mother said.

"You don't have to leave."

She made herself look at her mother's face, the discomfort creeping along her spine since this was one of the longest conversations she'd ever had with her; the longest she'd made herself stay in the same room, just the two of them. Still fighting the urge to leave, she glanced at the door, waiting for her grandmother to walk in and rescue her.

"There's no need for you to look for your own place. It's good that you're here, taking care of Grandma. I shouldn't have been rude to you when you came back, but I didn't know how long you'd stick around for, or what you wanted."

"I wanted to make up for—"

Mackenzie cleared her throat. "I've seen that you do a lot, and I'm sure Grandma appreciates it. I can't come over to see her as often as I need to, so you being here takes that worry away."

She'd been wrong. She's seen that her mother did a lot around the house. At first, Mackenzie had assumed it was because she'd been here, albeit for a temporary stay, but her grandmother had pointed out that her mom did the grocery shopping, cleaned the house, cooked and took good care of her, even when Mackenzie wasn't there.

"I don't want to get in the way." Her mother looked at her as if she were seeking her approval.

"You won't. I don't come around here that much—"

"But it's been so lovely having you here. Even just hearing your voice …" Her mother put her hand to her chest.

"I don't like the idea of Grandma being alone, and I'm sure she likes having company." Mackenzie finished filling up the bottle of water.

"I don't want to impose." She could hear the plea in her mother's voice. Even now her mother seemed afraid of her. Had she really been so rude and unwelcoming that her mother felt as if she were imposing in what had once been her childhood home?

"Talk to Grandma and see what she says. It's up to her, not me." She turned to leave. Her heart was racing, not in the way Adam made it race, but out of fearfulness. From stepping out of her comfort zone. She'd been used to keeping her mother at bay, and now the walls were starting to crumble. "And you don't have to sleep on the couch either. I can't believe you've been sleeping there the whole time."

"I couldn't walk back into your life and take your room. I've made a lot of mistakes in my life, and I will carry the regret of the things I said and did, the way I treated you, and how I made you feel—all of that is on my conscience. It's something I'll never be able to put right."

Mackenzie didn't speak, her head filled with snatched images from her past, feelings, smells, and sounds from her younger years; the scent of freshly cut grass, and summer and ice cream, the sounds of laughter coming from the play area at the park. Sounds of crying and shouting, dinner thrown against the wall, a broken glass on the floor. Stronger and more vivid, the memories crawled out of the basement where she'd hidden them, piling on top of each other. She'd buried them so far down, it was a miracle she remembered.

Examining her mother's face intently, a face she'd often turned her back on, she saw wrinkles lining her forehead, lines creeping out from the corners of her eyes and mouth. Her mother hadn't aged well, and the look of life gone by now haunted her sunken eyes.

Pity pooled inside her, along with the desire to forgive this woman, and to let her have a chance. But she couldn't speak.

"I'm sorry for what we did to you, Mackenzie. I should never have walked out, but I loved your father too much, and he ... he crushed me when he left me for–" Her mother's shoulders heaved, and she was losing her fight to hold herself together.

"It's not your fault, M-Mo—"

Mom.

It was still a struggle to say it.

"But it was, don't you see? Everything I was, everything I believed about myself, was rooted in what your father thought of me. I was weak and pathetic. I should have known better, but I couldn't see it then."

Pin-drop silence blanketed the air.

"I loved him too much. More than I loved myself. I was a terrible mother, I see that now. I saw it then, but I was in the wrong company, and your grandmother tried to get me to take responsibility for you, but I couldn't. I wasn't well after I had you. Nobody understood, Grandma tried, but I couldn't look after you, and she put all her time and energy into you. She had your best interests at heart, not mine. You were defenseless. A child, pure and innocent, and I should have known better than to pin all my hopes and dreams on a man."

This woman was broken, had been broken a long time ago. It would do no good to keep on punishing her. "I want us to try, Mom. We can both try," she said, feeling hopeful.

"I would like that. I've missed out on so much of your life, and I look at you now and my heart fills with pride. I just wish..." Her mother's chest started to heave, her voice broke as she struggled and failed to compose herself. "I just wish I'd been here to see my little girl grow up." Her mother sniffled into her tissue, trying to keep her voice low, as she glanced over towards the door.

"Don't cry ... Mom ... it's okay ..." Mackenzie felt powerless to do anything and held onto her drinking bottle as if her life depended on it, with the apple gripped tightly in her other hand as she watched her mother fall apart in front of her eyes. She wanted to make amends. This felt like the right time to start.

"I just ... I just want you to know that it fills my heart with happiness to see you all grown up into such a beautiful young woman. It will haunt me for the rest of my life that I abandoned you. I missed out on you growing up, and that's something that will hang over my head until the day I die."

"Maybe we can ... start from here?" She felt helpless standing in front of a woman whose heart was breaking, and not able to fully comfort her. She was there for her friends. If this had been Leigh, she would have had her arms around her in a heartbeat second. Doing nothing felt strange.

"Can we?" A silent plea fell from her mother's thin lips and she dabbed the corners of her bloodshot eyes. "Will you ever forgive me, Mackenzie?"

Mackenzie swallowed. Seeing this woman sobbing and asking her for forgiveness started to chip at some of the hardness inside her. "I forgot about you, Mom, because I had to, but ... I want you back in my life now, to stay. We've wasted too many years apart. Maybe we can try to make up for them."

"But will you forgive me?"

"There's nothing to forgive because you've suffered enough."

Her mother wiped her eyes again, then dried her cheeks with the back of her hands. "You're nothing like me. I'm so proud of you, Mackenzie. You getting away from a man who hurt you, you won't make the same mistakes I did."

Mackenzie blinked. "You mean Adam?" She hadn't told her mother anything about Adam, hadn't spoken to her at all about the reason she'd come here, but maybe her grandmother had. Her situation was so different from her mother's.

"Is he the one who helped you with those videos?"

"Yes."

"He seemed like a good guy. It's a shame," her mother commented. "The videos were so good. I can't stop watching them. Even now. It's what I do every day when you and your grandma sit and talk. I'd sit in the kitchen looking at jobs to apply for, but I'd also watch your videos, just because it felt like you were talking to me."

Her mother's words shot her like bullets, lodging deep inside her, shattering bone and muscle, making her bleed. The weight of guilt brought tears to her eyes. Any moment now, she was going to break apart. "I … I haven't … I haven't added any new ones," she managed to stutter, an expert at putting up a façade.

"Why not?"

"I don't know how to."

"I keep watching the same ones over and over. You're so good, Mackenzie. It fills me with so much joy. I didn't think I could feel like that again, but I do, seeing my little girl all grown up and running her own business. You should see if there's a way that you could get Adam to still help you with the business side of things until you get up to speed. I'd hate for your business to take a hit."

Mackenzie sighed heavily. She'd had the same thought. "I've asked him. He said he wants to help me, but I need to find someone else quickly."

"I don't really know what happened, your grandmother only said that you couldn't trust him." Her mother clasped her hands together, looking like an outsider, someone desperate to come back to the fold and be on the inside again. What would that look like, having a mother in her life again?

"I couldn't." Mackenzie stared at the floor, contemplating. Adam had lied to her about his role as the Love Doctor, but as far as she knew, he hadn't cheated on her.

Her mother's story was so different from her own. Her mother had suffered from depression, due to her pregnancy, but her husband had also cheated on her. It would have broken any vulnerable woman. To make matters worse, her mother had then discovered that she'd been lied to for all those years. The news had destroyed her. Mackenzie could see it in the cracks and lines of her mother's face.

Adam hadn't cheated on her. Not like that. She hadn't suffered from depression. What she had experienced had been nothing compared to what her mother had gone through.

For the first time, she suddenly saw her mother with new eyes. Setting her water bottle and apple down, she tentatively put her arms around this almost-stranger, making a new and uncertain move driven by the need to make amends. Her mother flinched at first, her body hard and small in Mackenzie's embrace, her arms limply hanging from her sides as if she didn't know what to do.

"I want us to try again, Mom," Mackenzie whispered, and slowly, inch by careful inch, her mother's rigid arms began to lift up and go slowly around her waist.

"Me too." A stifled sob followed, and then, "Thank you, Mackenzie."

They stayed like that for a moment longer, until she thought she heard a noise in the hallway. She half turned to glance at the doorway, expecting her grandmother to walk in, but no one did.

Tears trickled down her face. Tears of regret, and loss, and wasted time. She had been humiliated and hurt by Adam lying, but her mother had fared far, far worse. It was time to stop punishing her and let go of all the old hurt.

CHAPTER 39

"Have you read this?"

Leigh's jaw dropped open as she waved the paper at Mackenzie.

"No," she answered slowly, wondering who it was that had died. She'd only just opened the shop, and Leigh should have done the same but she'd come rushing over. It had to be something big and since nothing startling ever happened in Starling Bay, Mackenzie assumed that Leigh had just read someone's obituary. Her friend shoved the newspaper in Mackenzie's face.

Starling Bay's Matchmaker Explains Why He's Giving It All Up.

Her eyes widened in disbelief before skating over the rest of the article, gobbling up the words in big chunks. Adam talked about why he'd started his Love Doctor side business, only he referred to it as a 'joke' that got out of hand and earned him some 'big bucks'. He'd done it to help men, he said, men who were too shy and too timid, and lacking in confidence. Men who didn't look like movie stars.

He went on to explain that he knew what it was like to be one of these men, because he had once been a teen who had been laughed at. He'd gone unnoticed at school, and his awkward, geeky demeanor only got him the attention of awkward girls.

"The super-hot ones weren't interested in me. The cheerleaders definitely weren't," he went on to say, before admitting that he was shamelessly attracted only to looks at that age.

"But I grew up determined to change myself. And I did, turning myself into a Clark Kent figure, only without the Superman suit and cape. I reinvented myself by studying people, and their desires, and figuring out how to influence others."

"Well?" Leigh cried. "Say something."

But Mackenzie's eyes flew down the page. Adam went on to say that he later questioned what he was doing, the role he was playing. He considered himself as providing a service that some men needed, but it wasn't until he overheard the reactions of some women that he had any idea about the pushback to his book and his coaching.

In the final paragraph, he said, "My actions have hurt people, people I care very deeply for. I am sorry for the pain and distrust I have sowed, and for that reason, I shall no longer be continuing in that capacity. I've made a lot of money from the book, but I see that I've now also attracted a lot of copycats. Good luck to them. I want to focus more on my other role in helping small companies to market their businesses better."

Mackenzie looked up at the end. So, he was giving it all up, was he?

"Didn't he explain it so well?" Leigh cried, obviously championing Adam's cause.

"I haven't read it properly." Mackenzie's heart thundered loudly behind her rib cage and she was sure that Leigh would soon hear it. She had skimmed it quickly to see if there was anything in there about her. Adam hadn't mentioned her by name, for which she was grateful, but he had, it seemed, alluded to her. He had sounded almost apologetic.

She started to read it again.

"Don't you think it's sweet?" Leigh asked.

"I'm reading it carefully." She was reading it slowly, carefully, savoring every word. Adam sounded humble, sad even. Almost as if he was talking directly to her. He'd had to resort to going through a newspaper because she hadn't let him explain his side of the story. His friend had even come to the shop and made Adam out in a good light. Leigh was rooting for him. Even her mom and grandmother seemed to think he was a good guy.

She set the paper down when she had finished.

"Do you believe him now?" Leigh asked.

It was impossible not to. "I suppose so."

"He's giving up that Love Doctor business, even though it's been a success. Why do you think that is?"

Mackenzie shrugged. She didn't want to get pulled into a conversation where Leigh was extolling Adam's virtues and rubbing her face in it.

"I like him. He's one of the good ones," Leigh said.

"That's what my mom said."

"Your grandma is always right." Then, after a few seconds had passed, "Wait, your *mom?*"

Mackenzie's mouth twisted as she tried to find the words to explain. "We're … we're making an effort. We're trying."

Leigh's arms went around her in a tight bear hug. "Awww, really? That's just the best news." She pulled away and stared into Mackenzie's eyes, excitement overflowing in hers. "This has been a huge change in your life. Huge. This is good. This is really good. What made you want to try now?"

"I don't know." A shift in perspective. Seeing things from her mother's point of view. Listening. Realizing that her mother hadn't hated her, and that she had been a victim of circumstance. Learning to forgive and let go of her perceived ideas about the situation.

"I'm really happy for you." Leigh hugged her again. "Your mom thinks Adam was one of the good ones, too, huh?"

She didn't want to tell Leigh about Adam's friend, the coaching student who had come to her shop to tell her the same. What was it about Adam that a team of people, some of whom barely knew him, were vouching for him?

She had been hasty in not wanting to hear his version of events. He'd done a bad thing by lying to her. Trust was paramount in a relationship, and the blatant lying to her face had hurt her the most.

But the man had given up his side job career. She hadn't asked him to. The coaching student, who had refused to tell her whether Adam had coached him, gave her the answer. He had sung Adam's praises. He claimed that Adam had helped him.

Maybe she'd been guilty of letting her upset blindside her?

$\mathcal{A}$ knock at the door this late in the evening? He let out an exasperated sigh hoping that Patrick wasn't at the door.

The guy checked in on Adam every other day via a phone call or a text, but it had been a week or so since they'd last met. Adam braced himself. He wasn't in the mood to talk to anyone, least of all Patrick, who had been on a first date with his new girlfriend and was so happy, Adam could feel the happiness vibes bouncing off him on this side of the town.

Shamefully, he decided to play dead, and not answer the door. He didn't want to hurt Patrick's feelings by turning him away, or trying to get rid of him too quickly, but his energy was low, and during his empty evenings he sat and watched TV for hours.

Mind-numbing drama was a way for him to take his mind off the drama in his own life. He'd been about to go for a run, because that helped. But he was too scared to leave his place until the way was clear. He waited patiently, but a few moments later there was another knock.

"Go away, buddy," he hissed under his breath.

"Adam?"

The sound of her voice stilled him.

Mackenzie?

She was on the other side of that door? He strode to it in a heartbeat and opened it. "Mackenzie?" She was the last person he expected to see, but he'd never been happier to see anyone.

"Hi." Her large eyes stared at him.

"Hey." He didn't know whether to ask her in or not, didn't know what would be too much, or too little, didn't know how to be or what to say.

"Mind if I come in?" she asked finally, when they stood by the door, letting the few tight, awkward seconds stumble by.

"Sure, sure. Come in."

She seemed to notice only then that he was in his shorts and T-shirt. "Were you going somewhere? Or did you just come back?"

"I was about to go for a run."

She nodded. "Then I won't take up too much of your time."

That was always her line. Always afraid of imposing, and taking up too much time and energy and attention. Things which he'd give willingly and in truckloads—for her.

"I can go out later. It's no big deal."

"I don't want to stop you from—"

"You're not." His voice sounded harsher than he intended. "You're not," in a softer voice. "I'll always make time for you."

She barely balked at those words as she looked around his place, her gaze going to his corkboard in the corner. It was still blank, but his desk was neater. He was curious to see if she would mention it.

"I heard that you're not doing that stuff anymore." She made a vague reference to his previous side job.

"I decided to give it up. I was never really sure about it."

"But it was so successful. You could have retired on it."

He forced a laugh. "For a few months, maybe years. Those things don't last. There are already copycat books springing up."

Her eyes widened. "Really?"

He wasn't about to lie to her. "Yes. People like to make a quick buck, and copying someone's lucrative idea is a good way to try."

"But why did you give it up so soon? It's still doing well, isn't it?"

"It's making good money, but it never felt right. I felt like an imposter. What do I know about women and dating?"

She stared up at him through thick eyelashes, saying nothing.

"How did you know?"

"In the local paper. Leigh made sure I read the article."

He placed his hands on his hips, his gaze falling to the floor as he suppressed a smile. Thank goodness for Leigh. Hope wrapped around him for a fleeting moment.

"So, uh, I wanted to ask if you could maybe train me quickly to upload the videos for the paid site? The site goes live soon."

And just like that, his newfound hope vanished. She wanted his help, and that was the only reason she had come here. It wasn't to talk or to work through things.

"I said I'd help you. Of course I will."

She clasped her hands together, wringing them, a sign which indicated that she was nervous, even if she didn't look it. Glacial, is how she looked, and it made him wary of touching on any personal matters.

"When do you want to get together?" he asked.

"Whenever it's a good time for you. You let me know." She tucked a lock of hair behind her ear, something he used to do. She was being polite, civil and undemanding; like she'd been at the start when he first met her.

"Will it be awkward for you?" She gave him a smile which didn't reach the rest of her face.

"Awkward?"

"To work together, for a short while." She was setting boundaries.

He was grateful just to have her back in his life again. He shook his head. "It's not going to be awkward. Is it going to be awkward for you?"

"No. But I wasn't sure and I didn't know who else to ask. I've already looked around online for someone who could do this but it's not easy finding someone who you can trust."

Her words smacked him unexpectedly. She'd come to him after having no success anywhere else. "I said I'd help you, Mackenzie. I will. I'll teach you how to do it all yourself. You'll grasp it quickly. I know you will."

"Thanks, that's what I was hoping for." She made a move to leave.

"That's it?" he asked, saying out loud the phrase that screamed inside his head. "You're leaving already?" *We haven't talked about anything important.*

"I only came to ask. I felt I should at least make an effort and meet with you in person."

She sounded so formal. In retreat. Restrained.

"I've had 287 people sign up for the course," she announced proudly, her face lighting up for the first time.

His mouth fell open. "Two. Eight. Seven? That's insane!" Bordering on almost three hundred subscribers, when she was relatively unknown and had only just launched herself on the social media platform. This was truly amazing, and it boded well for her online course. "That's just fantastic, Mackenzie. Wow. Freaking amazing. I'm really happy for you."

"I thought it seemed good. I don't really know what to make of it. But I do need to get the site up as soon as possible."

Hence her showing up at his door now. She opened the door to leave. "You'll let me know when you're free to meet?"

"How about this weekend? Or tomorrow after work, at your shop?"

"I'm pretty busy on the weekends, but how about after work, in a few days' time? I'll call to confirm."

He was about to tell her again that he was sorry, that he never meant to hurt her, but she slipped away before he could say a word.

He was still crazy about this woman, and there wasn't a thing he could do about it.

CHAPTER 41

"*A*dam said he would help me." She was sweeping the shop floor, or trying to, when Leigh accosted her at the end of the next day.

"And?"

Mackenzie kept her focus on the floor, not daring to look at Leigh in case her friend saw right through her. "And that was it. He said he'd help me. I told him to let me know when he's available. I told him I was busy on the weekends—"

"Why did you say that?"

She stopped sweeping and then realized she'd swept the floor twice now. "I'm spending more time with my mom. Getting to know her—"

"I know, and I'm happy for you, but Adam will think you're seeing someone else."

Mackenzie put the broom to the side. She didn't want him to think that. But she also didn't want to waltz back into his life so easily.

"You can't let him just walk away," Leigh wasn't one to give up, but Mackenzie wished her friend would cut her some slack.

"I'm not. I'm seeing what happens. I know I can be quick to cut people off. I see that now, about how I was with my mom—"

"Your mom left you."

"She was depressed, and she wasn't right in the head. I should have cut her some slack."

"You were a child."

"Who then grew up and should have been more understanding."

"But your mother wasn't around much even when you were growing up, and it's only been a few years since she came back into your life in a permanent way."

Mackenzie shrugged.

"I'm happy that you're going to give her another chance," Leigh continued, "but I think you should do that with Adam, too. We both made fun of the Love Doctor, but I see what he was trying to do."

She moved over to her displays and started to tidy them up. "Don't push me, Leigh. I can handle this."

Her friend's arm came around her shoulders. "I know you can. I just don't want you to cut him out without giving him a second chance. You were happy together. You had a glow about you that I haven't seen before." Leigh kissed her on the cheek. "I'm going to stop hounding you, okay? Rourke and I are going to watch a movie, so I'll see you tomorrow."

"Have fun."

"Why don't you come with us?"

And be the third wheel with those two? No way. "I've got to finish up some content for the paid site and it's Halloween weekend. I've been crazy busy."

Leigh raised a disbelieving eyebrow. "It's just a few hours. It'll be fun. We're going to watch a horror flick."

"Then definitely count me out."

"Don't be by yourself. We were going to throw a Halloween

party, just a little get-together for our close friends, but Merry isn't up to it. But come over and we'll do a little something."

"I'm not feeling in the mood. Sorry. And the site is supposed to go live in a few weeks. I have hundreds of people waiting on it." The pressure hung over her head, making her anxious.

"Oooooh! Look at you. Hundreds of people? Mackenzie Jeffers live on the internet." Leigh turned her hand into a megaphone and spoke into it.

"It's not live."

Leigh swatted her playfully "You know what I mean. But still, you'll be teaching a class of hundreds. That incredible."

"I won't physically be standing in front of hundreds. It will just be me and the camera."

And Adam.

"Good luck. We should celebrate when it goes live. I don't understand the whole thing, but you said you were going to upload all the videos at once and unlock a new class every week?"

"Something like that." She wasn't sure. She needed to consult with Adam, because this was all so new to her. He'd already mentioned that she'd need to answer questions and emails as and when they arose. It was going to be extra work, but already she was beyond excited. The income from this class had already well exceeded what she made every month.

"We need to celebrate!" Leigh cried, with enough enthusiasm for the both of them.

"We will."

Leigh left and Mackenzie got back to cleaning up. But there was nothing much left to clean, she'd closed her shop over an hour ago and she'd twice given it a once-over. She was avoiding going home because at home she would be preparing content for the rest of the videos. She'd become adept at recording herself, but they all needed editing.

She was meeting with Adam to finalize everything. The next few weeks were going to be big, and the launch of her paid site couldn't go wrong. Adam had assured her he'd help her every step of the way, and while it was reassuring from a business standpoint, it also scared her.

Her life was changing. Good things were coming to fruition. Things she had never thought of before. Even her relationship with her mom was changing and for the better.

It was the part of her life with Adam that had fallen apart.

"Hey." He walked into her shop, the way he had done many times before, only this time he felt like a customer.

"Hi." Mackenzie let him in and then locked the door. "Shall we get to it? I've recorded everything, I just want to see how you edit a video and upload it, and then I can do the rest myself."

She was still adamant about wanting to do it all herself.

Well, so be it.

"Great." She had overlooked the fact that she needed to buy and install and learn how to use the editing software, and that wasn't easy. But he wasn't going to push it.

The atmosphere was charged, but this time with tension. Gone was the electric spark that had ignited the air between them.

Yet, seeing her, being here, remembering how things used to be, brought back a wave of sadness he'd tried to push away. He wondered how she felt.

She walked through to the back and sat down, opening up the screen of her laptop. "If you can show me how to edit the first video, then I can do the rest."

So much for making small talk. The chill in the air turned

sharper as the temperature plunged a few more degrees. He hadn't expected her to greet him with open arms, but they had been good together once, on the cusp of something great, and how they were just now seemed to him a great tragedy.

He took a seat next to her. "Do you have the video editing software?"

"No ... uh. I guess I should do that, huh?"

"Sure, go ahead." He waited.

She chewed her lip. "Which one do you recommend?"

"It's up to you. There are different price points, and different levels of complexity to learn."

"But what do *you* recommend?" She turned her face to him, her eyes flickering with anxiety, her mouth straight. She looked miserable, just the way he felt.

"I would suggest that you look at the top five, maybe narrow them down to the top three, and then get free trials. Most vendors allow you to test the software for free for a limited time period, and then you can go through each one and use them and decide for yourself which one you like the best."

"But ...that will take time."

"It will." She didn't like her answer, but he was giving her what she wanted.

Distance.

His advice.

His help.

He'd offered to take care of this for her, but she had always pushed back. She'd wanted to go do it herself, and he was letting her.

"I have twenty videos."

"Twenty? Did we decide on that many?"

"No, because ..." She pressed her lips together, not finishing the sentence. "I decided. I wanted to be thorough and give my customers good value for their money."

"That's commendable. I'm sure you did a great job."

"Now I need to edit them all."

"Yes, you do."

It was an effort not to give in and help her. He'd offered his help enough times, and she had pushed him back as many times. The only thing to do now was to sit back and let Mackenzie decide what she wanted, and to go with that. He clasped his hands together and waited.

She tapped away on her keyboard, the stubborn jut of her chin telling.

"These three?" she asked, turning her laptop towards him slightly so that he could see.

"Sure, go ahead." It was difficult sitting here, watching her flail, even though outwardly she was a picture of calm. He forced himself to watch and do nothing, not because he wanted to see her suffer, but because he needed her to realize for herself.

She typed away on her laptop and the minutes ticked by.

Many minutes.

"I'm going to install the first one. I don't have time to install three versions and learn all of them."

It was on the tip of his tongue to tell her she didn't need to learn all of them. But he just about managed to keep quiet.

As he waited, he pulled out his cell phone and checked for messages. Nothing urgent. And still nothing from McGregor. That opportunity was gone, and now that he had put a stop to the Love Doctor business, he needed to ramp up his marketing business even more because he'd gotten used to the easy money, and now he needed to make up for it.

"I've installed the software," Mackenzie announced, her cheeks pink, and her brow creased. "I didn't think it was going to take this long."

He had the software on his laptop, ready to use. He could have edited a video for her in the time it had taken her to do all of this.

"Nothing worth having comes easily," he told her. She stared at him. Those brown thickly lashed eyes burning a hole right through him.

Jesus, Mackenzie.

It had been a while since he'd stared directly at her face, or sat this close to her, and he'd forgotten the effect she had on him.

"Okay, so if I open my first video in this ... I guess we can edit it."

We? "Don't you want to run through a few of the online lessons and see how it works?" he asked.

Her brows pushed together even more. "I don't have time for this." He watched a tiny muscle twitch along the line of her clenched jaw. She was getting angry. "Can't you just show me?"

"Gladly. I'll need your laptop."

She pushed it towards him. He tapped a few keys. "This isn't the full version. I won't be able to use all the functionality I need."

"What?"

"You've downloaded a trial version."

"Because you told me to," she retorted.

"Because you said you didn't have a paid version and I suggested that you try a few different versions before you spent money on purchasing one."

She brushed a hand through her hair. "Why is it so complicated? I thought you would help me."

"I am. I offered, but you want to do it all by yourself."

"I don't want to rely on you." Her eyes blazed at him.

"I understand." He grappled to keep his voice level. "That's why I'm letting you do this your way, Mackenzie. I'm doing what you want."

"I want you to help me."

"I am helping, as much as I can. As much as you're letting me."

"How is this helping? We've been here for a while and I'm nowhere near getting this edited."

She was being unreasonable, and he had a hunch that she knew this. "You tell me how you want to do this. I can edit this for you. I can show you on my laptop. I have the software that I've used for years. I know what to do. I can teach you. This is what I offered as soon as I got here. You said you wanted to do it your way, by yourself. You didn't want to depend on me."

"Because I think that would be best for us." She stood up, startling him with her pent-up anger. Mackenzie usually kept it all in. She was the epitome of poise and calm. This was new.

"I don't want you to depend on me either. You're smart enough to be able to do this yourself, but you're facing a deadline, and you need to get these videos edited and uploaded. People have paid for this content, so it needs to be stellar."

Her lips flattened. She didn't like his answer, but he was giving her what she wanted. Or what she thought she wanted; him to back off.

"You don't want my help, Mackenzie. You've made that clear."

"I do want your help." The frustration in her voice seemed to melt, as she slipped back into her chair.

"Then, let me help you," he offered softly.

She turned to face him, and the anger in her eyes had started to fizzle away.

"I hate depending on you."

"You've told me, countless times. You don't need to keep emphasizing it. I can show you on my laptop, and with the software I recommend. Do you want me to show you on mine?"

"Okay."

He got his laptop out of the bag and powered it up.

"I hate that it's come to this, Mackenzie. I hate that this is how things are. I don't want the problems between us to get in the way of your success."

"I hate that you lied to me."

His finger stilled on the mouse and the hairs along his arms rose as he tried to focus on the screen in front of him. It was on the tip of his tongue to say it all over again, but he'd told her, once, twice. She wasn't ready to accept it. Common sense and experience told him that he needed to listen. It was obvious that Mackenzie needed to get things out of her system, and it behooved him to do nothing but listen to her and let her.

"I know." He fired up the software and got it ready. Venturing a glance at her, he found her soft eyes trained on him. Only the fight was gone, and in its place surrender. "I did lie. It's unforgiveable." So much for shutting the heck up and listening. "I need your video. Have you saved it to where I showed you?"

"It's all there, in the cloud, where you told me."

He found it and played the video. Much to his dismay, she didn't say anything further, so he watched, stopping and starting the recording as he edited it, showing Mackenzie what he did every step of the way.

She was a good student, and she made notes.

"And that is it." He turned to her at the end. "That didn't take too long. I like this software, and I recommend you—"

"Thank you."

He blinked.

"Thanks for helping me, Adam, even after everything, and with me being so irritable and demanding."

"You're not irritable and demanding."

"You're always so nice to me."

"Glad to be of help." They could talk about work, about the editing, but what he wanted was for her to tell him about her feelings, so that he could deal with them and put things right. She wasn't giving him a chance and it was the blanket silence he couldn't face. Yet, she still needed his help, and this was his short time window to try to get through to her.

"Do you want to edit the next video?" He slid the laptop sideways towards her, and then he watched as she started working. They both watched the next recording, and she edited parts of it, referring to her notes now and then. Occasionally, her finger would hover over the menu options when she wasn't sure what to do next.

But she wouldn't ask him. And that's what worried him.

Soon enough, she would not need his help, or him.

Adam was patient with her, and a great teacher. He was helpful and he tolerated her. These were all the things she loved about him, and she missed them.

It was one thing needing his help professionally, but she also needed him back. She wanted things to be the way they used to be.

The lack of trust, his lying, and the things he had hidden from her, she was learning to get over. Give him a second chance, perhaps. She had suffered no great hardship, nothing physical, but it had hurt. It would take time to get back to how things used to be, but this was what she wanted. It seemed that Adam did, too, but she needed to focus on the paid site and launching that, before she was in a good frame of mind to talk about them.

"Should we stop here?" She had edited a few more videos but there were still more than half to do.

"It's up to you," he said. "Do you want to call it a day? I can stay for longer."

With it being Halloween, she'd had a crazy week, making floral arrangements for a few big parties, and of course she had arrangements to make for a wedding reception and this online side of the business always consumed so much of her time.

"I've got lots to do, and I'm running behind. I should start on those now."

"Yeah, sure. Whatever you think is best."

Someone else would have told her to get lost. She'd been unreasonable earlier, but she couldn't help it. The frustration and miasma of despair she'd been surrounded by had made her moody, and still Adam had been so accommodating and helpful. She wanted to give him an out, in case he'd had enough of her, but his desire to want her to succeed got in the way. "I can edit the rest of the videos myself now. I think I've got the hang of it."

He was packing his laptop away. "But the software is on my laptop," he reminded her. He had a point. She could buy it herself, and install it and use it on her laptop, but it would be another obstacle to get over, and she was running out of time.

"So it is."

"The offer still stands. I'm happy to come over again." He shrugged, indicating that it didn't matter to him.

"I might just have to take you up on it, because I don't have much time."

"You don't. I can come by tomorrow after work," he offered. His desire to want the best for her showed in his eyes, his voice, in the slant of his head as he looked at her.

"I'd appreciate that very much."

If she didn't know it already, Adam was the type of guy who would drop anything for her.

True to his word, Adam came to her shop again as agreed, and let her use his laptop.

She had a delivery to make to a wedding reception later in the evening, but she could spare an hour on the videos before then. He'd brought a second laptop along with him which he worked on while she edited a handful of videos on his, stopping every so often to ask him when she was stuck.

They worked side by side, quietly and diligently. To unknowing eyes, it would have seemed that they were together, because they were in such unison, even in silence.

They couldn't have been further apart, and seeing this, feeling the space between them, saddened her.

The work was slow, and required her to watch each video, then make changes. It was nothing too difficult, especially since she was getting well versed in using the software, but it was laborious work. She sat back, unable to edit another video and found herself staring at Adam's side profile as he stared at his laptop screen. He typed away, unaware that he was being watched.

He looked busy. The entire time he'd been typing away, with a speed she found enviable. Poor man, he seemed to have enough things to deal with, yet here he was, sitting by her side, ready to help her.

"Can we do the rest tomorrow? There's only a handful of videos left."

He turned to her, his eyes raking over her face slowly as if he needed to remember every feature, every line, every inch of her face. "We don't have much time. You go live next week."

She let out an exhale, acutely aware of the ticking timepiece. So much was riding on her new venture, and everything was starting to pile up on top of her. "I have to deliver some flowers for a wedding reception."

"Now?"

She nodded, then yawned, putting her hand over her mouth.

"Why didn't you say so?" he asked. "I would have done this, and you could have gone to make the delivery."

"I can fit it all in. The reception isn't until eight, and if I leave now, I'll be fine."

"You work too hard, Mackenzie."

"So do you."

"But this is insane. You closed the shop, then worked on the videos, and now you're making a delivery. When do you rest?" The concern in his eyes, the way he looked at her, the way his voice lowered when he talked to her, made her melt. It had felt good, no, *great*, having someone. For the short time they'd been together, life had been about more than just work and TV dinners.

She missed that.

"Tomorrow, I'll sleep in until noon." She managed a smile.

"I worry about you."

Those words caressed her soul. This man was concerned about her. He cared.

"Thank you." It was heartfelt. From deep within. No matter

what he'd done in the past, this man's actions had vindicated him. She'd punished him enough.

But he hadn't said anything about getting back together again. She'd half expected him to, especially now that they'd been working closely for a few days.

He'd heeded her advice and backed off, he'd been all about the work and the paid site. He'd listened to her, and now she felt abandoned, and she had no one to blame but herself.

"Let's call it a day," she suggested, standing up and needing to get ready to drop the arrangements off to a wedding reception. "I can do this tomorrow. Shoot, I'll still need your laptop."

He stood up, watching her carefully. "You told me you were going to take it easy and sleep in late tomorrow."

She opened her mouth to protest.

"I can't come to the shop tomorrow, so you won't have use of my laptop. I have a … date."

"A … *date?*" His confession skewered a hole in her chest. She almost stumbled back in shock.

"I think it would be better to finish all the editing today, Mackenzie. I could get started on the rest while you're gone. Or do you still feel the urge to do these all by yourself?"

She was still reeling from his words. And struggling to speak, the breath constricting in her chest, as their recent conversations whizzed by in her mind. No wonder he'd been quiet and elusive, not venturing to talk much about them. Because he no longer was interested in there being a *them*.

"That would be a great help. Thank you."

"I'll get started."

She felt the color drain from her face, and hoped he hadn't noticed. "I'll only be a few hours," she managed to say, trying to steady her voice. "I don't have far to go, and I can race there and back. I should get going, but it will be quite late, Adam."

"It's okay. I want to help, and you've got a lot going on."

"Thanks. I really appreciate it." She walked out feeling shell-shocked, relieved to be out of the room, to not have to face him. A date?

Already?

Walking to her display stand where her arrangements were neatly lined up, she lifted two of them, carrying one in each hand, and walked out to her van.

When she turned around, Adam stood there with more of her arrangements in his hands. She took them from him.

"Thank you." But she couldn't bring herself to look at him, in case he saw how much he'd hurt her. He disappeared again, then reappeared with more arrangements until they were all stacked in her van.

There was no denying the fact that they made a good team.

~

Maybe this was the way to do it. He watched her drive the pink and black van away.

He'd lied again. A white lie. He had a date, with his family. For dinner. Obviously, it had had the effect he'd intended.

He worked quickly yet carefully, mindful that time was running out, and knowing that Mackenzie would return later than the hour she'd assumed she'd take, but she would be exhausted, and it would be late. She would be in no mood to edit, but she was also stressed. She had that drawn look about her, and he sensed it was the pressure of work and the online classes.

She didn't need to spell it out that she was starting to struggle He could see it for himself.

She needed to take it easy tomorrow.

Next week would have its challenges. He'd be by her side when her paid site went live, but these things never went smoothly. There were always glitches, and he was prepared for them. Mackenzie wouldn't be.

When she didn't return almost two hours later, he was glad, because he still had two more videos to edit.

When another hour had passed and she still didn't return, he got worried. He'd finished editing everything. All that was left was for the videos to be uploaded, and for him to show her a few last things on the subscription site software.

He called her but it went straight to voicemail.

And that was when he got *very* worried.

CHAPTER 44

The delivery had taken longer than she had expected.

She needed a helper. More than that, she needed someone to take over some of her deliveries sometimes, especially if her life was going to get even busier with the online classes. Then she would definitely need an extra pair of hands.

She was exhausted.

But she was used to the physical exhaustion, the standing and serving customers in her shop all day, then going out and delivering the arrangements to different venues. It was nothing new.

What was new was the mental exhaustion.

The up and down roller coaster ride with Adam.

Finding out that he had a date.

Those two words had scattered her emotions at a time when she had only recently, during these last few days with Adam, managed to get herself back to an even keel.

Adam had a date, with some other lucky lady.

She clamped her jaw tightly and climbed into her van, slammed the door. Inside, she leaned forward, her elbows on the steering wheel, her head in her hands.

She wanted to go home. Home to see Grandma and her mom. She wanted to retreat into her shell again.

But Adam was at her shop, editing her videos.

Adam, who had a date tomorrow.

She turned on the ignition, and slowly backed out of the hotel parking lot. From her rearview mirror, she saw that a van was indicating to turn in from the road, so she stopped.

But the driver sped around the corner, driving into the parking lot too fast. The neurons in her brain clambered frantically, and she drove forward, trying to get back into her parking space, but the van was too fast, and the driver was eating something. She felt the bang before she heard it. It rear-ended her. She jolted forward, miraculously avoiding hitting her face into the steering wheel.

The loud thundering crash and crumpling of twisted, folding metal screeched through the air.

Then silence.

He'd hit her. The van had rammed into the back of her.

"Hey!" The man, a burly, balding, thick-necked guy stuck his head out of the window. "What the hell?"

He had the audacity to make out that it was her fault. Simmering with rage, she climbed out to confront him.

"You went into the back of me," she yelled, fury coursing through her veins as she surveyed the damage to her van. "*You* did *that*!" she screamed, jabbing a finger at him. That's when she saw it, the half-eaten hot dog in the palm of his hand.

"It was your fault!" His face was red, his eyes bulging as he got out of the van, his worn-out scrappy jeans hanging low under his rotund belly.

"You hit me!" Her voice was a banshee's shriek. Loud and piercing. A warning sound, venting her frustration and anger.

A hotel valet came running over, as did some other people from the parking lot. She turned her back to them and examined her van again. The doors at the back were dented and caved in, and the panels were crumpled on either side. She thanked God that this had happened now, on her way home, and not before she'd delivered the flowers.

"You okay?" someone asked her.

It had happened in slow motion, and she was still in a daze. She heard someone ask her again if she was injured, the man peering intently at her face, asking her if she was hurt anywhere else.

Just my heart.

She shook herself out of that trance.

Adam had a date.

She'd just been in a crash.

This wasn't her fault.

But Adam was going on a date.

The man had no shame. Moving from her to someone else in the time it took to click one's fingers.

"Are you hurt, ma'am?" Another man, this time in a smart suit, with a badge, someone from the hotel, she assumed, was asking her.

Forget Adam.

Forget him.

She snapped her attention to the present. She'd been lucky. She wasn't injured. The van was damaged, but only at the back. It could have been worse.

By now, several witnesses had come forward, and the other van driver had calmed down. Not long after, a police officer appeared and took down details.

It was already so late, and all she wanted was to go home.

She and the van driver swapped insurance details, and after surveying the van doors again, she deemed that they looked solid and weren't about to fall off. She prayed they wouldn't. She took a chance and drove it home.

It wasn't until she was on the road that it occurred to her to call Adam and let him know why she was so late.

He'd been waiting a long time for her. The poor guy had a date and likely needed his beauty sleep.

Who was she?

Anger spiked in her bloodstream and she floored the gas pedal. No sooner had she parked outside the shop when Adam came running, his face distorted with worry.

"What happened?" He looked at her, then the van.

"Someone rear-ended me as I was pulling out of the hotel parking lot."

"What? Are you okay?" In a second, he was by her side, framing her face with his hands, examining it carefully. The aloofness and distance had vanished and in their place a triple shot of concern.

"Do you hurt anywhere?" he asked, peering into her eyes, tilting her face one way, and then the other. Apprehension masked his face, a hint of uneasiness flickering across his expression before his lips curved upwards at the corners into a false smile, when he caught her staring. The feel of his familiar hands, soft and warm, on her face comforted her. She didn't mind that he was manhandling her, examining her, inspecting her for signs of injury.

"I'm okay. You don't have to do this—"

"Hold still." He rubbed his finger gently over her eyebrow, then shook his head. "It's nothing."

"I told you. I'm not injured. I'm not hurting anywhere." But his hands were on her and they felt as if they belonged there. She didn't move and let him take a moment longer to make sure she hadn't cut her face or suffered an injury.

"Who was it?"

"A van driver. He was going too fast."

"Son of a bi—"

"It's all taken care of," she said wearily, feeling a tsunami of tiredness crash over her.

Adam put his hands down and listened, his hands holding hers as if she might crumble from the shock of what had just happened.

"Tell me what happened."

Confused, she scowled at him. "I just did. A guy rear-ended me."

"In detail."

So she did, telling him slowly what she could remember. "And then he shouted at me and tried to make out as if it was my fault."

"The son of a gun—"

Adam's anger was endearing. "It's on CCTV, and there were a lot of witnesses."

"We should go to the hospital to make sure there are no internal injuries."

"There aren't! I didn't hit anything. I'm not going to the hospital, Adam. I'm okay. I promise you I am. We need to finish editing—"

"It's done."

"What?" she asked, surprised. "All of it?"

"All of it. You were gone for so long."

"I didn't mean to—"

"You could have called."

"I remembered when I was on my way back." She also remembered what she'd been angry about. Adam and his date. She took a few steps back, the sudden rush of remembrance like acid to her face.

"I was waiting here for you," he reminded her. "I was worried."

"It all happened so fast. I just wanted to get back, and I was already on the road. I wasn't thinking straight. I was shaken from the crash. I didn't think to pull over to call you."

"You're back, and that's all that matters. I was worried, Mackenzie. I still care about you, no matter what you think."

She fortified her guard. "I rushed back. I'm sorry I kept you so late, I know you're busy tomorrow, with your date or whatever, so ... uh, you should go. Thank you, for everything you've done for me, Adam. I really appreciate it. I can take over from here. If you've edited everything, I can take it from here. I can manage."

He blinked at her, as if she was spouting nonsense which didn't make sense to him. Taking another step towards her, he closed the gap she'd left wide open. She backed away some more. And he closed that gap, too.

"Why does this sound like goodbye?" he asked, a melancholy gloom in his expression.

"I'm going to buy the software and I know how to use it now because you've shown me."

"You don't know how to upload it to the internet," he commented, taking another step closer.

She would have stepped back, but he was right. She didn't know what happened next. She still needed him. His help, more like it. The thought of having to sit by his side and be with him, while he walked her through the launch of the new site, it would kill her now, knowing he had someone. And that it wasn't her.

"Did you play by your rules from your book?" she asked, wanting to fire her arrows. Needing to cause some pain.

"Who?"

"Your date."

"You mean the woman?"

She frowned. "Yes, the woman. Who else?"

"She thinks so, but I didn't."

He moved another step closer.

She didn't want to talk to him about his new lady friend. "It's late, Adam. You should leave."

"You sound annoyed, Mackenzie. Are you?"

Yes, god damn it, she was annoyed. The whole time when she'd had him by her side, she hadn't appreciated him, and now that he was with someone else, she wanted him back.

The heart always wants what the heart can't have. Her heart wanted Adam back.

"I've just been in an accident. I want to go home. I'll get in touch next week."

He took another step closer, and this time she had no place to back into except the wall of her shop. She leaned against it, her breath coming fast and furious. Anger and jealousy mixing with the short, sharp breaths.

He took her hand, placed his other one on the wall, by the side of her head, semi caging her in. She swallowed, feeling unsure, not knowing what to make of this. His boldest move yet.

"You have a date tomorrow," she murmured, her voice oddly raspy.

"With my parents. Meeting them for dinner."

"But you said—"

"I had a date, and I do. With my parents."

"But I thought—"

"I know. I wanted to see your reaction. See if you cared."

Her mouth fell open. "You don't have a date with a *woman*?"

"I very much would like a date with a woman." He pressed his forehead against hers. Her heart rate rocketed inside her chest. "But I'm not sure if this woman wants a date with me. I'm praying she'll give me a second chance."

He's talking about me. He is. Is he? Just to make sure. "Are you talking about me?"

"Yes, Mackenzie. I'm talking about you. Are you done being

angry? I don't mean done forever, because we need to talk about some things. But are you done pushing me away?"

She couldn't articulate her thoughts, her feelings, couldn't find the words under the night sky, pushed up against a wall with this wonderful man pressed against her. Looking at him, so close to her she could smell his sweet breath and a hint of his aftershave, she saw a man who always helped her. His so-called ten rules hadn't even been radical rules, as Leigh constantly reminded her. He'd always been there for her in her time of need. He wouldn't have done anything to hurt her willingly.

"I want you back, Adam. I want us back together."

He cocked his head, as if he didn't quite believe what he was hearing. "Are you sure you don't want me to take you to the hospital for signs of concussion?"

"I don't have a concussion."

"No?" He stayed where he was, his face inches from her, but he seemed to be cautious, still reeling from her words. "Then tell me again what you want?"

"I want you, Adam. I've missed you."

His head dropped to her shoulder, and she raised a hand, raking it through his hair. He hugged her for a moment, and her arms went around him as they held one another, savoring the closeness that they had denied each other.

He lifted his head, his eyes burning into hers with need. "I've missed you. I didn't think you'd let me come back to you again."

"I want you back." The void in her life had been too large, too all-consuming, too lonely.

He kissed her then, suddenly and quickly, taking her by sweet surprise as his lips melted against hers. Closed lips which darted over her cheeks, and cheekbones, then her forehead and nose. Touching everywhere but where she wanted him the most.

Disappointment settled in her chest before his mouth clamped over hers. That's when her heart danced for joy, and her pulse followed.

His lips brushed against hers briefly before he deepened the kiss, gaining access and claiming her mouth, claiming her. She clutched his shirt, her need for him burning down her defenses, and speeding up her heart.

Da-doom, da-doom, da-doom, her heartbeat boomed, as he framed her face with his soft, large hands. They moaned in unison. She wasn't sure where his voice ended and where hers began; wasn't sure where his mouth ended and hers began. Looking back, she would see that this makeup kiss would imprint itself on her skin forever.

The *coming back* kiss. The one that made her feel like she was coming home again. Being so close to him reminded her of all the things she'd lost but had now found. Belonging, being wanted, meaning something to someone.

Adam was what she needed.

EPILOGUE

"You're working too hard, Adam. I feel bad, this being the weekend and all. Let me help you."

Mackenzie's mother reached for the spare paint roller; the one Mackenzie had been using until she'd had to rush off back to Bloom.

"No, ma'am. I've got this. It's almost finished and there's no reason for you to get paint all over your clothes."

"But I feel like I'm doing nothing."

"It's just this wall left. It won't take me long to finish it, ma'am."

"Call me Amanda," her mother said. "It sounds downright formal, you calling me ma'am all the time."

He laughed. "You're always plying us with food."

"You have to eat, Adam, painting all day. It can't be easy."

Mackenzie's mother could not do enough for them. She baked cakes, cooked lunches and dinner, and plied them with food. He dipped his roller into the paint tray, getting ready to paint again. Hopefully, after this wall was done, Mackenzie's mom's room would be complete.

He and Mackenzie had been coming to her grandmother's

house for the past few weeks to help with a little DIY on the house. Mackenzie had told her family of her grand plan to redo parts of the house. Mackenzie was eager to convert the downstairs utility room to a bathroom for her grandma who was finding it difficult to climb the stairs. She had insisted on paying for this from the income from her online lessons. And she could, quite easily. Work was due to start on the utility room conversion in a month or so.

She'd expressed a desire to make life easier and more comfortable for her grandmother because she wanted to repay her for all the love and kindness she had shown her, and after discussing the idea with her family, she'd decided to also update the decor. A priority was painting the bedrooms, mainly her grandmother's and her own, which she now wanted her mother to have.

It was illuminating to see the relationship change between Mackenzie and her mother. At first the two were awkward around one another; Mackenzie's mother more so, but over time, things had started to blossom, like Mackenzie's flowers that were all closed up then, slowly starting to open, petal by petal.

Her soft eyes stared up at him. "I worry about Mackenzie. She's always working too hard and she doesn't take proper care of herself. I'm just so glad the two of you are back together."

He smiled and nodded. He was too. Life was better when shared with someone special.

"Where is that girl?" Grandma shuffled into the room, her crinkly eyes wide with wonder as she looked around, obviously happy with the results of his hard labor. "A fresh lick of paint has made this room as good as new. It's like we moved and went to a new place," she chuckled.

"I'm glad you like it." He set down his roller in preparation. Mackenzie's grandmother passed by a couple of times during the day, and often stopped to talk for a good while.

She gave him an approving look. "You're a man of many talents."

"He certainly is," Mackenzie's mother agreed.

"The Love Doctor knows no limits," her grandmother winked mischievously.

"Mom, would you stop that!" Mackenzie's mother chided her.

"Mackenzie isn't here." Grandma slowly walked over and looked out of the window. "No sign of her van either." She turned around to him. "You can take a bit of ribbing, can't you, Adam?"

"Yes, ma'am."

"I hope you're staying for dinner." Amanda picked up the empty plate. She would return with it in due course, refilled with more snacks.

"Uh, no, ma'am. We've got plans for later." Mackenzie had gone to her shop to pick up a couple of things for her friend's baby shower later today. Why she couldn't have done that on the way back from here, he didn't know, and he wondered how much longer she would be.

"Plans for later?" Grandma winked at him. "I like the sound of that. Our girl did nothing but work until you came along. Work, work, work, work, work."

"He gets the message, Mom." Amanda gave him an apologetic smile.

Just then, the sound of a vehicle outside made him walk over to the window and look out.

"Mackenzie's back. I'd better get finished up. She said she needs to go home and get changed. She's going to her friend's baby shower," he explained.

"It's nice for her to take some time out and enjoy life," Mackenzie's mother remarked.

"Is this for Merry?" Grandma asked.

"I believe so." He'd heard the name, but he hadn't met anyone other than Leigh, and Rourke more recently. Leigh constantly threatened to arrange a dinner so that 'they could all get to know one another,' but Mackenzie seemed reluctant for that just yet. She'd told him she wanted him all to herself for now.

He understood. They needed to spend more time together, and with the success of her online lessons, carving time out for just the two of them to enjoy life wasn't easy.

Mackenzie's slow footsteps up the stairs were followed by her appearing at the door, a smug grin on her face as she stood, looking odd with her arms behind her back.

"What are you all doing in here?" she asked.

"Admiring all your hard work," her grandmother replied.

"I was about to get him some more snacks," her mother said, still clutching the empty plate in her hands.

Mackenzie looked at her mother. "I wanted to put this up, so that you could see it on the wall first."

"Put what up?" Her mother's brows wrinkled. Adam had a feeling he knew what it might be. Mackenzie pulled it out carefully from behind her back.

"What is that?" Grandma asked, squinting. "I can't see anything."

Mackenzie turned it over so that it faced them. Her mother gasped and set down the plate she'd been holding, her hands going to her chest as if she was struggling to keep the emotions in place.

She'd finally bought the painting.

Once, when they'd been walking to Roxy's Diner, she'd stopped and looked through the windows of the shop a few doors down from her. She'd told him about it.

"You didn't..." her mother voice was soft and low, falling from her lips like a shaky whisper.

"What's going on?" Grandma asked, looking from daughter to mother. Mackenzie pressed her lips together, as if she couldn't contain the happiness that was about to burst inside her.

"I did."

"You bought that for me?" Tears glistened in her mother's eyes.

"You said you liked it, Mom."

"I did. You used to wear a dress that had red poppies all over it."

"I remember that dress," Grandma cried, her jowls wobbling as she examined the painting. "You made that, didn't you, Mandy?"

"Do you like it?" Mackenzie asked, the eagerness in her voice sounding like a child who wanted to please her mother.

"I love it." A fat tear rolled down her mother's cheek as she took the painting in her hands and surveyed it.

"It's not supposed to make you cry, Mom!"

Her mother wiped her cheek. "I love this. It makes me happy, looking at these bright flowers bursting with color, but most of all, it makes me happy because it reminds me of you, in that dress. I always used to remember you in that dress. You must have been three, or four?" Mackenzie's mom looked at her own mother for clarification.

"She was around that age," Grandma agreed. "You'd do her hair up in bunches. You went looking for hair clips that had poppies on them. Took you a while, but you finally found them."

Her mother nodded, then sniffled. "Thank you."

"We'll put that up for you, won't we?" Mackenzie asked him.

"Sure we will." He'd put it up before they left, depending on which wall Mackenzie's mother wanted it on, and if it was dry or not.

Things were changing, and for the better, not just between him and Mackenzie, and her and her family, but for him in his life, too.

Jake Parnell was a remnant from of the Love Doctor era, though the guy had done him a favor by revealing his secret. He'd made Adam see that in this day and age, he couldn't do what he was doing and keep his identity under wraps.

Patrick was in love with the fancy notebook woman, and Sean McGregor had contacted him only a few days ago. The person he had hired didn't turn out to be as great at the job as he'd claimed during the interview. McGregor was beginning to lose patience and was still interested in Adam. He'd asked him to come in and do his presentation again.

Here, standing in this room, watching the love and trust slowly flow back into Mackenzie's and her mother's lives, it was priceless, and it meant so much more to him because of the woman he was falling so hard and so fast for.

If anyone deserved all the good things, it was this woman he'd found face down in a flower pot.

~

"That was sweet, what you did for your mom." Adam looked up from his laptop and watched her as she lightly primped her curls with a small smattering of serum.

"She was really surprised, wasn't she? I think she liked it."

"She didn't just like it, Mackenzie. Your mom absolutely loved it. You could see it written all over her face."

She swallowed and continued smoothing her wild hair down. Her mother had been speechless, more so than Mackenzie would have thought. She'd been in tears. Hearing her mom and grandma talking about the dress she'd worn as a child, discovering that her mom had been on a hunt to find matching hair clips complete with little poppy plastic cutouts, it had made her heart ache. Sadness for the time gone by commingled with a burgeoning sense of hope for the new future she was determined to create with the woman who had given birth to her.

Unfortunately, her mom hadn't gotten the job she'd set her

heart on, but she had a few more interviews lined up and she remained optimistic. She had taken control of her life again and was determined to make a new start.

It was a start that Mackenzie wholeheartedly believed in.

If recent months had taught her anything, it was that there was only one life, and it was short and unpredictable. Anything could happen, so it was better to make the most of the opportunities one was given.

She was going to hold onto her mother and never let her go.

She felt the same way about Adam.

Moving on from the past meant overcoming her own insecurities and fears. She'd finally pushed them away, not allowing herself to wallow in them. Now, she wanted to grab all the good things and hold onto them forever.

She had softened because she had found love. She'd met a man who adored her, who made her feel as if she mattered.

He loved her. He hadn't told her in words, but she didn't care about words. It was actions that mattered and everything about Adam Hartman told her he loved her fiercely and passionately.

Someplace deep inside her, Mackenzie had found the strength to reach out to her mother, and to start building bridges. Feeling loved in such a way had given her the power to forgive and heal all wounds.

"Are you almost ready?" Adam came up behind her as she finished putting on her mascara.

"Almost. Could you help me with this?" She held up the necklace she always wore when she wanted to look a bit more dressed up. Adam stood inches taller than her, looking at her in the mirror, not saying anything.

"Could you?" she asked again, putting it on and holding the two ends behind her neck for him to fasten. She frowned, unsure of his silence.

"I hope you like it."

"Like what?"

She looked at the reflection in the mirror, confused, unsure. He held out his hand and lying in the middle of his palm was a small, black shiny box.

"What is it?"

"Why don't you take a look and see?"

She turned, then lifted the box out of his hand, slowly prizing the lid open. Inside, nestled in soft, black tissue paper, lay a thin gold chain, with the letter M hanging so that it was slanted.

"Adam!" An arrow of surprise shot through her chest, her insides aflutter. She lifted the chain out carefully. It was so delicate and thin in her hands that she was afraid it might break. "I always wanted a slanted letter chain. How did you know?"

"I didn't. I saw it and I really liked it. I thought you might like it, too."

Her brows lifted in delight. "I love it, Adam. I so, so, so love it."

"You sure?"

"Yes. Thank you." She tiptoed up and kissed him.

"I wanted to give you a little something."

"If anyone needs to give someone something, it's me, after all you've done for me."

He put a finger to her lips. "Shhh. I wanted you to have something to wear around that beautiful, elegant neck of yours."

He'd listened and heard her. He never stopped trying to erase the bad words and memories, and instead seemed to have taken it upon himself to paint them over with new ones.

"Thank you so much." This gift touched her heart in a way she couldn't even begin to express. "Fasten it for me?" She placed it around her neck and waited. He moved her hair to one side, his fingers warm and electric, causing her skin to prickle with anticipation. This man affected her in so many ways, it was sometimes scary.

He fastened the lock, and as she stared at her reflection, her fingers tracing the letter M, his lips feathered light kisses along her nape.

She turned to face him.

"I'm in love with you, Mackenzie," he whispered, making the breath hitch in her throat and her eyes pop wide open.

"I'm pretty crazy about you, too," she murmured. He linked their fingers, the touch of his hands multiplying the chaos he elicited inside her when their lips joined again.

This time he kissed her slowly, his mouth slanting over hers, warm, and sweet, and urgent, all at once. She fell into him, pressing her body against his, forgetting everything and everyone.

But creeping up from the back of her mind were the arrangements she'd made for Merry's baby shower. Leigh had told her to get there early. "I should go," she whispered, dragging her lips away from his and not wanting to leave, not now that they had just started an intimate conversation.

Jenna was having the baby shower at Reed's mansion which was at the other side of town. She'd claimed that Reed had the staff to cater and take care of such an event. Leigh called her a mistress of the manor.

"I hate that you have to go, but you have to, before Leigh shows up and drags you there." He pressed his lips against hers again, teasing her to the edge of giving up and giving in to another smoldering kiss.

He placed his finger over her lips, thumbing her lower lip gently. "We'll continue from where we left when you get back." She sighed, wishing time would stop and freeze and hold this moment forever.

A short while later, as they drove onto Reed's sprawling driveway, she saw Dylan helping a heavily pregnant Merry out of a car.

"You go over and see them," Adam told her. "I'll get the arrangements out."

She got out and rushed over to Merry's side. "You look like you're about to burst." The women kissed and hugged one another.

"I'm scared she might pop any minute." Dylan planted a welcoming kiss on Mackenzie's cheek before slipping his hand in Merry's. He stared at his wife in complete adoration.

"You worry too much." Merry swatted him with a playful wave of her hand.

Mackenzie glanced over her shoulder, conscious that Adam would need a hand with bringing the arrangements inside. She had created two large floral displays, one with blue flowers and the other with pink. Interspersed among the flowers were animal pictures that she'd drawn, cut out and colored with gel pens. She'd also put together an enormous bunch of balloons in pastel pink and blue colors.

"Did you make those?" Merry cried, following her line of sight. "They're gorgeous."

Mackenzie winced with guilt. "They should have been a surprise. I was supposed to come in early and set up." She watched Adam struggle to get the balloons out.

"I should help." She made a move to go to him.

"Is that the Love Doctor?" Merry asked, giggling. "Sorry, I shouldn't call him that. We need introductions."

"The Love Doctor?" Dylan's brows shifted north towards his hairline. "Reed mentioned something about that. I thought he was joking."

"Come over," said Mackenzie. "I'll introduce you." It was about time she showed her new boyfriend off to her friends.

"This is Merry and Dylan," said Mackenzie, making introductions.

"It is true?" Dylan asked, shaking Adam's hand.

"Do you have to bring that up?" Merry asked her husband, but her attention was quickly diverted to the arrangements. "These are *so* pretty, Mackenzie."

"Thank you. I really wish I'd come earlier and set them—"

"You're late!" A cry from another corner made them turn heads to find Jenna and Leigh marching over.

"What time do you call this?" Leigh asked her, as they hugged and kissed one another.

Mackenzie grimaced. "Sorry. I know I was supposed to get here before Merry."

"I love that chain." Jenna's eyes lasered in on the new necklace Adam had given her. The women craned their necks to take a closer look.

"Adam gave it to me just now." Mackenzie felt shy all of a sudden.

"Just now?" Leigh winked. "Is that why you're late?"

Jenna chuckled. "We'll discuss this in depth later. That's *soooo* pretty." Jenna marveled at the necklace again, before introducing herself to Adam. "I'm Jenna, and I know exactly who you are. I've have heard things about you." She waggled a finger at him.

Adam shook his head but he was wearing a smile. Mackenzie felt sorry for him being ganged up on like this, but at least he'd now met this group of people who were starting to mean a lot to her.

If Leigh had her way, Mackenzie and Adam would be sitting at a dinner table at one of their houses in the not-too-distant future.

"Let me give you a hand with those," she heard Dylan say, while she caught up with the women, all of them still talking at once.

"Are the men staying?" Mackenzie asked. She wasn't sure of the arrangements for men.

"Oh, my goodness, I hope not!" Merry looked at Jenna for guidance.

"They're going to the bar," Jenna replied.

Merry looked relieved. "Good, because Dylan is reading every baby book under the sun. He's been putting together timetables—"

"Timetables?" asked Leigh. "Whatever for?"

Merry patted her huge bump. "He thinks the baby will get up and feed and sleep at strict times. He has no idea. He needs to loosen up a little."

Leigh put her arm around Merry's shoulder. "Don't worry, Rourke and Reed have got this." They laughed and headed towards Reed's mansion.

Mackenzie had been here before on a few occasions, but even so, her mouth still fell open as she surveyed the decorations and banners in the huge hallway.

"I thought this was a baby shower for a few select guests," she whispered to Leigh.

"It is, but this is Jenna, and I swear to God, sometimes I think she's competing with the ghost of Olivia for throwing big parties."

"Olivia? Wasn't she the—?" Mackenzie started to ask.

Leigh put a finger to her lips. "Yes."

Adam and Dylan had set down the arrangements where Jenna had directed them to. Reed was hovering by their side when Mackenzie walked over to them. "What are you guys going to do?" she asked Reed.

"Jenna's throwing me out. Dylan needs to enjoy his last month of peace and quiet, and Adam says he's happy to join us. Rourke is already at the bar, waiting for us. I believe he's already ordered the drinks."

"This early in the afternoon?" Mackenzie asked.

Reed chortled. "You ladies are having your fun, and we'd like to have ours, right, Dylan?"

"Are you sure you'll be okay?" Dylan asked Merry.

"My waters aren't going to break just yet. Please go and stop worrying about me."

Mackenzie pulled Adam to the side slightly. "Are you okay to go with them?" She didn't want him to feel as if he'd been forced into this.

"Sure, why not? They seem like a nice bunch of guys."

"But do you *want* to go?" Mackenzie whispered. It was one thing Adam meeting everyone. It was quite another him going out for drinks with the guys when he barely knew them. She had a good idea what the main topic of conversation would be.

"We're going to the Blue Velvet Bar, it seems. Yeah, I'm up for it."

"They'll want to ask you about the Love Doctor," she cautioned.

"And I'll be happy to answer all questions." He put his hands out, and then reeled her into his arms, not caring where he was or who was watching. "I'm going to be fine. You ladies have fun." He kissed her, nothing too hot or sensual, but a teasing kiss, short and sweet, and one that left her wanting more.

She heard whistling around them, and they both ignored it, looking at one another as if it were only the two of them here.

"They're going to grill you," she said, tapping his nose lightly, before pulling away.

"They can grill me all they want. I was the Love Doctor. Maybe I can teach them a thing or two? Bore them with a few rules."

She looked at her friends and their partners. "I think they're doing just fine."

"Like us." He slowly unfurled his fingers from hers as he started to walk away. "I'll see you later?"

She nodded, watching Adam leave with Dylan and Reed. She would go home after this baby shower, to Adam. Not to an empty place, with just a laptop and her dreams for company. Not just to a dinner eaten alone in front of the TV.

But to Adam.

Her life was so much richer now. She had so much more; so many special people and so much love. She mattered, she was wanted, she belonged.

Thank you for reading A BOUQUET OF CHARM! I hope you enjoyed Mackenzie and Adam's story, and I'm sorry that this one took me so long to release. Thank you so much for your patience.

A CHRISTMAS WISH is the next standalone romance. It's Christmas in Starling Bay, which means that Hyacinth Fitzsimmons is on a mission to ensure that the Christmas pageant goes ahead, no matter what.

It's Christmas in Starling Bay but the season of joy is not without its problems …

Leah Shriver's world has been turned upside down and, much to Hyacinth's dismay, plans for the annual Christmas pageant are in jeopardy. Merry and Dylan are having their baby, so Dylan can't help either.

All is lost. Or is it?

If this is the first book you've read in the STARLING BAY SERIES, you might want to read the first book, WINTER'S KISS. This is about a sexy gift store owner, a jaded widow and a Great Dane. Or you can get the boxed set, Escape to Starling Bay.

SIGN UP FOR MY NEWSLETTER to find out when new books release and also get the prequel to the series, WHIRLWIND KISSES for free!

http:/www.siennacarr.com/newsletter

I appreciate your help in spreading the word, including telling a friend, and I would be grateful if you could leave a review on your favorite book site.

Thank you so much!
Sienna

BOOKLIST

Starling Bay: Come to Starling Bay, a small coastal town with lots of lovely places, and meet memorable people you'll want as your friends. Small town. Big Romance.

Whirlwind Kisses

Winter's Kiss

Maid for Him

Love Letters

Escape to Starling Bay (Books 1-3)

From Faking to Forever

Winter's Vow

Guarded Hearts

Table for Two

A Bouquet of Charm

A Christmas Wish

The Rose Sisters: Meet Ashleigh, Eloise and Ginny, the Rose sisters, who run a bridal boutique in Whisper Falls. Sibling rivalry, forgotten dreams, new challenges.

The Bridal Shop

ACKNOWLEDGMENTS

I would like to thank my amazing group of proofreaders who check my manuscript for errors, typos and inconsistencies.

I am eternally grateful for their help and support:

Marcia Chamberlain
Dena Pugh
Charlotte Rebelein
Carole Tunstall

I would also like to thank Tatiana Vila of Vila Design for creating this awesome cover.

ABOUT THE AUTHOR

Sienna Carr is a pen name for an author who has been writing romance since 2013. She lives in the UK with her husband, three children, and a parrot.

Connect with Me

I love hearing from you – so please don't be shy!
You can email me at: sienna@siennacarr.com